# ALFRED HITCHCOCK'S
# HOME SWEET HOMICIDE

# ALFRED HITCHCOCK'S HOME SWEET HOMICIDE

## STORIES FROM *ALFRED HITCHCOCK'S MYSTERY MAGAZINE*

Edited by Cathleen Jordan

**WALKER AND COMPANY**
**NEW YORK**

First published in the United States of America in 1991
by Walker Publishing Company, Inc., 720 Fifth Avenue, New York, NY 10019.

Published simultaneously in Canada by Thomas Allen & Son
Canada, Limited, Markham, Ontario

Library of Congress Cataloging-in-Publication Data
Alfred Hitchcock's home sweet homicide: stories from Alfred
Hitchcock's mystery magazine / edited by Cathleen Jordan.
p. cm.
ISBN 0-8027-5798-7
1. Detective and mystery stories, American. I. Jordan, Cathleen.
II. Alfred Hitchcock's mystery magazine.
PS648.D4A3435 1991
813'.087208—dc20
91-14989
CIP

Printed in the United States of America

2 4 6 8 10 9 7 5 3 1

# CONTENTS

# FOREWORD

Home is good (broadly speaking).

Home is happiness and security and the people you love.

Home is also the stuff of the cosiest of crime fiction.

The body on the library carpet is the very essence of the tradition. The family, at least, is in residence; often a house party is in progress. The manse is snowed in, or otherwise secured from the outside world. The evil sister-in-law, the degenerate brother, the too-proud mother of the lot, the penurious cousin—we know them all well. And those who aren't related by blood but are still "family": the lawyer, doctor, curate, best friend.

Another subgenre—a big one—is the spouse murder tale. The biter-bit story. These abound, as any editor of mystery short stories can tell you. "Doreen must go," they say at the beginning. And Martin or Harry or whoever scavenges around for a plausible means. Doreen, of course, gets him in the end.

In the pages that follow, all manner of homes are represented. Stately homes and shabby ones and those in between. A nursing home, as well. And all manner of families, from the family of the street to those tightly knit upper-class enclaves that mystery fiction so loves to make frail. There is much puzzlement and much humor, and there is also a thread of sadness. Robert Frost said that "home is where, when you have to go there, they have to take you in," bespeaking pain and tensions and passions running deep.

But you, dear reader, are in good hands. Some of our finest authors are gathered here to give you laughter, insight, glimpses of other lives, people we know or might have known, and, above all, the unparalleled quest for the solution. Our stories range from England to New England to California, from sad to stern to straightforward to exasperated to funny.

It seems that, after all, home *is* where the heart is—but watch out. Some hearts are in the wrong places.

And stay away from house parties.

—Cathleen Jordan

# ALFRED HITCHCOCK'S HOME SWEET HOMICIDE

# MARCIA MULLER

# DEADLY FANTASIES

"**M**s McCone, I know what you're thinking. But I'm not paranoid. One of them—my brother or my sister—*is* trying to kill me!"

"Please, call me Sharon." I said it to give myself time to think. The young woman seated across my desk at All Souls Legal Cooperative certainly sounded paranoid. My boss, Hank Zahn, had warned me about that when he'd referred her for private investigative services.

"Let me go over what you've told me, to make sure I've got it straight," I said. "Six months ago you were living here in the Mission district and working as a counselor for emotionally disturbed teenagers. Then your father died and left you his entire estate, something in the neighborhood of thirty million dollars."

Laurie Newingham nodded and blew her nose. As soon as she'd come into my office she'd started sneezing. Allergies, she'd told me. To ease her watering eyes she'd popped out her contact lenses and stored them in their plastic case; in doing that she had spilled some of the liquid that the lenses soaked in over her fingers, then nonchalantly wiped them on her faded jeans. The gesture endeared her to me because I'm sloppy, too. Frankly, I couldn't imagine this freshly scrubbed young woman—she was about ten years younger than I, perhaps twenty-five—possessing a fortune. With her trim, athletic body, tanned, snub-nosed face, and carelessly styled blond hair, she looked like a high school cheerleader. But Winfield Newingham had owned much of San Francisco's choice real estate, and Laurie had been the developer's youngest—and apparently favorite—child.

I went on, "Under the terms of the will, you were required to move back into the family home in St. Francis Wood. You've done so. The will also stipulated that your brother Dan and

1

sister Janet can remain there as long as they wish. So you've
been living with them, and they've both been acting hostile
because you inherited everything."

"Hostile? One of them wants to *kill* me! I keep having
stomach cramps, throwing up—you know."

"Have you seen a doctor?"

"I *hate* doctors! They're always telling me there's nothing
wrong with me, when I know there *is.*"

"The police, then?"

"I like them a whole lot less than doctors. Besides, they
wouldn't believe me." Now she took out an inhaler and
breathed deeply from it.

Asthma, as well as allergies, I thought. Wasn't asthma sometimes psychosomatic? Could the vomiting and other symptoms
be similarly rooted?

"Either Don or Janet is trying to poison me," Laurie said,
"because if I die, the estate reverts to them."

"Laurie," I said, "why did your father leave everything to
you?"

"The will said it was because I'd gone out on my own and
done something I believed in. Dan and Janet have always lived
off him; the only jobs they've ever been able to hold down have
been ones Dad gave them."

"One more question: Why did you come to All Souls?" My
employer is a legal services plan for people who can't afford
the going rates.

Laurie looked surprised. "I've *always* come here, since I
moved to the Mission and started working as a counselor five
years ago. I may be able to afford a downtown law firm, but I
don't trust them any more now than I did when I inherited the
money. Besides, I talked it over with Dolph, and he said it
would be better to stick with a known quantity."

"Dolph?"

"Dolph Edwards. I'm going to marry him. He's director of the
guidance center where I used to work—still work, as a volunteer."

"That's the Inner Mission Self-Help Center?"

She nodded. "Do you know them?"

"Yes." The center offered a wide range of social services to a mainly Hispanic clientele—including job placement, psychological counseling, and short-term financial assistance. I'd heard that recently their programs had been drastically cut back due to lack of funding—as all too often happens in today's arid political climate.

"Then you know what my father meant about my having done something I believed in," Laurie said. "The center's a hopeless mess, of course; it's never been very well organized. But it's the kind of project I'd like to put my money to work for. After I marry Dolph I'll help him realize his dreams effectively—and in the right way."

I nodded and studied her for a moment. She stared back anxiously. Laurie was emotionally ragged, I thought, and needed someone to look out for her. Besides, I identified with her in a way. At her age I'd also been the cheerleader type, and I'd gone out on my own and done something I believed in, too.

"Okay," I said. "What I'll do is talk with your brother and sister, feel the situation out. I'll say you've applied for a volunteer position here, counseling clients with emotional problems, and that you gave their names as character references."

Her eyes brightened and some of the lines of strain smoothed. She gave me Dan's office phone number and Janet's private line at the St. Francis Wood house. Preparing to leave, she clumsily dropped her purse on the floor. Then she located her contact case and popped a lens into her mouth to clean it; as she fitted it into her right eye, her foot nudged the bag, and the inhaler and a bottle of time-release vitamin capsules rolled across the floor. We went for them at the same time, and our heads grazed each other's.

She looked at me apologetically. One of her eyes was now gray, the other a brilliant blue from the tint of the contact. It was like a physical manifestation of her somewhat schizoid personality: down-to-earth wholesomeness warring with what I had begun to suspect was a dangerous paranoia.

Dan Newingham said, "Why the hell does Laurie want to do that? She doesn't have to work any more, even as a volunteer. She controls all the family's assets."

We were seated in his office in the controller's department of Newingham Development, on the thirty-first floor of one of the company's financial district buildings. Dan was a big guy, with the same blond good looks as his sister, but they were spoiled by a petulant mouth and a body whose bloated appearance suggested an excess of good living.

"If she wants to work," he added, "there's plenty of positions she could fill right here. It's her company now, dammit, and she ought to take an interest in it."

"I gather her interests run more to the social services."

"More to the low life, you mean."

"In what respect?"

Dan got up and went to look out the window behind the desk. The view of the bay was blocked by an upthrusting jumble of steel and plate glass—the legacy that firms such as Newingham Development had left a once old fashioned and beautiful town.

After a moment Dan turned. "I don't want to offend you, Ms . . . McCone, is it?"

I nodded.

"I'm not putting down your law firm, or what you're trying to do," he went on, "but when you work on your end of the spectrum, you naturally have to associate with people who aren't quite . . . well, of our class. I wasn't aware of the kind of people Laurie was associating with during those years she didn't live at home, but now . . . her boyfriend, that Dolph, for instance. He's always around; I can't stand him. Anyway, my point is, Laurie should settle down now, come back to the real world, learn the business. Is that too much to ask in exchange for thirty million?"

"She doesn't seem to care about the money."

Dan laughed harshly. "Doesn't she? Then why did she move back into the house? She could have chucked the whole thing."

"I think she feels she can use the money to benefit people who really need it."

"Yes, and she'll blow it all. In a few years there won't *be* any Newingham Development. Oh, I know what was going through my father's mind when he made that will: Laurie's always been the strong one, the dedicated one. He thought that if he forced her to move back home, she'd eventually become involved in the business and there'd be real leadership here. Laurie can be very single-minded when she wants things to go a certain way, and that's what it takes to run a firm like this. But the sad thing is, Dad just didn't realize how far gone she is in her bleeding heart sympathies."

"That aside, what do you think about her potential for counseling our disturbed clients?"

"If you really want to know, I think she'd be terrible. Laurie's a basket case. She has psychosomatic illnesses, paranoid fantasies. She needs counseling herself."

"Can you describe these fantasies?"

He hesitated, tapping his fingers on the window frame. "No, I don't think I care to. I shouldn't have brought them up."

"Actually, Mr. Newingham, I think I have an inkling of what they are. Laurie told her lawyer that someone's trying to poison her. She seemed obsessed with the idea, which is why we decided to check her references thoroughly."

"I suppose she also told her lawyer who the alleged poisoner is?"

"In a way. She said it was either you or your sister Janet."

"God, she's worse off than I realized. I suppose she claims one of us wants to kill her so he can inherit my father's estate. That's ridiculous—I don't need the damned money. I have a good job here, and I've invested profitably." Dan paused, then added, "I hope you can convince her to get into an intensive therapy program before she tries to counsel any of your clients. Her fantasies are starting to sound dangerous."

Janet Newingham was the exact opposite of her sister: a tall brunette with a highly stylized way of moving and speaking. Her clothes were designer, her jewelry expensive, and her hair and nails told of frequent attention at the finest salons. We met at the St. Francis Wood house—a great pile of stone reminiscent of an Italian villa that sat on a double lot near the fountain that crowned the area's main boulevard. I had informed Laurie that I would be interviewing her sister, and she had agreed to absent herself from the house; I didn't want my presence to trigger an unpleasant scene between the two of them.

I needn't have worried, however. Janet Newingham was one of those cool, reserved women who may smolder under the surface but seldom display anger. She seated me in a formal parlor overlooking the strip of park that runs down the center of St. Francis Boulevard and served me coffee from a sterling silver pot. From all appearances, I might have been there to discuss the Junior League fashion show.

When I had gotten to the point of my visit, Janet leaned forward and extracted a cigarette from an ivory box on the coffee table. She took her time lighting it, then said, "*Another* volunteer position? It's bad enough she kept on working at that guidance center for nothing after they lost their federal funding last spring, but this . . . I'm surprised; I thought nothing would ever pry her away from her precious Dolph."

"Perhaps she feels it's not a good idea to stay on there, since they plan to be married."

"Did she tell you that? Laurie's always threatening to marry Dolph, but I doubt she ever will. She just keeps him around because he's her one claim to the exotic. He's one of these social reformers, you know. Totally devoted to his cause."

"And what is that?"

"Helping people. Sounds very sixties, doesn't it? That center is his raison d'être. He founded it, and he's going to keep it limping along no matter what. He plays the crusader role to the hilt, Dolph does: dresses in Salvation Army castoffs, drives a motorcycle. You know the type."

"That's very interesting," I said, "but it doesn't have much bearing on Laurie's ability to fill our volunteer position. What do you think of her potential as a counselor?"

"Not a great deal. Oh, I know that's what she's been doing these past five years, but recently Laurie's been . . . a very disturbed young woman. But you know that. My brother told me of your visit to his office, and that you had already heard of her fantasy that one of us is trying to kill her."

"Well, yes. It's odd—"

"It's not just odd, it's downright dangerous. Dangerous for her to walk around in such a paranoid state, and dangerous for Dan and me. It's our reputations she's smearing."

"Because on the surface you both appear to have every reason to want her out of the way."

Janet's lips compressed—a mild reaction, I thought, to what I'd implied. "On the surface, I suppose that is how it looks," she said. "But as far as I'm concerned Laurie is welcome to our father's money. I had a good job in the public relations department in Newingham Development; I saved and invested my salary well. After my father died, I quit working there, and I'm about to open my own public relations firm."

"Did the timing of your quitting have anything to do with Laurie's inheriting the company?"

Janet picked up a porcelain ashtray and carefully stubbed her cigarette out. "I'll be frank with you, Ms McCone: It did. Newingham Development had suddenly become not a very good place to work; people were running scared—they always do when there's no clear managerial policy. Besides . . ."

"Besides?"

"Since I'm being frank, I may as well say it. I did not want to work for my spoiled little bitch of a sister who's always had things her own way. And if that makes me a potential murderer—"

She broke off as the front door opened. We both looked that way. A man wearing a shabby tweed coat and a shocking purple scarf and aviator sunglasses entered. His longish black hair was windblown, and his sharp features were ruddy from the cold. He pocketed a key and started for the stairway.

"Laurie's not here, Dolph," Janet said.

He turned. "Where is she?"

"Gone shopping."

"Laurie hates to shop."

"Well, that's where she is. You'd better come back in a couple of hours." Janet's tone did little to mask her dislike.

Nor did the twist of his mouth mask *his* dislike of his fiancée's sister. Without a word he turned and strode out the door.

I said, "Dolph Edwards?"

"Yes. You can see what I mean."

Actually, I hadn't seen enough of him, and I decided to take the opportunity to talk to him while it was presented. I thanked Janet Newingham for her time and hurried out.

*  *  *

Dolph's motorcycle was parked at the curb near the end of the front walk, and he was just revving it up when I reached him. At first his narrow lips pulled down in annoyance, but when I told him who I was, he smiled and shut the machine off. He remained astride it while we talked.

"Yes, I told Laurie it would be better to stick with All Souls," he said when I mentioned the context in which I'd first heard of him. "You've got good people there, and you're more likely to take Laurie's problem seriously than some downtown law firm."

"You think someone *is* trying to kill her, then?"

"I know what I see. The woman's sick a lot lately, and those two—" he motioned at the house "—hate her guts."

"You must see a great deal of what goes on here," I said. "I noticed you have a key."

"Laurie's my fiancée," he said with a puritanical stiffness that surprised me.

"So she said. When do you plan to be married?"

I couldn't make out his eyes behind the dark aviator glasses, but the lines around them deepened. Perhaps Dolph suspected what Janet claimed: that Laurie didn't really intend to marry him. "Soon," he said curtly.

We talked for a few minutes more, but Dolph could add little to what I'd already observed about the Newingham family. Before he started his bike he said apologetically, "I wish I could help, but I'm not around them very much. Laurie and I prefer to spend our time at my apartment."

I didn't like Dan or Janet Newingham, but I also didn't believe either was trying to poison Laurie. Still, I followed up by explaining the situation to my former lover and now good friend Greg Marcus, lieutenant with the SFPD homicide detail. Greg ran a background check on Dan for me, and came up with nothing more damning than a number of unpaid parking tickets. Janet didn't even have those to her discredit. Out of curiosity, I asked him to check on Dolph Edwards, too. Dolph had a record of two arrests involving political protests in the late seventies— just what I would have expected.

At that point I reported my findings to Laurie and advised her to ask her brother and sister to move out of the house. If they wouldn't, I said, she should talk to Hank about invalidating that clause of her father's will. And in any case she should also get herself some psychological counseling. Her response was to storm out of my office. And that, I assumed, ended my involvement with Laurie Newingham's problems.

But it didn't. Two weeks later Greg called to tell me that Laurie had been taken ill during a family cocktail party and had died at the St. Francis Wood house, an apparent victim of poisoning.

I felt terrible, thinking of how lightly I had taken her fears, how easily I'd accepted her brother and sister's claims of innocence, how I'd let Laurie down when she'd needed and trusted me. So I waited until Greg had the autopsy results and then went to his office at the Hall of Justice.

"Arsenic," Greg said when I'd seated myself on his visitor's chair. "The murderer's perfect poison: widely available, no odor, little if any taste. It takes the body a long time to eliminate arsenic, and a person can be fed small amounts over a period of two or three weeks, even longer, before he or she succumbs. According to the medical examiner, that's what happened to Laurie."

"But why small amounts? Why not just one massive dose?"

"The murderer was probably stupid enough that he figured if she'd been sick for weeks we wouldn't check for poisons. But why he went on with it after she started talking about someone trying to kill her . . ."

"He? Dan's your primary suspect, then?"

"I was using 'he' generically. The sister looks good, too. They both had extremely strong motives, but we're not going to be able to charge either until we can find out how Laurie was getting the poison."

"You say extremely strong motives. Is there something besides the money?"

"Something connected to the money; each of them seems to need it more badly than they're willing to admit. The interim management of Newingham Development has given Dan his

notice; there'll be a hefty severance payment, of course, but
he's deeply in debt—gambling debts, to the kind of people who
won't accept fifty-dollar-a-week installments. The sister had
most of her savings tied up in one of those real estate investment partnerships; it went belly up, and Janet needs to raise
additional cash to satisfy outstanding obligations to the other
partners."

"I wish I'd known about that when I talked with them. I
might have prevented Laurie's death."

Greg held up a cautioning hand. "Don't blame yourself for
something you couldn't know or foresee. That should be one of
the cardinal rules of your profession."

"It's one of the rules, all right, but I seem to keep breaking it.
Greg, what about Dolph Edwards?"

"He didn't stand to benefit by her death. Laurie hadn't made
a will, so everything reverts to the brother and sister."

"No will? I'm surprised Hank didn't insist she make one."

"According to your boss, she had an appointment with him
for the day after she died. She mentioned something about a
change in her circumstances, so I guess she was planning to
make the will in favor of her future husband. Another reason
we don't suspect Edwards."

I sighed. "So what you've got is a circumstantial case against
one of two people."

"Right. And without uncovering the means by which the
poison got to her, we don't stand a chance of getting an
indictment against either."

"Well . . . the obvious means is in her food."

"There's a cook who prepares all the meals. She, a live-in
maid, and the family basically eat the same things. On the night
she died, Laurie, her brother and sister, and Dolph Edwards all
had the same hors d'oeuvres with cocktails. The leftovers tested
negative."

"And you checked what she drank, of course."

"It also tested negative."

"What about medications? Laurie probably took pills for her
asthma. She had an inhaler—"

"We checked everything. Fortunately, I caught the call and
remembered what you'd told me. I was more than thorough.

Had the contents of the bedroom and bathroom inventoried, anything that could have contained poison was taken away for testing."

"What about this cocktail party? I know for a fact that neither Dan nor Janet liked Dolph. And according to Dolph, they both hated Laurie. He wasn't fond of them, either. It seems like an unlikely group for a convivial gathering."

"Apparently Laurie arranged the party. She said she had an announcement to make."

"What was it?"

"No one knows. She died before she could tell them."

Three days later Hank and I attended Laurie's funeral. It was in an old-fashioned churchyard in the little town of Tomales, near the bay of the same name, northwest of San Francisco. The Newinghams had a summer home on the bay, and Laurie had wanted to be buried there.

It was one of those winter afternoons when the sky is clear and hard, and the sun is as pale as if it were filtered through water. Hank and I stood a little apart from the crowd of mourners on the knoll, near a windbreak of eucalyptus that bordered the cemetery. The people who had traveled from the city to lay Laurie to rest werc an oddly assorted group: dark-suited men and women who represented San Francisco's business community; others who bore the unmistakable stamp of high society; shabbily dressed Hispanics who must have been clients of the Inner Mission Self-Help Center. Dolph Edwards arrived on his motorcycle; his inappropriate attire—the shocking purple scarf seemed several shades too festive—annoyed me.

Dan and Janet Newingham arrived in the limousine that followed the hearse and walked behind the flower-covered casket to the graveside. Their pious propriety annoyed me, too. As the service went on, the wind rose. It rustled the leaves of the eucalyptus trees and brought with it dampness and the odor of the nearby sea. During the final prayer, a strand of my hair escaped the knot I'd fastened it in and blew across my face. It clung damply there, and when I licked my lips to push it away, I tasted salt—whether from the sea air or tears, I couldn't tell.

As soon as the service was concluded, Janet and Dan went back to the limousine and were driven away. One of the Chicana women stopped to speak to Hank; she was a client, and he introduced us. When I looked around for Dolph, I found he had disappeared. By the time Hank finished chatting with his client, the only other person left at the graveside besides us and the cemetery workers was an old Hispanic lady who was placing a single rose on the casket.

Hank said, "I could use a drink." We started down the uneven stone walk, but I glanced back at the old woman, who was following us unsteadily.

"Wait," I said to Hank and went to take her arm as she stumbled.

The woman nodded her thanks and leaned on me, breathing heavily.

"Are you all right?" I asked. "Can we give you a ride back to the city?" My old MG was the only car left beyond the iron fence.

"Thank you, but no," she said. "My son brought me. He's waiting down the street, there's a bar. You were a friend of Laurie?"

"Yes." But not as good a friend as I might have been, I reminded myself. "Did you know her through the center?"

"Yes. She talked with my grandson many times and made him stay in school when he wanted to quit. He loved her, we all did."

"She was a good woman. Tell me, did you see her fiancé leave?" I had wanted to give Dolph my condolences.

The woman looked puzzled.

"The man she planned to marry—Dolph Edwards."

"I thought he was her husband."

"No, although they planned to marry soon."

The old woman sighed. "They were always together. I thought they were already married. But nowadays who can tell? My son—Laurie helped his own son, but is he grateful? No. Instead of coming to her funeral, he sits in a bar. . . ."

\* \* \*

I was silent on the drive back to the city—so silent that Hank, who is usually oblivious to my moods, asked me twice what was wrong. I'm afraid I snapped at him, something to the effect of funerals not being my favorite form of entertainment, and when I dropped him at All Souls, I refused to have the drink he offered. Instead I went downtown to City Hall.

When I entered Greg Marcus's office at the Hall of Justice a couple of hours later, I said without preamble, "The New-ingham case: You told me you inventoried the contents of Laurie's bedroom and bathroom and had anything that could have contained poison taken away for testing?"

"Right."

"Can I see the inventory sheet?"

He picked up his phone and asked for the file to be brought in. While he waited, he asked me about the funeral. Over the years, Greg has adopted a wait-and-see attitude toward my occasional interference in his cases. I've never been sure whether it's that he doesn't want to disturb what he considers to be my shaky thought processes, or that he simply prefers to leave the hard work to me.

When the file came, he passed it to me. I studied the inventory sheet, uncertain of exactly what I was looking for. But something was missing there. What? I flipped the pages, then wished I hadn't. A photo of Laurie looked up at me, brilliant blue eyes blank and lifeless. No more cheerleader out to save the world—

Quickly I flipped back to the inventory sheet. The last item was "1 handbag, black leather, & contents." I looked over the list of things from the bathroom again and focused on the word "unopened."

"Greg," I said, "what was in Laurie's purse?"

He took the file from me and studied the list. "It should say here, but it doesn't. Sloppy work—new man on the squad."

"Can you find out?"

Without a word he picked up the phone receiver, dialed, and made the inquiry. When he hung up he read off the notes he'd made. "Wallet. Checkbook. Inhaler, sent to lab. Vitamin cap-sules, also sent to lab. Contact lens case. That's all."

"That's enough. The contact lens case is a two-chambered plastic receptacle holding about half an ounce of fluid for the lenses to soak in. There was a brand-new, unopened bottle of the fluid on the inventory of Laurie's bathroom."

"So?"

"I'm willing to bet the contents of that bottle will test negative for arsenic; the surface of it might or might not show someone's fingerprints, but not Laurie's. That's because the murderer put it there *after* she died, but *before* your people arrived on the scene."

Greg merely waited.

"Have the lab test the liquid in that lens case for arsenic. I'm certain the results will be positive. The killer added arsenic to Laurie's soaking solution weeks ago, and then he removed that bottle and substituted the unopened one. We wondered why slow poisoning, rather than a massive dose; it was because the contact case holds so little fluid."

"Sharon, arsenic can't be ingested through the eyes—"

"Of course it can't! But Laurie had the habit, as lots of contact wearers do—you're not supposed to, of course; it can cause eye infections—of taking her lenses out of the case and putting them into her mouth to clean them before putting them on. She probably did it a lot because she had allergies and took the lenses off to rest her eyes. That's how he poisoned her, a little at a time over an extended period."

"Dan Newingham?"

"No. Dolph Edwards."

Greg waited, his expression neither doubting nor accepting.

"Dolph is a social reformer," I said. "He funded that Inner Mission Self-Help Center; it's his whole life. But its funding has been cancelled and it can't go on much longer. In Janet New-ingham's words, Dolph is intent on keeping it going 'no matter what.'"

"So? He was going to marry Laurie. She could have given him plenty of money—"

"Not for the center. She told me it was a 'hopeless mess.' When she married Dolph, she planned to help him, but in the 'right way.' Laurie has been described to me by both her brother and sister as quite single-minded and always getting what she wanted. Dolph must have realized that too, and knew her money would never go for his self-help center."

"All right, I'll take your word for that. But Edwards still didn't stand to benefit. They weren't married, she hadn't made a will—"

"They *were* married. I checked that out at City Hall a while ago. They were married last month, probably at Dolph's insistence when he realized the poisoning would soon have a fatal effect."

Greg was silent for a moment. I could tell by the calculating look in his eyes that he was taking my analysis seriously. "That's another thing we slipped up on—just like not listing the contents of her purse. What made you check?"

"I spoke with an old woman who was at the funeral. She thought they were married and made the comment that nowadays you can't tell. It got me thinking. . . . Anyway, it doesn't matter about the will because under California's community property laws, Dolph inherits automatically in the absence of one."

"It seems stupid of him to marry her so soon before she died. The husband automatically comes under suspicion—"

"But the poisoning started long *before* they were married. That automatically threw suspicion on the brother and sister."

"And Dolph had the opportunity."

"Plenty. He even tried to minimize it by lying to me: he said he and Laurie didn't spend much time at the St. Francis Wood house, but Dan described Dolph as being around all the time. And even if he wasn't he could just as easily have poisoned her lens solution at his own apartment. He told another unnecessary lie to you when he said he didn't know what the announcement Laurie was going to make at the family gathering was. It could only have been the announcement of their secret marriage. He may even have increased the dosage of poison, in the hope she'd succumb before she could reveal it."

"Why do you suppose they kept it secret?"

"I think Dolph wanted it that way. It would minimize the suspicion directed at him if he just let the fact of the marriage come out after either Dan or Janet had been charged with the murder. He probably intended to claim ignorance of the com-

munity property laws, say he'd assumed since there was no will
he couldn't inherit. Why don't we ask him if I'm right?"

Greg's hand moved toward his phone. "Yes—why don't we?"

When Dolph Edwards confessed to Laurie's murder, it turned
out that I'd been absolutely right. He also added an item of
further interest: he hadn't been in love with Laurie at all, had
had a woman on the Peninsula whom he planned to marry as
soon as he could without attracting suspicion.

It was too bad about Dolph; his kind of social crusader had
so much ego tied up in their own individual projects that they
lost sight of the larger objective. Had Laurie lived, she would
have applied her money to any number of worthy causes, but
now it would merely go to finance the lifestyles of her greedy
brother and sister.

But it was Laurie I felt worst about. And it was a decidedly
bittersweet satisfaction that I took in solving her murder, in
fulfilling my final obligation to my client.

# CHARLOTTE MACLEOD

# THE UNLIKELY DEMISE OF COUSIN CLAUDE

You know how it is around a medical research laboratory about half past five on a Friday afternoon. Or maybe you don't, but it certainly is. So when Carter-Harrison emerged from the fastness wherein he does whatever he does and suggested a spot of research involving a couple of boiled lobsters and a seidel or two, I cheerfully acquiesced.

We were nicely settled in a booth at Ye Old Lobster Trappe, a Boston landmark since 1973, with our paper bibs around our necks and our nutcrackers at the ready when Carter-Harrison remarked, "You ought to taste a real lobster, Bill."

"I'm about to," I replied as the waitress, whose name is neither Marge nor Myrtle but in fact Melpomene, set one in front of me. My companion, a man of science first and foremost, reached across the table and tore off one of its claws, which he proceeded to excavate and consume the meat thereof.

"Not bad, considering," he admitted, wiping melted butter off his chin. "But wait till you toss a bicuspid over a genuine Beagleport lobster, hauled from the briny blue Atlantic about fourteen minutes before you get your grubhooks into it."

"You owe me a claw," I said. "Where's Beagleport?"

Carter-Harrison ate one of his own claws—or, to be scientifically accurate, one of his own lobster's claws—and wiped more melted butter off his chin. He has one of those long, bony New England jaws ideally adapted for getting dripped on. Then he punctiliously gave me his other claw. Then he uttered.

"Did I ever tell you about my family?"

"I never knew you had one," I replied. "I thought you sprang full-armored from the brow of Dr. Spock."

He thought that one over for a while. "Ah, I see. One of your jokes. No, Williams, I was born pretty much according to normal procedure, of not exactly poor and almost ridiculously honest parents, in the village of Beagleport, Maine."

"I'll bet you were a beautiful baby," I said with my mouth full of tail meat.

"My mother always thought so. That's why she insisted on splicing her maiden name of Carter to the parental cognomen. My parents have now passed to the Great Beyond, namely Palm Springs, but the old family homestead is still occuped by my Aunt Agapantha and my cousins Ed and Fred. I was thinking we might take a run up there this weekend."

"Are you sure this is the right time of year to go?" I asked, gazing out the window at the lashing sleet that gives our city so much of its gentle springtime charm.

"The perfect time," he assured me. "We won't run into any tourists."

"I wouldn't mind running into some tourists," I said, but he wasn't listening. These excessively brainy types never do.

And that's why, some three hours later, we were groping our way up the Maine Turnpike in my old Chevy. I was groping, anyway, trying to sort out the road from the surrounding frozen wastes by the occasional glimpses I was able to get through my slush-caked windshield. Carter-Harrison was thinking deep thoughts. At least I assumed he was. He never said.

By ten o'clock, I'd had it. We found a motel open somewhere between Kittery and the Arctic Circle, and turned in. I woke expecting more of the same, but Saturday dawned crisp and clear. We got out of the motel early—there wasn't much there to hang around for—and fetched Beagleport around the middle of the morning.

Carter-Harrison started barking orders like, "Left at the fire station," and "Right at the general store." At last he sat back with a sigh of relief. "Now, we're on the home road."

"This is a road?" I cried in startled disbelief.

He didn't answer. He was busy sniffing, his bony nose straight forward like a bird dog's at the point, his bony cheeks flushed, the way they get when he's about to give birth to another bright idea. I felt an ominous twinge.

"What's eating you?" I said.

"It's the air," he replied.

There sure was a lot of it. I tried a few sniffs myself, a rich blend of salt, pine trees, and ancient vehicles. We sniffed our way along until we came to two houses, one of them painted baby blue with scalloped pink shutters. The other was merely white. It was when we reached this latter that Carter-Harrison yelled, "Starboard your helm."

"Huh?" I said.

"Turn right. This is our driveway."

And so it proved to be. Ah, I thought, civilization at last. Then a powerful voice welled up from the bulkhead and ricocheted off my eardrums.

"What in time are you settin' there for like a pair o' ninnies?"

Carter-Harrison leaped from the car. "Hello, Aunt Aggie."

"Well, James. I might of known. Couldn't you of wrote first?"

A woman of uncertain years wearing an awfully certain kind of expression emerged and confronted her nephew. She was almost as tall as he, though not so skinny. After a certain amount of glaring back and forth, he bent his head to kiss her on the cheek. She let him. Neither of them appeared to enjoy it much. I thought I might as well join the party, so I got out of the car and Aunt Aggie turned her glare on me.

"Who's the young 'un?"

"My colleague, Dr. Bill Williams," Carter-Harrison told her. "I brought him up to see the place."

"Doctor, eh?" She hauled a pair of gold-rimmed spectacles out of her sweater pocket, gave them a wipe with her apron, put them on, and looked me over. "Huh, he don't even look dry behind the ears yet. 'Least he ain't all skin an' bones like you, James. Ain't enough meat on you to grease a griddle with. Well, come on in. Can't stand here lollygaggin' around the dooryard all day. Oh, drat an' tarnation! Go on, git! Scat! Shoo!"

At first I thought Aunt Aggie meant us, but it soon became clear she was addressing a large brown goat with white spots. As she pursued it across the yard, we could see the creature was chewing on a piece of rag. She made pretty good time, but the goat was faster. At last she came back, her apron at half-mast, her expression one of mingled fury and despair.

"There went the last o' my good pillowcases. I'd like to wring that critter's neck."

"Then why don't you?" asked her nephew, ever the keen, inquiring mind.

" 'Cause he ain't my goat, that's why."

"Ergo, why do you let him into the yard?"

"I don't let him, you dern fool. He comes."

"Isn't there any way to keep him out?"

"Might try a deer rifle, but I misdoubt he'd just eat the bullet an' want another."

"Have you thought of building a fence?" I asked her.

She gave me a look. "Ed an' Fred spent fifty-two hard-earned dollars on barbed wire, an' three days' worktime stringin' it. He'd et his way through an' bit the tail off Fred's Sunday shirt before they'd got the posthole digger put away."

"You ought to sue his owner for damages."

"That's real bright o' you, Willie."

"Well," said Carter-Harrison, "why don't you?"

"Because," said Aunt Aggie, "that's why."

She nodded over toward the baby blue house with the pink shutters. A fluffy little blonde with a fluffy pink coat on was tripping winsomely down the steps. The goat ran to meet her, and she flung her arms around its neck.

"Oh, you naughty Spotty," we heard her coo. "What have you got in your mouth?"

She came across the yard to us, snugging the goat against her pink fluff. "Has Spotty been a bad boy again, Auntie Agapantha?"

I expected Auntie Agapantha to snap the blonde's head off and swallow it in one gulp. Instead, she only shrugged.

" 'Twasn't nothin', Lily Ann. Just an old dishrag."

"I've told him and told him." Lily Ann gave her curls a sad little shake. "I've said time and time again, Spotty, if you don't leave Auntie Agapantha's clothesline alone, I'll have to give you a spanking. But he never pays a mite of attention."

"Now, don't you fret yourself," Aunt Aggie insisted. "Lily Ann, I don't believe you've met my nephew James that's a doctor down to Boston. An' this here's his friend William that helps around the hospital some. Lily Ann's the one that married Cousin Claude, James. You remember I told you Claude got married?"

"Yep," said Carter-Harrison. "And killed. Did they ever find the murderer?"

Lily Ann burst into tears. Carter-Harrison began to look uncomfortable but didn't drop the subject.

"Stands to reason, doesn't it?" he said. "Claude was supposed to have caught his necktie in the cream separator and been strangled to death. Whoever wore a necktie separating cream? Claude wouldn't have known how to tie one anyway, even if he'd owned a necktie, which he didn't."

"He did s-so," sobbed Lily Ann. "He w-wore a tie at our wedding."

"Rented it with the suit," snorted Carter-Harrison.

"And I g-gave him another one for Christmas. He w-wore it because he l-loved me."

The young widow settled down to some serious bewailment. Aunt Aggie gave her eminent nephew what can best be described as a look.

Then she put her arm around Lily Ann's shoulders and led her away toward the baby blue house with the pink shutters. We two were standing there feeling like a nickel apiece when an old pickup truck clunked into what I had been assured was the driveway. Two men got out, one a clone of the other, though it would have been impossible to say which was the original and which the copy. They were both wearing ragged blue work shirts, ragged gray work pants, and ragged navy blue pea jackets. Both looked a lot like Carter-Harrison.

"Hahyah, James," said one.

"Hahyah, James," said the other.

"Hahyah, Fred. Hahyah, Ed," said James, as I may as well call him. "This is Bill Williams, a friend of mine from the lab. My cousins Ed and Fred, Bill."

"Hahyah, Ed. Hahyah, Fred," I replied. "Mind my asking which is which?"

"We don't mind," said Ed, or Fred.

"But it wouldn't do no good," said Fred, or Ed.

"You'd mix us up anyway."

"Folks always do."

"So do we, sometimes."

"What ails Lily Ann?"

"She's cryin' again."

The first part of our conversation had been amiable enough, but these last two remarks were made in definitely accusatory tones. It was clear that both Ed and Fred had strong feelings about Lily Ann.

"It's because I just happened to ask who murdered Claude," James explained.

"Some Boy Scout, maybe," said one twin.

"Doin' his good deed for the day," said the other.

"Lily Ann done all right out of it."

"Got rid o' Claude."

"Got his folks' house."

"An' the farm. Fifty acres, prime land. Prime for Beagleport, anyways."

"Seaweed makes good top dressin'. Lot o' seaweed been spread over them acres down through the years."

"Raise anything you've a mind to."

"Lily Ann's not farming it herself, is she?" James broke in.

"Nope. Rents it to Abner Glutch."

"Abner Glutch? I thought he owned the hardware store."

"Does."

"Owns the fillin' station, too."

"Gets men to run 'em for him."

"Got eight, nine workin' for him now."

"Makin' money hand over fist."

"Come to think of it," said James, "didn't I hear something about his trying to buy Claude out when his parents died?"

"Ayup. Claude wouldn't sell."

"Claude would of sold." It was the first sign of disharmony between Ed and Fred. "Mother wouldn't let 'im. Told 'im he'd blow the money in two, three years, then where'd he be?"

" 'Bout where he is now, like as not. Damn shame the poor bugger never got the chance to spend it."

"Would of left Lily Ann holdin' the short end o' the stick."

"Then she'd of needed a new husband, wouldn't she?"

Aha, I thought. Now we were getting to the crux of the matter.

"She could hardly have picked a worse one than Claude," said James. "I can't imagine why she'd cry over a clown like that. Claude had an I.Q. of about fifty-six and looked just like that blasted goat. Beats me what she ever saw in him."

"Beats me," Ed affirmed.

"Beats me," Fred agreed.

At least they both said it beat them, though I'm not sure of the order. I was comparing one craggy face with another, and it appeared to me that they all three looked about equally besotted with Lily Ann.

You may argue that it was impossible for Dr. James Carter-Harrison to have become smitten by a fluffy blond head and a weepy blue eye in so short a space of time, but that's because you don't know Dr. James Carter-Harrison. He'd already fallen in love three times during that same week, all three with semi-disastrous results. Maybe this was a family trait. Anyway, it made me nervous.

"Let's go take a look at that clothesline your aunt was complaining about," I suggested, to divert his attention. "It's cold standing here."

None of the three cousins answered me, they just wheeled and stomped around behind the house, two of them wearing seaboots and the other walking as if he did. I was a little surprised they'd been so willing to let the subject be changed, then I wasn't. If in fact Claude Harrison had been wilfully done to death by the unlikely instruments of a necktie and a cream separator, it was not beyond the bounds of possibility that one of Lily Ann's lovestruck neighbors might have had a hand and possibly even a cravat in his sudden demise.

Since I was going to be their houseguest, I thought it would be rude to pursue the matter. Instead, I joined the cousins in grim contemplation of Aunt Aggie's clothes reel.

"Pitiful," was my diagnosis, and nobody disputed it. The upper halves of various items were hung on the lines that stretched among the various poles that poked out from the center like the ribs of an umbrella only less so, if you get my drift. You've seen the things, you know what I mean. Anyway, the bottoms of said items were either hanging in shreds or missing altogether. Around the pole lay the remains of attempted fortifications: shattered picket fencing, tangles of chicken wire, oil drums, and suchlike futile measures.

"Have you tried land mines?" I suggested.

"Can't do that," said one twin.

"Lily Ann wouldn't like it," said the other.

"Can't say I'd go for 'em much myself," snapped a now-familiar voice behind us.

"Oh hello, Aunt Aggie," said James. "Have you tried cayenne pepper in the rinse water?"

"He found it appetizin'. Speakin' of which, I s'pose you're hungry as usual."

"We had a snack at the motel."

"Huh."

She tossed her head toward the kitchen. We followed. This turned out to have been the correct move. She fed us home-cured ham, new-laid eggs, home-grown and home-hashed potatoes, homemade biscuits with homemade jam, and a few other odds and ends. I attempted a little light conversation to be polite, but James sat lost in thought. At last he quit chewing and spoke.

"Aunt Aggie, is there any place around here we could buy one of those supersonic dog whistles?"

"Ed got me one. Spotty swallered it."

"Well, I'll think of something," he muttered, absentmindedly helping himself to a few more biscuits.

He continued to ponder. You could practically hear the brains churning, or maybe it was the biscuits. At last, as his aunt was making a pointed remark about did we think we was going to set here all day, he leaped from his chair like Archimedes from his bath.

"I've got it! Mind if I borrow your truck, boys?"

"We was goin' to pick up a mess of lobsters," one of them demurred.

"Thought Bill here might like 'em," added the other.

"Might get a few extra."

"Ask Lily Ann over."

"We can go in my car," I said.

So we did, all but James, who drove off in the truck by himself whistling "I'm a Yankee Doodle Dandy."

His aunt followed his departure with a jaundiced eye. "Got another of his fool notions, I'll be bound. Been like that ever

since he was knee-high to a sculpin. Beats me how\
lived to grow up."

She was off on a stream of reminiscences. James l
been an ingenious little cuss, it appeared, right from
he'd tried to hatch a clutch of duck eggs in his Sunday rompers.

"But he's one of the most respected men in his field," I
protested. "We consider him a genius."

"Genius is as genius does," she sniffed.

They steered me down the shore road so I could view the
breaking waves dashing high on a stern and rockbound coast;
then we went back to the house, arriving in a dead heat with
James.

"Ah, good," he said. "I can use some help unloading."

"Go ahead, fellows," I said, quick-thinking as always. "I'll take
care of the lobsters."

Aunt Aggie had taken advantage of my good nature to make a
few extra stops, but I didn't care. There was a lot of nautical
language coming from the back yard and I figured I'd got the
best of the bargain. After I'd lugged in her manifold purchases,
though, she remarked that if there was a worse nuisance than a
man around the kitchen, she didn't know what it might be and
I better go see what them three out there was up to, so I went.

One of the twins was up on a ladder screwing a pulley into
the side of the house. The other was threading a vast amount of
new manila rope through some more pulleys that had been
attached to the center pole of the clothes reel. Carter-Harrison
was horsing around with one of those heavy gas cylinders we
see so many of back at the lab.

"Great idea," I exclaimed. "You're going to anaesthetize the
goat."

"I don't think Lily Ann would go much for that," said the twin
on the ladder.

"Me neither," said the one on the ground.

The goat wasn't saying anything, just sitting there waiting to
see where his next meal was coming from.

"Then what's in the tank?" I asked. "Oxygen? Isn't there
enough of that floating around up here already?"

"It's helium," Carter-Harrison explained. "Would you mind
stepping over to the truck and bringing us that brown baglike

object we took the precaution of leaving locked in the cab? Got the keys, Ed?"

"Fred's got 'em," said the man on the ladder.

Ah, at last I knew which twin was which. Provided Ed stayed up on the ladder, anyway. I took the key, said, "Thanks, Fred," to flaunt my newly acquired knowledge, and went to get the brown baglike object, still unscathed by goatly tooth. I could swear Spotty snickered when he saw it.

When I got back to the scene of the activity, Carter-Harrison had both hands full of rope and an end between his teeth. "Gaha bawoo? Gooh!"

Being expensively educated, I was able to translate. "Balloon? Is that what this is? What do you want it for?"

He spat out the rope end. "Elementary, my dear Williams. We hitch the balloon to the top of the clothes reel, Aunt Aggie hangs out her wash, we inflate the balloon with helium from the tank, then pay out enough line to raise the reel out of the goat's reach. The ropes will be fastened to those cleats up beside the window where she has her washing machine, so she needn't even go outdoors to raise or lower the reel, just haul it in as far as she wants."

By this time, his aunt's face had in fact appeared at the aforesaid window. Carter-Harrison hitched a short length of hose from the tank to the balloon, let the brown bag fall, then started paying out the guy ropes.

"See, Aunt Aggie, we've got 'er ballasted, and you can adjust the ropes to keep the pole upright. When you want to reel in, just give a tug on this hunk of fishline. That will pull the stopper out of the balloon and let the gas escape slowly. You just haul in your lines and she'll come up all standing."

He raised the reel about fifteen feet above the ground, then handed the guy ropes to Ed, who fastened them to the cleats beside the window, came down, and took away the ladder. Spotty made a few frantic leaps at the clothes flapping high above, then fell back, a shattered goat.

"I do declare, James," cried Aunt Aggie. "I b'lieve it's goin' to work. But what happens when that there gas tank gits empty?"

"Take it to Lem Maddox and he'll give you another."

"An' charge me a fortune for it, I'll be bound."

"Oh no. You're not paying for the tank, you know, just the gas."

"Huh. Forkin' out good money for a passel of wind."

Spotty made another futile leap.

"But I guess it'll be wuth it. You know what? I'm goin' upstairs an' get that old dress suit Uncle Hector wore to Warren G. Harding's inauguration. It ain't had a good airin' since Lily Ann got that dratted goat. Could you just haul that reel down for a minute an' let it up again without emptyin' the balloon, James? No sense wastin' gas when you just filled it."

"I expect we can manage. Go get the suit, Aunt Aggie."

By the time she returned, we'd collected an audience. Lily Ann was back, pinker and fluffier than before, and she had a man with her. Quite a large man, who looked a lot like Teddy Roosevelt in his later and portlier years. His name was Abner Glutch and he was wearing a necktie. In fact, as Aunt Aggie remarked, he was all togged out like a hog goin' to war.

"How come you're so fancy, Abner? It ain't Sunday till tomorrow, in case you lost count."

"Nope," he told her, "I ain't lost nothin'. I have gained me a helpmeet. Me an' Lily Ann just snuck off quietly by ourselves an' tied the knot."

"We didn't want any fuss," Lily Ann explained, "out of respect for Claude." She strove manfully, or rather womanfully, to keep the quiver out of her voice.

"Well, I swan!" cried Aunt Aggie.

I swanned, too. So Abner Glutch had found a way to get his pudgy mitts on the late Claude's ancestral acres, Aunt Agapantha notwithstanding. I looked at his necktie and wondered where he'd been when Claude got snarled up in the cream separator.

Now, it appeared, all we could do was celebrate the event. As soon as she'd finished hanging up her Uncle Hector's dress suit, to the admiration of all present except Spotty, Aunt Aggie invited everybody into the front parlor for tea and cake. The goat stayed outside, banging one of the oil drums around in hopeless frustration. Ed and Fred had been made to take off their seaboots before they joined the party, but I didn't think this was what made them so glum. They sat chomping down cake and looking as if they'd rather be out back with Spotty, banging oil drums around.

No doubt to disarm us into believing he loved Lily Ann for herself alone, Abner insisted on telling us what he was giving her for wedding presents. He'd already insured his life in her favor and deeded over both his store and his filling station.

"And I'm going to deed over the farm to Abner," said Lily Ann, sweet innocent that she was. "It's the least I can do."

"Not that I exactly what you'd call need it," said Abner, toying with his new wife's hand so everybody could get a good look at the sparkler she was wearing. "Business ain't been so bad."

He proceeded to tell us how good it was while Ed and Fred ate more cake and Aunt Aggie grew restive. As soon as she could get a word in, she started dropping a few hints about her own family.

"Well, us Harrisons ain't much on braggin' about what we got. Let's talk about somethin' more int'restin'. What was that you was tellin' me, Willie, about James flyin' clear out to California because all them bigwigs out there wanted to hear about the research he's doin'? Even paid 'is fare for 'im an' put a big piece in the paper, didn't they?"

"James, you never told us," cried Lily Ann.

"Oh, one honor more or less doesn't mean much to James," I said. "He's always winning some award or having some head of state or delegation of scholars drop in to offer him another research grant." That was true enough, Carter-Harrison's activities being more inscrutable than anybody else's and scholarly veneration for those great brains who are doing that which nobody else can figure out the whereof or whyfor being ever immense.

"Can't be much money in it," Abner snorted, "or he wouldn't be drivin' that rattletrap out there."

"Oh, that's mine," I said. "My kid brother's, I mean." I felt I owed this to Aunt Aggie. "My Ferrari's in the shop. James never drives himself. It wouldn't be quite the thing, you know, for a man in his position."

That was true enough, anyway. Carter-Harrison was too subject to sudden fits of cerebration to be allowed behind a wheel, but I didn't explain that bit. I was enjoying the smug look on Aunt Aggie's face. Lily Ann was impressed. Abner was irritated. Ed and Fred said they had to go an' practice.

"Practice what?" snapped their mother.

"Pistol shootin'. Volunteer police. You shoot, James?"

James said no, but he wouldn't mind trying. Lily Ann said if there was any shooting she was going home and hide under the chesterfield because guns scared her silly.

"Let's not even talk about horrid old guns. Let's go look at the balloon again."

So we all trooped out to look at the balloon, Ed and Fred strapping on their holsters in a what-the-heck sort of way as we went. As we stood goggling at James's latest miracle of science, Abner Glutch expressed the opinion that it struck him as a mighty bothersome sort of way to hang out a few duds. Furthermore, he didn't see why all that foolishness about letting out the helium was necessary. Why couldn't they just pull it down?

"They did," Aunt Aggie told him. "Ed an' Fred got on one rope an' Willie an' James on the other—"

"Huh! Seems to me a man with a little beef to his bones could do it single-handed."

"I'll bet Abner could," cried Lily Ann.

"He's welcome to try," snarled Carter-Harrison.

"Yep," said Ed and Fred in unison.

So Abner took off his jacket, revealing a pair of lavender suspenders with baby-blue forget-me-nots on them, no doubt a gift from Lily Ann, and hauled. By George, he was a powerful cuss at that. In no time flat, he had Uncle Hector's pantlegs dragging on the ground. Lily Ann applauded enthusiastically, then halted in mid-clap.

"Spotty, you bad boy! What are you—"

She got no further. A shot rang out. Abner Glutch sprawled on the ground. Uncle Hector's dress suit, released from his lifeless grasp, soared again skyward.

As doctors, Carter-Harrison and I dropped at once to our knees beside the fallen man. Diagnosis was no problem. There's something all too obvious about a bullet through the back of the head.

"We'll have to call the police, Aunt Aggie," said Carter-Harrison.

"We're the police," said Ed, or Fred.

"Sort of, anyways," said Fred, or Ed.

"Yes, well." Carter-Harrison groped for words to explain tactfully that it wasn't the done thing for suspects to arrest each other. Before he'd succeeded, Lily Ann screamed and fell into a swoon beside her dead bridegroom.

Aunt Aggie took over. "Pick 'er up, Fred. Take 'er in the house. Step lively. Ed, you call the state troopers. Some dern fool hunter takin' a potshot at that balloon to be cute, I'll be bound."

If I were a mother who had two sons with revolvers strapped to their waists and a grudge against the man who'd married the object of their combined affections, I might have said the same thing. But why would the hunter have waited till the balloon was on the ground with a group of people clustered around it before he shot?

I was cursing myself for not having made Ed and Fred drop their guns before they took off when I noticed Spotty. Be cussed and be darned if that goat hadn't rolled his oil drum up against the house, directly under the cleats from which Abner hadn't bothered to cast off the guy ropes. He was on top of the drum with his forehooves braced against the clapboards and his neck stretched out like a camel's, yanking down lengths of that new manila line and gobbling them up as if they'd been spaghetti.

"Hey," I yelled, but too late. The balloon was free, traveling low and fast over the treetops on an offshore breeze, carrying with it the clothes reel and Uncle Hector's dress suit. Carter-Harrison leaped to his feet.

"Williams, got your car keys?"

"Yes, but—"

"No buts. Come on."

"The police will think we're running away," I protested as he hustled me into the Chevy.

He didn't bother to answer, just licked his finger and held it out the car window to see how the wind was blowing. "South-southeast by a half east. She can't be more than three knots. Full speed ahead to the harbor."

"But if it's blowing out to sea—"

"Step on it."

I could see why he wanted me out of the way. I'd seen gunshot wounds enough during my internship in the emergency room. Abner had been shot from only a short distance, obviously by either Ed or Fred. It didn't matter which. The twins would both ditch their guns before the state troopers arrived, get hold of two others—it wouldn't be hard in hunting country—and swear those were the ones they'd been carrying. Aunt Aggie would back them up. Lily Ann wouldn't know the difference. The bullet would never be traced. Aunt Aggie's yarn of somebody taking a wild potshot at the balloon would hold. I was abetting a murder.

I knew it, and I kept going. I gunned that old can for all she was worth, praying the tires wouldn't pop or the engine fall out. We hurtled over rock and sand, through potholes and ditches, finally made it over the rise, and spied the balloon.

"Thar she blows!" cried Carter-Harrison. "Faster, Williams."

There was nothing ahead of us but a sharp slope and a lot of water. I whizzed downhill with my foot on the gas and my heart in my brakes, skidded out onto a wooden deck, and managed somehow to stop two feet from the end. Dead ahead of us, Uncle Hector's clawhammer coat was skimming the wavetops. Beside us, a lone lobsterman was standing in his boat with his mouth wide open and his eyes bulging. Again, Carter-Harrison grabbed my arm and hurled me aboard.

"Follow that clothes reel," he barked.

The lobsterman stared at Carter-Harrison, at the balloon, and at the twenty-dollar bill which I, with a flash of psychological insight, was waving under his nose. I added a second twenty. He nodded once, and cast off.

Out we pounded, into the chop. The clothes reel skipped along in front of us. Sometimes it was almost within our reach, then a ruffle of wind would send it skimming on ahead.

"Uncle Hector always was an exasperating old devil," muttered Carter-Harrison.

"I think I'm getting seasick," I said.

"Comin' on to blow," said the lobsterman.

With that, Carter-Harrison grabbed a boathook, poised it like a harpoon, and let fly. There came a giant pop, then a tangle of canvas and clothesline lay sprawled on the water.

"Oh, jolly good shot," I yelled.

"She's goin' down," grunted the lobsterman.

"Pole's too well balanced," groaned Carter-Harrison. Waiting not to repine, he tore off his windbreaker, kicked off his boots, and dived. Seconds later, his hand popped up among the wreckage, waving Uncle Hector's clawhammer coat like a soggy banner.

"Catch, Williams," he shouted. "I'm going down for the pants."

I retrieved the coat, laid it over a lobster trap, and stood by to help him aboard. As he reappeared, dripping and triumphant, I held out my hands.

"Take these first," he spluttered.

I grabbed the pinstriped bundle, tossed it behind me on the floorboards, and hauled him over the gunwale. "Got a blanket or something?" I asked the lobsterman.

He didn't speak or move, just stood there gaping down at Uncle Hector's trousers.

"Great balls of fire, they're alive!" Carter-Harrison bent and snatched up the writhing garment. Out of the left leg slithered a six-pound haddock.

"Don't s'pose you'd care to set 'em again?" suggested the lobsterman.

"No," said Carter-Harrison through chattering teeth. "I think we've caught what we're after."

He shook the pants again. Out of the hip pocket dropped a gun, one like Ed's or Fred's, but it wasn't Ed's or Fred's. On the butt were carved in fancy letters the initials C.H.

"C.H.," I gasped. "Not—not Carter—"

"No, not Carter. Claude. Claude Harrison."

"You don't mean Lily Ann—"

"Oh yes." Carter-Harrison had got his windbreaker around him now, and taken a medicinal snort out of a flat bottle the lobsterman produced from behind the bait tub. "It was obvious from the start. Lily Ann, as you must have noticed, is a remarkably attractive woman. I asked myself what somebody like her could see in an oaf like Claude."

"You asked Ed and Fred, too," I reminded him.

"So I did. They didn't know, either. Therefore, there could be only one reasonable answer."

"Fifty acres of prime seaweed," I cried.

"Precisely. Claude then died under circumstances that would have been considered mysterious if Claude hadn't been such a clumsy lout and Lily Ann such a persuasive weeper. The widow was free to reopen negotiations with Abner Glutch, which she now believes herself, no doubt, to have concluded satisfactorily. She probably didn't intend quite such a brief honeymoon, but the chance came up and she took it. We needn't waste any blame on ourselves for providing the opportunity, Williams. If the fortuitous combination of the clothes reel, the balloon, and Uncle Hector's dress suit hadn't provided her with a way to get rid of the murder weapon, she'd have thought of something else."

"I don't doubt it," I agreed. "Lily Ann must be a pretty darn smart operator, to have hauled out that gun and shot Abner, then ditched it in the old man's suit and kicked the oil drum over to where the goat could reach the ropes, all without anybody's noticing."

"I expect she had the gun already in her hand," said Carter-Harrison. "I noticed she had her hands tucked up inside the sleeves of that loose, fluffy coat she was wearing when we went outside. It's a natural thing for a woman to do on a chilly day, so why should anyone have thought anything of it? Then she yelled at the goat, and we all automatically turned our heads to look at him. That gave her a chance to shoot Abner. Of course he became the center of interest while she did her other little chores and pulled a faint so we wouldn't find her lacking in properly wifely concern. Well, we'd better get back to the house before she marries Ed or Fred."

I shook my head. "It won't be Ed or Fred. If you ask me, Lily Ann's looking forward to marrying a rich and famous doctor from Boston. Maybe I laid it on a bit thick."

"Good God!" Carter-Harrison picked up the haddock, wrapped it thoughtfully in Uncle Hector's coat, laid it back with the pants, and took another swig from the lobsterman's bottle.

"Well," he sighed, "someday perhaps I'll meet a woman who loves me for myself alone."

He was moody all the way home, sitting there with the haddock, the pistol, and Uncle Hector's suit in his lap. When we got there, Aunt Aggie was still doctoring Lily Ann for hysterics while the state troopers stood around looking helpless. When we showed them the revolver that had come out of Uncle Hector's hip pocket, though, and explained the modus operandi by which we believed it to have got there, Lily Ann recovered fast and demanded to be allowed to call her lawyer. They said she could do it from the station. She began to cry again, but it didn't seem to be helping her much. State troopers are smarter than men like Claude and Abner Glutch.

As they departed, Aunt Aggie faced her nephew, tight-lipped.

"Well, James, you've really done it this time."

"But, Aunt Aggie," he protested, "what else could I do? That woman would have wiped out half of Beagleport and never batted an eyelash if somebody hadn't stopped her."

"I ain't sayin' you was wrong. I'm just remindin' you of how Claude's father's will was wrote. When he died, the farm went to Claude. When Claude died, it went to Lily Ann. But a murderer ain't allowed to profit from 'er crime, which means Lily Ann never inherited at all. An' that means it comes back to us. An' that means the whole shebang, includin' that gol-dern goat."

"Oh gosh, Aunt Aggie," cried Carter-Harrison, as well he might. "Well, never mind. I'll think of something."

"Do me a favor," said his aunt. "Quit thinkin'. Now git on upstairs an' take off them wet clothes."

So that was that and there we were: Ed and Fred out in the back yard building a goat house for Spotty, James crouched beside the stove wearing an old flannel nightshirt of his Cousin Raymond's and soaking his feet in a pail of hot water and mustard, Aunt Aggie boning the haddock for chowder. Nobody was saying anything. I felt uncomfortable.

Finally I broke the silence. "Say, James, you know those things they have at the laundromat, that you put a quarter in and—"

He was alive again, his eyes flashing, his flannel-clad arms flailing, his feet spraying mustard water all over the carpet.

"That's it! Aunt Aggie, have you a mail order catalogue in the house?"

"I expect likely." She rubbed the fish smell off her hands with a hunk of cut lemon and went to get it. "Goin' to order yourself a new brain, James?"

"No, by thunder, I'm going to order you an automatic clothes dryer."

"A clothes dryer? Why, I never—well, now, that just might— you know, James, I always did suspicion there might be a speck of common sense under all that intellect of yours. Willie, go call in the twins an' tell 'em to get cleaned up for supper. I think it's about time we cooked you city folks a decent lobster."

# NANCY PICKARD
## I, WITNESS

Steve Krebs was stopped at a traffic signal on Ward Parkway, in the middle of three lanes of cars heading into Kansas City, when he happened to glance out his rolled-up window, through the rain, at the torrent pouring down Brush Creek. In that instant, he saw a man run to the edge of the flooding stream. What happened next was so shocking to Steve, and occurred so quickly, that he nearly didn't believe it, or even that he had seen it.

Between the changing of the traffic signal and the first surge of vehicles through the water in the intersection, Steve saw the man step to the very edge of the water.

Between the lifting of Steve's foot from the brake to the gas pedal, the man bent his knees, flung both of his arms back, and leaned forward at his waist.

Between the refusal of Steve's mind to believe what it was seeing and then its stunned acceptance, the man flung his arms straight out in front of him. His feet left the ground. Between the honking of the car behind him and Steve's responding pressure on his gas pedal, the man dived into the water that looked ten feet deep and twenty feet out of its banks—deadly, urgent water that was furiously propelled by six days of rain.

No. Steve's mind recoiled, rebelled. No. No!

He unconsciously turned his steering wheel in the same direction he was looking, and nearly sideswiped the car to his left. The driver leaned on her horn and stared at him before shooting ahead, away from the threat of his car. Shaking now, Steve straightened the steering wheel and pulled his car back between the white lines of the middle lane.

Hadn't anybody else seen it?

He risked a glance at the driver in the car to his right, but she was talking to her passenger, and laughing. He glanced across Brush Creek, to the traffic going in the opposite direction on the other side of the flooding waters, but nobody had stopped over there, either. Nobody was getting out of their cars and racing down the banks to the creek. Nobody honked frantically. Nobody in any of the cars surrounding him looked over at him in shared, stunned shock. Didn't anybody else see it? he wondered again.

His mind tried to refuse it again: Why would anybody dive into that flood? Nobody would do that. It was suicide. He'd never make it to the other bank. Steve felt helpless and shocked. People had been swept into Brush Creek and died in other floods. God. Oh, God. He should stop and go back and try to help, his emotions cried. But how could he stop, his mind argued, with so much traffic around him? In this rain, in rush hour, there was no place to pull over. And what would he do if he did stop? He couldn't dive in after the man because then they'd both drown. In a small corner of his mind a voice murmured, two minutes ago you were just a tired man driving home like everybody else. If you'd kept your eyes on the road, you wouldn't even have seen it.

But he had seen it. In that moment, when the traffic had slowed down, he had looked to his left to check the progress of the flood in the creek, and he had seen it. It was terrible, and terrifying, how a person's whole life could change completely in just a single moment, in just a moment! One minute you were alive, the next minute you were dead, one minute you had a job or a wife or a home, and the next you were fired or divorced or homeless, one minute you were safe, the next you weren't . . .

There was no red speck in the side mirror now as he approached the curve that led to the Alameda Plaza Hotel—only cars, rain, and more cars.

With a shaking right hand, Steve turned down the sound of the newscaster on National Public Radio and rolled his window down a couple of inches, letting in a cold spray that wet the side of his forehead, but outside there was no sound of shouting in the rain.

What can I *do?* he thought. But he knew it might be too late for that question, and that the more accurate one was: What could I have done?

In a couple of blocks he would reach the lower entrance to the hotel parking lot. He would stop there and call 911, he decided. But as he drove on, prevented from hurrying by the traffic, he thought: In a couple of blocks, that man could drown. He could be dying now. He could be dead. God. Help him. But as much as he meant that, Steve also meant: Help me!

The north entrance to the hotel was now half a block ahead of him. He managed to slide over to the right-hand lane and then to turn into the lot. Once inside the covered entrance, he parked in the circle drive and raced into the lower level of the hotel. He felt like shouting, "Help! Somebody's drowning! A man dived into the creek!" But figuring that would be more dramatic than efficient, he ran to the public phones, endured a strange, surrealistic moment of searching for a quarter's worth of change in his pockets, and punched in the emergency number.

"Nine-one-one."

"I just saw a man dive into Brush Creek." He tried to sound calm but urgent. "Has anybody called you about this?"

"No, sir."

"Oh. Well, I saw him dive in and it's really flooded there, I mean the water's going incredibly fast, and it's, uh, I don't know exactly where to tell you, but you know where the creek runs out of Kansas onto the Missouri side?" He didn't wait for her to affirm it. "Well, it's just west of the Plaza, you know? Between State Line and, uh, I think the first bridge, I guess. That's where he went in, although, God, he'd be a lot farther downstream by now if he didn't manage to get out. He was a white man." Steve felt self-conscious saying that to the operator, who sounded black to him. "He was wearing blue jeans and a red shirt, I think it was red, and he wasn't real tall, and he was maybe youngish, I don't know, maybe in his twenties." He was beginning to feel foolish in the face of her silence. "Uh, do you need to know anything else?"

"No, sir."

"Do you want my name, or my address?"

"No, sir. Thank you."

"Oh, well, you're welcome."

He hung up, feeling unsatisfied. Had she grasped the urgency of the situation? Maybe she didn't think it *was* urgent. Maybe people jumped into Brush Creek all the time, five or six a day, and they came out of it alive. Maybe this was no big deal to the cops, nothing even for him to be so concerned about. No, that couldn't be true. She was just used to life and death emergencies, and he wasn't.

Steve breathed deeply, stuck his hands in the pockets of his raincoat, and walked self-consciously back to his car. He wondered if any of the other people in the reception area had overheard him. He felt kind of important, although he also felt like ducking his head and running out before anybody got a good look at him. He wondered whether they thought he was a good citizen for reporting the incident. A lot of people wouldn't have done that much. Think of all those cruel people in New York who'd ignored that poor woman who was being killed. Or would they think he was a coward because he only called for help, because he hadn't actually tried to rescue the man who dived into the creek?

I couldn't stop! he wanted to protest.

Instead of getting back into his car, he walked up to the edge of the sidewalk outside the hotel. From there, he could see the traffic and the Country Club Plaza shopping center on the far side of Brush Creek, but he couldn't see the creek itself. He could hear it, though, even over the noise of the rain and the traffic. It was a frightening sound, he couldn't imagine diving into that sound. Normally, Brush Creek was only a trickle of water in the manmade storm drainage system that bisected Kansas City. It was a strangely beautiful creek for one that ran in a cement bed and was basically only a storm sewer. In the Plaza area where he stood, it was arched by elegant bridges and lined by gentle, green, tree-lined slopes. There were tennis courts along the banks of the creek, and playgrounds. On summer Sundays families brought their blankets and thermoses to listen to free concerts in the creekbed that was now under swiftly rising water.

A few years before, the creek had climbed so far out of its banks that it flooded the stores across the street, and had even flooded down into the hotel where Steve had placed his call. Cars had washed into the creek. People had drowned. He himself had been prevented from reaching home that terrible night because of flood waters in his path, and he had spent the night at a friend's house north of the Plaza. He remembered how disorienting it had been to see waters like lakes in the intersections where he usually drove home from work. And how terrifying it had been to think that he could have been washed out of his car and drowned, just trying to get home.

Home. Mirian would be wondering where he was by now. Not worrying, necessarily, or caring, but maybe wondering. He should have called her, too.

Hunching down into the collar of his coat, he stepped out onto the sidewalk, into the rain, and then kept walking until he could see the flood waters.

Cars splashed by him, their occupants staring at him.

I must look like a lunatic, he thought, standing out here in this downpour. He searched for a red shirt floating by, or a man in a red shirt clambering up on the banks of the creek, soaked but safe. The only red he saw was in the stop lights at the intersection of Brush Creek and Wornall Road. After they changed three times, he turned around and walked back to his car. On the drive home, he turned up the heater full blast to dry his shoes, socks, and pantlegs. Eventually, they stopped dripping, but they stuck to his skin and felt clammy.

Is he dead? Steve wondered, while a smaller, more urgent voice wondered, am I a coward?

When he opened the door from the garage, Mirian Krebs lowered the evening newspaper onto her lap. She watched him remove his raincoat, which looked soaked, and hang it over the edge of the door.

With fast strides, he crossed the hall, then the den, and walked into the screened-in porch where she sat in an armchair, her feet propped up on a hassock.

"Where have you been, Steve?"

"I saw a man jump into Brush Creek, Mirian!" It excited him to tell her, as if he had brought home a trophy to display to her. "I couldn't believe what I was seeing!" His hands and arms were moving in excited accompaniment to his words. "There I was, just driving along in the middle lane of Ward Parkway, and the traffic was so bad and the rain was pouring down, and I just happened to look at the creek. I mean, I just happened to look! And there he was, this guy in a red shirt and blue jeans, and he dived in the creek. I couldn't believe it, Mirian. It was insane. The water's rushing down there, it's so deep and there are whitecaps, you know how it gets, it's just going unbelievably fast. He just dived in!"

She looked at him as she always did lately, which was without expression except for a cynical, wary twist to her mouth. In the face of that intimidating show of indifference, Steve blinked and looked away from her.

"What are you doing out here?" he asked.

"Why not?" she said in a bored tone. The newspaper rustled in her lap as she crossed her legs at the ankles. "It's dry on this side of the pool. I like the rain. I like the thunder and lightning. It's warm enough to sit out here."

"It's kind of weird, don't you think?" He could barely hear her words over the clamor of the rain. "I mean, to sit on a screened-in porch during a thunderstorm?"

The silence with which she greeted that remark lasted long enough for one long rumble of thunder and a crash of lightning. Their screened-in porch was a large one, built more like Florida than Missouri, and big enough to contain their swimming pool. Outside, the rain poured off the two patio umbrellas in solid sheets that looked like cellophane wrappers. We should have lowered those umbrellas, he thought. Down the block, an electric transformer crackled; a blue glow flashed briefly around it. I hope we don't lose our power, he thought.

Finally she answered him, in a dry monotone in which each word sounded compressed with emotion, "Do you want to talk about weird, Steve?"

He stepped to the edge of the swimming pool and looked into the too-blue water. The rain blew through the screens just to the far side of the pool. That was funny, he thought—they could stay dry while going swimming. Steve turned around to face her, putting his back to the pool and the storm.

"Mirian, I keep thinking that I should have done something to help the guy, but I don't know what it would have been." He started pacing the side of the pool while she watched him, expressionless but for the twist to her mouth. "I couldn't very well stop the car in the middle of all that traffic, I might have caused a wreck, and then somebody would have been hurt for sure. And you know, there are only those big houses on the other side of the street, and maybe nobody was home for me to use their phone . . . So I had to go all the way to the Alameda to call 911 . . ."

She shrugged, the single gesture that chilled him the most, and said, "I think you did more than most people would have done, Steve."

He would have felt good about that if she hadn't then added, "You did what you could."

He knew that in her estimation that wasn't much.

"Have I missed the news?" he asked, looking at his watch at the same time. "No, good, maybe there'll be something on the news."

"I doubt it," she said.

"Why?" He crossed in front of her to turn on the set. "If somebody drowned or got rescued in Brush Creek, that would be big news. Look . . ."

She folded her hands on top of the newspaper with a resigned air and watched with him as the newscaster briefly summarized the major stories that would be covered. There was no mention of a rescue or a drowning in Brush Creek.

Steve switched to Channel 5, but found a weatherman talking about inches of rain and storm systems out west. There wasn't any mention of the story on Channels 9 or 41, either.

"Well, that's good," he said, turning down the sound.

"It is?" She sounded amused. "Why?"

"Because nobody drowned, Mirian."

"Maybe they haven't found him yet. *Steve."*

There it was again, that sudden, vicious edge to her voice. He should ask her about it, he knew he should, maybe she was even trying to goad him into confronting her about it, but he was afraid of that viciousness, he was afraid of how it might change his life.

He didn't want his life to change, so he looked away from her direct, level, waiting, brown-eyed gaze, and said, "Maybe there'll be something on the news tonight."

"There usually is."

Mirian! he thought.

"Are you hungry?" he asked.

"I thought we'd have chicken noodle soup and BLT's."

"That sounds good."

He wondered if that meant she would fix it. He was afraid to ask, for fear she'd say, "You break your arm? You can't open a can of soup?" But he was also afraid to start fixing it himself because she might say, "I can *fix* it. I was going to *fix* it, Steve."

He turned back around to face the pool, and tried to imagine it a torrent, and himself diving into it. She stared at his back.

"Why would anybody try to cross that creek, Mirian?"

"To get to the other side?"

"Very funny."

She sighed. "I don't know. Maybe he was drunk. Maybe he was high. Maybe he was crazy. Maybe he wanted to kill himself. Maybe he was diving for sunken treasure. Maybe he got tired of sitting in rush-hour traffic and decided to swim . . ."

Steve turned around suddenly, his face tense. "What would you have done, Mirian?"

"I would already have been home from work, Steve," she said with a sarcasm that started out slow and light and dry, but then built with each word into something as heavy and full and angry as the storm outside. The words seemed to get away from her, to get out from under her control so that each one was louder than the last, and by the end, she was screaming at him over the thunderous, pounding sound of the rain. "So I wouldn't have seen it at all, Steve. I wouldn't have been driving around aimlessly, pretending to be doing something, when in reality, I hadn't done anything at all, all day. For days. Weeks. Months! I wouldn't have seen it. I would have been too *busy.*"

Her last word was like a wasp driving its stinger into him, and he flinched with the pain of it. The force of her anger would have driven him back if he hadn't already been standing on the edge of the swimming pool. He stared at her, feeling a terrible desperation and thinking: Here it comes, here it comes.

She got up from the chair and advanced toward him.

"What did you really do today, Steve? While you weren't rescuing drowning men, I mean? Drive around? Have coffee?

Pretend to look for a job? Think up wild stories to come home and tell me, to justify your existence? Well, you don't exist any more. Not for me. Not for yourself. Not for any reason that I can detect. You don't live, you don't feel, you don't think, and God knows, you don't work!"

He turned around to look at the pool.

"Face me!" She walked up to him, put her hands on his shoulders, tried to turn him around. "Face yourself. Please, Steve, for God's sake . . ."

Carefully, he edged away from her. Without looking at her, he said, "I'll start the soup," and walked into the kitchen to prepare their dinner. The transformer down the street crackled, spit, and flashed blue. The lights went out and the television went dead.

He turned around to smile ruefully at her, and to shrug.

"Great," Mirian said, gazing hopelessly out at the rainy night. "Perfect."

There was nothing on the ten o'clock news about a drowning or a rescue, or even about anybody reported missing. The man must have climbed out on the other side and survived, Steve decided. He was ashamed of how let down he felt. He also felt embarrassed that he'd gotten so excited over nothing. But it could have ended differently, he told himself, it could have ended tragically.

Earlier, he and Mirian had eaten peanut butter sandwiches and fruit salad by candlelight in the dining room, not saying much. A few times Mirian had tried to raise the topics of paying bills or selling the house or seeing a counselor, but each time Steve had brought the subject back to the man in the creek until finally she had given up.

"You're not only out of a job," she had said, "but also out of touch with reality. We can't stay here, Steve, we can't keep this up. Things have got to change."

But he didn't want anything to change, except the subject of her conversation. After the news, he asked her if she'd like to go for a swim in the pool.

She looked at him as if he were crazy. "There's a thunderstorm, Steve, in case you hadn't noticed. No, thank you. People don't usually go swimming in electrical storms." She laughed, a sound full of sarcasm. "Except maybe your man in the red shirt and blue jeans."

So he waited until after she'd gone to bed before he took his swim. He stood at the edge of the deep end of the pool for a long moment, then he flung his arms behind him, bent his knees, leaned forward at the waist, and pushed off into a dive. He was fully clothed. The water was warm and it dragged at his clothes and he felt his shoes filling with it. He dived deep, until he touched the bottom with the fingertips of both hands, and then he surfaced quickly, pushing his head above the surface as if there were waves to surmount. He swam the length of the pool in quick, strong strokes, and then reversed his course. Again, again. He continued doing laps while the rain poured outside, and now and then the thunder rumbled and the lightning brightened the dark porch.

"*Steve!* What are you doing! Get out of there!"

Under his arm, he saw Mirian standing at the edge of the pool in her nightgown. She looked frightened. He pulled himself to the edge of the pool where she stood staring down at him.

"What's the matter with you?" She began to cry, and he reached out tenderly to touch her bare ankle. He was so grateful for this display of emotion, of kind emotion, for him. "Oh, Steve," she cried, "look at you, you still have all your clothes on."

Mirian bent down to hold her hands out to him, to help him out of the pool. Gratefully, he placed his weight in her small, shaking hands, allowing her to tug at him. Rescue me, he thought, rescue me. She pulled, but he was too heavy and the tile around the pool was too slick. Mirian slipped, falling not into the pool with him, but onto the side of it. Her head struck the tile, bounced, struck it again, and then fell into the water in the deep end of the pool. Mirian lay on her back, her head half under water, her hair floating. There was no choking, no attempt to breathe. She lay still. The water distorted things, making the top of her head look too large for her chin, which was out of the water. Her blood trickled into the swimming pool, turning the artificial blue a strange dark purple. Steve recoiled from it. He climbed out of the pool quickly before it touched him, and then pulled her out of the water by her feet. She wasn't breathing. He was sure she wasn't ever going to breathe again. He ran dripping into the kitchen to dial 911. But with his hand on the receiver, he looked down at himself.

They would ask why he had gone swimming with his clothes on. It would seem crazy. They would think he was crazy, that he had killed Mirian, that he had pulled her down on purpose.

"Oh, Mirian," he wept to the dial tone. "I'm sorry."

He couldn't let it happen. His life would change too much, and he didn't want his life to change.

Steve hung up the phone without calling 911. He walked, dripping, into their bedroom and rummaged through her closet. He didn't want the police seeing her like that, wearing that nightgown. He thumbed the hangers until he found a nice pair of blue jeans that she looked good in and a pretty red plaid shirt and her tennis shoes, and he carried them back onto the screened-in porch. After he had cleaned her and dressed her, he carried her to his car and laid her down gently in the back seat. Then he drove through the rain to the far east side of Kansas City, Missouri, where Brush Creek empties into the Little Blue River.

The next morning he called the police.

"Please." His voice shook with tears and exhaustion. He hadn't slept but had spent the rest of the night draining the pool, cleaning it, covering it with its canvas top. Outside, it was still raining. "My wife didn't come home from work last night, and I'm so worried about her. She's been depressed lately. The last time I saw her, she was wearing blue jeans and a red shirt. Have you . . . have you . . . had any reports of anybody fitting that description?"

# HERBERT RESNICOW
## THE MOONSTONE EARRINGS

I was in my pajamas, ready to settle down with a new whodunit—what else would I be doing on a Saturday night, no boy in Ethan Allen High would dare date me—my face covered with white goop guaranteed to remove all the freckles and make my skin like alabaster, when the phone rang. "Patsy, I need you desperately." Angela Phillips sounded hysterical. "Please come to my house right away. *Please.*"

*Angela Phillips?* Who—even though she was only a soph, like me—was positively going to be voted Most Beautiful and maybe also—though not with me—Most Popular? Who had practically never spoken one word to me from kindergarten on? And who always referred to me, even when I was close enough to hear, as Carrots? Not just because of my name, Patricia Carin Campbell—I'm proud of it, like Mom said I should be—but because in the first grade I played a carrot in the class play and my hair sort of matched the costume. Not really "sort of"; more like exactly. Now I'm "Patsy," huh? And *she* needs *me?* Boy, she had to be in real *big* trouble. "Why me?" I asked.

"You're the only one who can help me." She was almost crying. "Please, Patsy. *Hurry!*"

"What about Andy Besser?" I asked. Andy was a shoo-in for Class Brain, but he was pretty stupid in other ways. Important ways. "He's your date for tonight, isn't he?" I don't keep track of *everything* he does, only certain things.

"I absolutely *can't* ask him, and you read all those detective stories, Patsy, and you're so smart and strong and you can make people . . . Everybody *respects* you."

Oh, great. Just what I wanted: Most Respected. It was more than a year ago that I turned fourteen, when Mom revoked her permission for me to play intramural football, but they still remembered what I was like. At that time Mom also got me dresses and heels. Even in sneakers I was taller than most of the boys, but did Mom listen? "They'll soon outgrow you," she swore. She even made me wear a bra, an A cup, which I definitely didn't need then, and it ruined my life still further. Wearing clothes like that, I couldn't kid around with the other jocks any more. In jeans and sneakers, it was okay to be one of the boys, but once I put on dresses and heels, even low ones, I was the opposition sex. The girls were even worse. To them I was practically a traitor.

"Andy Besser is even smarter than I am," I pointed out, "and he reads whodunits too." How she ever got a boy as intelligent as Andy to date her, and as shy, I'll never know. I'd have to observe her more closely.

"I can't. He may be—uh—*involved.*" She said that last part as though . . . Could she be . . . ? And didn't know which boy . . . ? If that was it, why did she need me? What could I do? And why whodunits? Nope, it wasn't that.

"Why should I help you, Angela?" I asked. "I don't even *like* you." Probably the first time in her whole life anyone ever said that to her, and it felt real good to say it.

"I don't care." She was definitely hysterical. Everybody *had* to like Angela Phillips; it was her whole purpose in life.

"What do I get out of it?" Not that I'd ever go, but just to twist the knife. I'd never have a chance like this again.

"Just because everybody thinks my father is rich . . ." What a mind; she'd offer to go shopping with me next. "I have almost sixty dollars saved up that my father doesn't know about. You can have that."

I didn't want anything from her. We sure could use the money but—but suddenly I knew what to do. It was perfect. I could get what I really wanted and, at the same time, I could give Angela what she really deserved. Besides, I wanted to see how she was able to get Andy Besser to date her on a Saturday night at her house, instead of going to see one of his favorite old detective movies. And sit in the tenth row, on the aisle. And eat popcorn. Not that I *always* checked; just enough to confirm the pattern. Besides, I liked old detective movies, too, though he didn't seem to notice that. I was also dying to find out what horrible thing Angela had done that only I could save her from. And that Andy was involved in.

"Get a pen and paper," I said, "and write what I tell you: 'I promise to give Patricia Carin Campbell, on demand, anything she wants, provided that she—' and fill in what you want me to accomplish. Sign it and date it."

Of course it could all be a very funny joke: Angela bet her friends that she could get me to run over to her house on a Saturday night. "She never has a date," I could hear her say, "so she'll be home for sure." If that was it, no problem. I'd just punch her head in, period. Andy's too, just for being there. And for being so stupid. And shy. He was an inch and a quarter taller than me now, but I was stronger and much better coordinated, so that would be no trouble. In fact, I'd enjoy doing it.

"Come in the back door," Angela said. "I'll be waiting in the kitchen. I don't want the others to see you." Well, hired help uses the service entrance, I guess.

"I'll be over in seven minutes," I said, and hung up. Hard. I got my jogging shoes and wiped the freckle cream off my face. It wouldn't have worked anyway; nothing I'd tried did. Once when I rinsed my hair blond, so people would look at my hair instead of my freckles, I looked like the Bride of Frankenstein. Maybe I should rinse it darker? The freckles might be less noticeable that way. Very dark red? Almost auburn? I looked in the mirror. Useless. Too curly; practically frizzy. And wigs were *out.*

I held out my hand, palm up, as soon as Angela let me in. For a moment, she didn't catch on, but then she gave me the promissory note. I didn't bother reading it—she wouldn't dare try to cheat—just put it in my pocket. The paper was damp and crumpled and Angela's eyes were red and she looked real worried. What did she think I was going to ask for, her hand in marriage? In spite of everything, she looked absolutely terrific. All in white, with lace all over, a low-cut cocktail dress—and she was wearing her mother's moonstone jewelry! Mrs. Phillips *never* let anyone, *anyone,* even touch her moonstones, and I don't blame her.

It was the most romantic thing that had ever happened in

Rockhill. In all of New Hampshire, I bet. Everybody knows the
story. When Mr. Phillips was overseas—he wasn't rich then—
he saved all his pay and secretly bought moonstones, one by
one, matching them according to his dream. Moonstones were
pretty cheap in the olden days, but not on a soldier's pay, so he
just bought exactly the ones he needed. They don't look like
much; just smooth, oval pieces of dull glass. But when you put
them against black velvet, the way Mrs. Phillips wears them
once a year on her wedding anniversary, in candlelight, they
become beautiful, with a soft, light-blue glow inside, like—like
true love, soft and fine.

When he was discharged, Mr. Phillips got off in New York
instead of making his plane connection to Manchester. He went
to the jewelry district and found an old Yemenite silversmith, a
Jewish refugee whose dark eyes glowed when he saw the
moonstones and who knew exactly what to do with them. The
silversmith made heavy antique Middle Eastern settings for the
stones, and fashioned them into a set exactly as Mr. Phillips had
envisioned them in the jungle: a three-tiered necklace with a
teardrop pendant at the bottom, a heavy ring with a single huge
moonstone parallel to the finger, and a pair of earrings, with a
small circular stone at the top and a drop-shaped moonstone
hanging. It was the most beautiful loving thing I had ever seen.

Although he thought the jeweler charged him less than the
cost of the silver alone because he was a soldier, Mr. Phillips
spent every cent he had for the setting and for some food while
he was waiting, so he had to hitchhike home and he couldn't
buy anything to eat on the way. It took two days to get back.

Even though he didn't have a job yet and her father didn't
like him, he and Mrs. Phillips were married a month later. At
the reception, right after they cut the cake, Mr. Phillips asked
his bride to turn around and close her eyes. Right there, right
in front of everyone, he hung the moonstone necklace around
her neck, slipped the ring on her right ring finger, and handed
her the earrings to put on herself. Mrs. Phillips almost fainted
and fell into his arms and started crying. My mother told me it
was the most beautiful thing she had ever seen, and I don't
think she meant the moonstones. I would give anything if that
would happen to me, but it won't. Ever. I'll be lucky to even . . .

Ever since then . . . Moonstones are soft and delicate; they not only scratch easily, they wear and get dull. So Mrs. Phillips puts them on only once a year, on their wedding anniversary. They give a party and invite everyone who was at the original wedding, and their families. Mrs. Phillips wears a high-necked black velvet gown and her wedding ring. Nothing else; she never got an engagement ring. At the end of the evening, Mr. Phillips asks her to stand up and turn around and close her eyes. Then he hangs the necklace around her neck, slides the ring on her right ring finger, and hands her the earrings to put on herself. She falls into his arms—and it isn't fake—and starts crying, and every woman in the house is crying too, and wishing . . . But for them, it's too late. For me too, I guess.

"Are you crazy, Angela," I screamed. "Why are you wearing the moonstones? If your mother ever finds out . . ."

"The others promised not to tell. I just wanted, just this once, to feel . . . to be . . . The moonstones are so beautiful and they're just right for my dress and my hair and—and I thought if I put them on tonight, I would be . . ." She started crying again.

How could I explain to her that the moonstones weren't magic, that you couldn't just put them on and become instantly loved? Or lovable? Or that wearing them would make you *able* to love? Didn't she understand that it was love that made the moonstones magic, not the other way around? The deep love, the true love her mother and father had for each other? That without that love the moonstones were just pretty pebbles? The moonstones looked just as beautiful on Angela's creamy skin as they did on black velvet and Angela could have been just then, if she hadn't been crying, the most beautiful sixteen-year-old girl in the whole world. Only not quite. Something was wrong, something was missing. The earrings! I pointed to her ears. "I can't find them," she sobbed. "You have to find them. Please, Patsy. My mother will kill me. And my father . . . I don't know what he'll do."

"Did you look all over?" I asked. "Get the others to help?" Then I realized: You don't lose *two* earrings; when one falls off, you know it. "Where did you leave them?"

"They're not there. Somebody took them."

"Tonight? One of your friends? That's why you told me Andy might be involved?"

She nodded miserably. "I can't even ask them. Whoever took them . . . It was purposely; it couldn't have been an accident. They were *stolen.* If I accuse anyone, and it isn't him—or her—I'll lose all my friends. I could even get into worse trouble."

"So you can't call the police either, otherwise your father will find out?" Angela nodded again. "And you want me to find who took the earrings and make him give them back?"

"Tonight. It must be tonight, before twelve, before my parents come back. I don't even care who took them. Yes, I do, I want to know, but I don't want to make trouble, not in front of everybody so my father will find out."

"This is really going to cost you, Angela." I could just imagine how she'd feel when I got done with her.

"I don't care. Just *hurry.*"

"Who's here besides Andy and you?"

"Just two couples." As I suspected; it was a couples party. And she and Andy were the third couple; the poor wimp didn't have a chance. "Jerry Sanders with Beverly Waldron, and Howard Kemp and Lucy Muller." Boy, what a selection. Jerry and Howard were varsity football players; nice guys, but linemen, if you know what I mean. Big, strong, and that's it. Beverly was Angela's best friend, pretty and *very* popular, the only girl who could possibly get more votes than Angela, and I could easily guess why if I wanted to. Lucy was head cheerleader and starred in all the annual musicals; very talented, but she never started a sentence without an "I." Andy wouldn't be able to talk to anyone in the place including Angela, whose brains were all in her you-know-what. Poor Andy.

"Do you do this often, Angela? Were any of them in your house before?"

"None of the boys, my father doesn't like football players, but the girls have been over lots of times."

I thought for a moment. "Show me where you put the earrings."

Her father's study was lined with books, shelves from floor to ceiling all around the room. A beautiful big walnut desk was near the far wall, a big leather couch on the right, and two leather wing chairs on the left. There were small round tables at the ends of the couch and next to each chair, each with good reading lamps. If the books had all been whodunits, I could have lived in that room for the rest of my life.

Angela walked over to the big couch and put her hand behind the pillow at the end. "Here. I put them right here."

"Why there? Why did you come in here in the first place?" It wasn't to read, that was for sure, but let her tell me.

"I . . . It was Andy's idea. We wanted a little privacy, a place where we could talk." I'll bet. And Andy, who had never been in that house before, knew exactly where to take her? Hah! You have to be pretty dumb to tell such an obvious lie to a whodunit reader.

"Whatever for?" I asked. I may never have had a date, but I read a lot and I wanted her to say it out loud; you never know what you can learn from an investigative interrogation. "Weren't you the hostess? Supposed to entertain *all* your guests?"

"They wanted to be alone, too. Jerry and Bevvy stayed in the living room, and Howard and Lucy went out on the back porch."

"You and Andy were on the leather couch?"

"We were just sitting there talking." Would *anyone* believe that? "Then he got very romantic and started kissing me passionately. I was so surprised and he was so—so *forceful* that I fell over backwards." Andy is so skinny she didn't have to pull him very hard was what I figured.

"Then how did the earrings get behind the couch pillow?"

"Well . . ." Trying to figure out how to say it. "Andy was a little—uh—inexperienced—" not any more, I bet "—and he didn't give me a chance to . . . to get ready. He started kissing me so fast and so hard that . . . I reached up with my free hand and took off my earrings."

"Why?"

She looked at me as though I was retarded. Luckily for her, she didn't make any cracks. "My earlobes are very—very *sensitive,* and when a boy discovers that, he just kisses them and kisses them and . . . and he could swallow an earring." From *kissing?* Come on, Angela! but this could be useful; if I ever started getting kissed, I'd make sure: *no earrings.* Angela isn't

the only one who has sensitive earlobes, I'll bet. "So I pushed
the earrings down between the back of the couch and the
pillow. For safety." And to free her hand, right?
"When did you discover they were gone?"
"About a half hour later. I didn't want things to get *com-
pletely* out of control, so we went back into the living room."
"You didn't look for the earrings before you left the study?"
"I was a bit . . . My mind wasn't on it." Mind? Hah!
"Didn't you disturb Jerry and Bevvy?"
"Oh, no, I wouldn't do a thing like *that.* I peeked in first, but
they were just getting up from the couch, like they were going
to go somewhere."
"So you and Andy went into the living room and sat on the
couch?"
"Oh, no, that would have been almost as bad as . . . I took
him into the kitchen and gave him a cold drink." Cold drinks
don't work. Not even cold showers. I know.
"After that, when we were all gathered in the living room, I
had to fix my hair, so I went to the powder room. When I
looked in the mirror, that's when I noticed."
"You went back to the study and checked the couch?"
"All over. I almost went crazy. They weren't *in* the couch, or
*near* the couch or around in the study, or *anything.* That's
when I panicked and called you." Thanks heaps, Angela.
"And I'm not allowed to accuse your friends? Or even upset
them?"
"They're my friends, my guests. Can't you do it without
making any trouble?"
I thought for a while. Alexander Magnus Gold had never
faced a problem like this with such a handicap, nor had Giles
Sullivan. They, at least, could accuse the guilty perpetrator.
What would they do in my shoes? Go crazy, I guess; men are so
weak. Morally, that is. Then I had it. A flash. It had to work. It
had *better* work; there was no other way to do it. It *would*
work. The thief couldn't tell anyone not to give me the right
answers because, when it all came out, as it had to if the
earrings weren't returned before Mr. and Mrs. Phillips came
home, it would prove that the thief, just by telling . . . What I
mean is, the thief had to give the wrong answers and the others

had to give the right answers, so . . . Then I would—I'm not
sure what, but I had to get Step One done first. If it worked.

"Get me a notebook and a pen," I told Angela, "and send
them to me, one at a time, in any order. Here, in the kitchen."

"But what should I tell them?"

"Say I'm conducting a psychological experiment, and you
promised me I could do it and you'd get everyone to cooperate.
It'll only take a minute each."

"They'll never believe that I . . ." She looked ready to start
crying again. "Just to help *you?* On a Saturday night? With my
folks away? Couples?"

Unbelievable. That moron . . . Here she was, an hour away
from being sent to a convent, and she was worried about what
her friends, one of whom was a thief, would think? "You better
make them believe it, Angela," I said firmly. "Because if you
don't, you'd better start thinking of a good story to tell your
father. About how this gang of thieves broke in and chloro-
formed you all, including two big linemen, and then went right
to where the moonstones were hidden and took only the
earrings and left the necklace and the ring and all the other
really expensive jewelry your mother has and—"

"All right." She put her hands over her ears. "I'll make them
do it. But how will that . . ."

"Let me worry about it," I said. "Besides, it's our only
chance." Angela turned blue. I shouldn't have said that; sometimes honesty is not the best policy. "Go." I had to push her.
"Tell them you did your quiz already."

Andy came in first. I had him sit opposite me at the kitchen
table. He started to say something to me, sort of friendly like,
but I stopped him. Any other time, I would have been thrilled,
but now? A detective has to be professional, to put his—her—
client's interests first. "Just tell me," I said, "the item of furnishings that impressed you most in each room of the house. Only
the downstairs part. Not the lavatories or the kitchens or the
halls; only the major rooms."

"In the living room," he said thoughtfully, "it has to be the
piano. It's a Bösendorfer Concert Grand, and I have a record at
home that—"

"No details; just what it is. Keep going."

He looked at me oddly, so I wrote his name on the paper, and "piano." "In the dining room, the carved sideboard. In the study, the Persian rug." I'll *kill* him. Her. Both. If they rolled off the couch onto the rug . . . "In the TV room, the multiamped stereo. And in the playroom, the Ping-Pong table."

I finished writing and sent him away. "Send in the next subject."

It was Jerry Sanders. "The soda fountain, that was real neat. And the big fireplace in the living room. All those shelves of books, just like a library." He thought hard. "The built-in barbecue on the back porch. The big dining room table; you could put the whole team around it. The giant speakers; boy, that bass really shook the floor. And the bearskin rug in the den."

Lucy Muller was dressed dramatically, as usual. A simple black dress with a big Dayglo yellow lightning flash set in jaggedly across the front, running from her left breast to her right knee. I guess she wanted to make sure she wouldn't get hit by a car if she decided to walk home. Which, according to the best rumors, hadn't happened yet, so there was no need to worry about cars. Getting hit by one, I mean. She selected—it might have been a good psychological test at that—the netsuke cabinet with the big glass front in the living room. The china closet, with all that Royal Doulton china. The big walnut desk. The ballet barre in the playroom. The African violets with the special lighting on the porch. And the TV sound camera setup.

Howard came in next, and he really concentrated. "The size of the living room, does that count? It's as big as my whole house. How about those hanging lights over the dining room table? And those big wing chairs; I could really be comfortable in one of those." Howard was even bigger than Jerry. "The multigym; you could get a workout right in your own house. The swinging seats on the porch; my grandmother had one of those."

Beverly was dressed to kill. Her mother would have had a fit if she saw her only daughter like that. A tight red dress, strapless, held up by glue or prayers or something, an innocent little red ribbon holding her hair back, and black net stockings. She must have seen my jaw drop and thought it was envy; glad to have made your day, Bevvy. "The needlepoint-covered couch in the living room is just perfect," she said. "And the slim, delicate dining room chairs. The recliner in the den is really comfortable and looks just right. The wall of mirrors in the playroom gym area. And the huge movie screen." I finished making notes and told her to send in Angela.

Angela had fixed her face during the interrogations, but she dropped her false brave smile the minute she came into the kitchen. "What do I do next?" she asked.

"Nothing," I said. "It's over."

"You failed," she moaned, her lower lip trembling. "My father will kill me, and my mother will throw me out."

"Relax, Angela," I reassured her. "I know who did it." Her eyes opened wide. "I just have to figure out how to get the moonstone earrings back. Quietly." I sat for a moment thinking. Simple. It was simple, really, from the right approach. "Take me into the living room." Angela looked worried, probably afraid I might embarrass her innocent little seraphim friends. Tough. Let her worry; might do her some good.

The five of them were sitting quietly talking. They knew something was wrong, even the football linemen. "Oh, I forgot to tell you," I said to Angela casually, "when we were in the kitchen, Bevvy told me she found your earrings. Right, Bevvy?"

Beverly Waldron turned white, then as red as her dress. "That's right, Angela," she said in a choked voice, taking the earrings out of her clutch bag and handing them to Angela. "I was going to tell you before, but when Carrots—Patricia—came I forgot all about it." Nobody believed her.

Angela was red, too. She took the earrings, but didn't put them on. Instead she took off the ring and the necklace and held the moonstone set in her hands. "My parents will be home soon," she said, without looking at her watch. "Will you boys take the girls home now?" Jerry and Howard nodded. As they were leaving, Angela turned to go upstairs. To her mother's bedroom, I guess.

"Wait," I called her back. "We have an agreement, remember?" Angela turned back. She looked all worn out. "You have to give me whatever I want, Angela." She nodded dully. Now was the time. I had it all planned. Everything memorized. I was going to tear the promissory note into tiny little pieces, drop them on the floor, and say, in front of her friends—it would be all over the school on Monday—"The trouble is, Angela, you don't have *anything* I want." But I looked at the poor frightened soul, the empty little doll whose whole life was in her looks, and I saw, clear as in a crystal ball, that her husband might buy her a diamond and platinum necklace for their anniversary, but he would never put a cheap-but-oh-so-precious handmade moonstone necklace that he had dreamed of for two years, and spent his last penny on, around her neck on their wedding day. And Angela would never look as beautiful as her mother did that first time I saw Mr. Phillips put the moonstone necklace around his wife's neck: so much love, so much.

I saw that Angela—it was such a surprise to me, and an even bigger surprise that I had not seen it sooner—that Angela wasn't beautiful, she was just *pretty.* And I understood that . . . that I was alive and she . . . she had never lived. Not really. I realized that I didn't have to hurt her, that instead I should feel sorry for her, for what she had done to hurt herself. I saw that I should give her not what she deserved but what she needed.

"I want you," I measured my words carefully, "I want you to give a hundred hours of your time this year, two hours a week, working in the Home for the Blind. They can't see what you look like there, but they can see very clearly what you are. At the end of the hundred hours, if you've become beautiful, really beautiful, they'll know. And you'll know, too. It's your last chance, Angela. Do it yourself. For yourself. I won't check up on you." I turned to go.

"Wait," Andy said, when I reached the door. "I'll go with you."

Outside, he asked, "How did you know?"

"The questions I asked. It wasn't really a psychological test, it was a—a criminal investigation."

"I knew it couldn't be a psychological test," he said. "I'd never heard of anything like that before. How did it work?"

"Take you, for example. You didn't mention any item of furnishings from the den or the back porch."

"Because I was never in either place. Angela just showed me—"

"Never mind," I interrupted. "I have a very good idea of what she showed you. Anyway, Howard didn't mention anything in the den, and he really tried to remember, which means he was never in the den. Lucy didn't mention anything from the den either, though she'd been in Angela's house many times and must've seen the room. I figured it was because she hadn't been in the den tonight and anything she's not in doesn't exist for her. On the other hand, Jerry was very impressed by all the shelves filled with books; he was in the study tonight. Since he was with Beverly all night—I'm sure she didn't leave him wandering around alone—she must've been in the study with him. Knowing Beverly's reputation, I'm sure they were sitting on the couch."

"I guess so, but what does that have to do with it?"

"That's where Angela left the earrings. But although Beverly had been in the study tonight, she didn't mention anything from there. Why didn't she? It was full of beautiful and impressive things, and she'd been in the house before."

" 'The wicked flee when no man pursueth,' " Andy quoted. "I thought it would be something like that." He was quiet for a moment, then said, "That was a pretty neat way you got Beverly to give Angela back the earrings."

"We detectives," I tossed off lightly, although I was really glowing, "work quietly our wonders to perform." Not like Gold or Sullivan; we don't brag. Women are nicer about practically everything.

"I don't understand," Andy said, "why Beverly stole the earrings. She couldn't even wear them. Even if she took them home, Mr. Phillips would have called the police and she'd have been arrested within an hour. After all, it took you only twenty minutes."

"The police couldn't do it my way," I pointed out. "They would have questioned everybody until someone confessed. But Beverly didn't intend to steal the earrings; she only wanted to wear them for fifteen minutes when she was all alone, to see if they would work their magic on her the way she thought they did on Mrs. Phillips. She would have put them back where she found them and nobody would have known. But Angela discovered they were missing, and then it was too late."

"How did Beverly know . . ."

"Did you see the way Angela looked when she came back from the study?"

"Yeah, sort of—wild."

"Beverly knew what that meant. She had to keep the earrings in her bag until she figured out what to do with them. But she's not very bright, and when Angela panicked and called me in . . ."

"Why didn't she just drop them on the floor or leave them in the girls' lav?"

"If she dropped them just anywhere, they might have gotten stepped on and the whole story would've come out. If she put them in an out-of-the-way place, Angela might not have found them before her parents got home. If Beverly left them in the lav and Lucy found them, Angela would know Beverly had stolen them. So she just kept her mouth shut and prayed for a miracle."

He took my hand in his—just took it; so masterful—and we walked quietly for a few blocks. As we were approaching my house, he stopped me. "You know, Pat," he said. "I've always thought it would be—uh—fun to know you, to be your friend. I've always wanted to, but I was afraid. You were so beautiful and funny and smart and strong and confident and . . . that I . . . I didn't want you to laugh at me. But I'd like . . . There's an old Sherlock Holmes coming at the Film Society. Basil Rathbone and Nigel Bruce. It's really great. Would you mind going with me? Next Saturday? Eight o'clock?"

Beautiful, huh? Me? "I'll think about it," I said. "I'll let you know."

"And if you ever have another case . . . I'm very interested in mysteries, you know. I'd really like to . . ."

"I'll think about that, too," I said.

# JOSEPH HANSEN
## THE OWL IN THE OAK

Alice Donovan was a small woman, past forty but brisk, with an open way about her, a smile and a perky word for just about everybody. She called her shop Ye Olde Oak Tree for the very good reason that an old oak sheltered it. Like a good many shops in Madrone, a tiny foothill town on California's central coast, hers had been converted from a spindly frame dwelling with jigsaw-work porches and bay windows. Most of these places sported fresh paint nowadays. Ye Olde Oak Tree was green with yellow trim.

The last time Hack Bohannon had noticed, Alice sold cheap china and pewter knickknacks, T-shirts and souvenir scarves, picture postcards, sunglasses, snapshot film, chewing gum, cigarettes—and cookies, when she felt like baking. She kept antiques that needed work. Bohannon recollected a treadle sewing machine in the front yard, an old wooden Maytag with hand-cranked wringers. A wagon wheel had leaned against the trunk of the oak. Bad oil paintings slumped on the porch, seascapes mostly—the ocean was over yonder, on the far side of the highway.

All this was gone now. Neat beds of pansies and petunias lay to either side of the footpath. Bohannon's boot heels knocked across an empty porch. And when he opened the door and stepped inside, he didn't recognize the place. New paint, wallpaper, carpet on the floor. The antique rockers, highboys, commodes were sleekly refinished. Not a postcard rack remained, no T-shirts, visor hats, suntan lotion. Good Mexican terra-cotta pots stood on shelves. Fine baskets occupied corners. Soft serapes in natural wool colors hung against the walls. On velvet in glass cases lay bracelets, necklaces, rings in hand-wrought silver set with turquoise and jade.

The shop took up the two front rooms of the little house, parlor, sitting room. He stepped behind a counter and opened

63

an inner door. Built-in diamond-paned sideboards said this had
been a dining room. Magazines, books, cassettes, a camera and
boxes of film crowded them now. The room had only space
enough for two wing chairs, a coffee table, a television set—
and these were all it held. He pushed a swinging door and was
in the kitchen. A deputy had used a black magic marker on the
pale vinyl tile of the floor to outline where and how Alice
Donovan's small body had lain when her hulking son Howard
had found it last night. Next to a glass of white wine on a
counter, slices of apple and a wedge of yellow cheese lay on a
saucer, a paring knife in the sink.

The back door stood open, and he frowned at that. Gerard
ought to have posted an officer here. Bohannon squinted at the
door and the frame. A deadbolt had been broken. Someone had
wanted badly to get in. Early this morning, as soon as news of
the murder got on the radio. A size twelve shoe had forced the
door, a shoe muddy from the dew in the brush out back. He
scowled around him. Had bigfoot found what Bohannon was
here to look for? That would be a hell of a note.

Morning sunlight came cheerfully through a window over
the sink and slanted onto the place where Alice Donovan had
died. The patch of dried blood there was the size of a dinner
plate. Someone had smashed her skull in, unhooked a cast-iron
skillet from its place in a row of pans over the stove and hit her
from behind. Lieutenant Gerard of the Madrone sheriff's office
figured big, shambling Howard had done it. Howard was sitting
in a cell. He claimed he had been on the beach, alone all
evening, thinking. He had killed eight cans of beer. The empties
were there, bobbing in the surf among the rocks to prove it, if
anyone cared to check.

"And many more besides," Gerard grunted, "I have no doubt.
Christ, people love to make the world ugly, don't they?" He
wadded the last bite of a cruller into his mouth and washed it
down with coffee from a chipped mug. "No, Howard and Alice
had been on a collision course since he was born. She babied
him through years one to thirteen, then made him the man in
her life, right? Except he could never do what he wanted, only
what she wanted."

"You could say—" Bohannon tilted back in a straight oak

chair "—he went direct from the nursing bottle to the whisky bottle."

Howard had spent times away from Madrone in hospitals that promise to cure addictive personalities and sometimes succeed—though not with Howard. He wasn't much more than twenty, but no peace officer who'd ever had to deal with him, Bohannon not excepted, figured him for less than a dangerous drunk for life—or at least for as long as he lasted. He was quite a driver when he drank. He had totaled two cars of his mother's, and others that had belonged to former friends.

"His buddies don't want him around," Bohannon said.

"Except Beau Larkin," Gerard said. "Worse than Howard. Beau'd be in Folsom if his dad wasn't a San Luis cop."

"Howard never got violent with Alice. Not once."

"There's always a first time." Gerard crumpled the white paper sack the cruller had come in and dropped it into a wastebasket. "Nothing was stolen, Hack. Whoever did it didn't have to force entry. No, Howard came home drunk, and they had another argument—their last one."

"Fred May doesn't think so," Bohannon said.

"Right. And that's why you're here." Gerard pawed the files, photographs, reports on his desk and found cigarettes. He lit one and looked at Bohannon through the smoke. "Fred wants you to find evidence that somebody else killed Alice Donovan." He gave a thin smile. "You do as much police work as you used to when you were on the payroll here, Hack. Why don't you just come back, and stop being so stubborn?"

Bohannon had been a deputy for fourteen years; then it had gone sour for him, he'd quit, and opened boarding stables up Rodd canyon. He liked the company of horses better than that of men, but people in trouble kept coming to him for help, so he'd taken out a private investigator's license. He didn't know how to turn folks away. But he would never come back to work here. He hated the very sounds and smells of the place, the desks, files, jangling phones, even the lighting. He and Gerard had been partners, friends. They weren't enemies now, but they'd never be the same again.

"Give me the keys," Bohannon said. "I'll go see if Fred's got a case or not."

When Bohannon passed it, May came waddling out of his office and walked beside him down the hallway. May, on the staff of the county attorney, was a public defender when the need arose. He was no paper-shuffler but a bright lawyer with a belief in justice nothing could shake—certainly not offers of money. He would have been better paid almost anyplace else. Luckily, his wife and kids were as decent as he was. If a battered VW bug was wheels enough for him, if he could get through the days in sweatshirts, cheap jeans, and worn-out tennis shoes, so could they, and cheerfully. Bohannon pushed open the side door of the substation, and the fat man followed him out to the parking lot where patrol cars stood collecting leaves and pods from the towering eucalypts that hedged the tarmac. May said: "You know what bothers me? Not that nothing was stolen. What bothers me is that Alice Donovan had anything worth stealing. Where did she get the money to upgrade the place so suddenly?"

"Why not from the bank?" Bohannon had lately wrecked his faithful old GM pickup, and the one parked out here now was new, shiny, apple green. He pulled open the door and climbed up into it. It didn't smell of alfalfa and dried manure yet. It still smelled new. He kept thinking it didn't belong to him. "She owned the property, didn't she? Why didn't she take out a loan on it?"

"I don't know—" May's moon face winced up at him "—but she didn't. Not in this area. We checked it out. See what you can find, Hack. There's an answer someplace."

"She didn't tell Howard?" Bohannon slammed the door of the pickup and slid the key into the ignition. "Or is he too hung over to talk?"

"He's not hung over, but she said it was a secret. She teased him, like he was five years old: 'I've got a secret, I won't tell—' "

"Don't sing, Fred," Bohannon said.

"Sorry about that. But he did say something interesting. Said he saw her hide something. If it was money, Howard wanted it. For booze, right? When he thought it was safe, he dug it out, but she caught him before he could open it."

"So he doesn't know if it was money or what." Bohannon started the truck.

Over the smooth hum of the engine May said: "A cardboard box with rubber bands around it. He looked for it again, every chance he got, but he never found it."

"Maybe I'll have better luck." Bohannon released the parking brake. "I won't have to worry about Alice walking in on me, will I?" He lifted a hand, and drove off.

Now, in the silent kitchen, he got down on hands and knees to probe low cupboards that smelled of soap powder. He climbed a flimsy aluminum step stool to grope on high shelves among cobwebby cut glass, cracked plates, forgotten gift boxes of fancy teas. In a shadowy hallway he unloaded sheets, pillow-cases, towels from a linen closet. Nothing. He got the step stool and poked his head through a ceiling trapdoor. Nothing but rafters, dust, and heat.

Alice Donovan's bedroom was neat and smelled faintly of sandalwood perfume. He found nothing that didn't belong there. She wouldn't hide whatever it was in Howard's room, but he searched that anyway. Empty pint vodka bottles rattled among the cleated shoes on the closet floor. The closet smelled of the sweaty jeans, shirts, jackets that hung there. On the shelf lay shoulder pads, helmets, a catcher's mitt, and a stack of dog-eared magazines with photos of naked young women. The bed was unmade. In the dustballs under it lay empty beer cans and crumpled potato chip bags.

The bedside stand held a lamp and a digital clock whose red numerals read 3:00. Plainly Howard hadn't bothered setting it again after the last power outage. Maybe time, along with everything else but his thirst, had ceased to have meaning for Howard. Bohannon opened a drawer in the table. Candy bar wrappers, scratched California lottery tickets, rubber bands, a broken pencil. And photographs. Half a dozen. Of a red-haired young woman who looked tall. Taken someplace among boats—Morro Bay? She wore tight jeans, a striped tank top, sunglasses that didn't hide her exceptional good looks. He tucked the photos into a shirt pocket and went to check out the bathroom.

It was shiny clean, and Alice Donovan had not hidden any-thing there. Back in the kitchen, he opened the refrigerator.

He'd never seen so many cans of beer outside a market. He took one, figuring Howard wouldn't mind, since Bohannon was trying to save his sizeable hide. A noise came from the shop. He must have left the door unlocked. He set down the beer can and jogged for the front rooms. A large, expensively dressed woman was peering into one of the glass cases. She turned and stared at him in surprise. He understood. In his Levi's, cowboy boots, sweaty stained Stetson, he plainly was no dealer in jewelry and antiques.

"Who—who are you?" A thick envelope was in her hand. She poked it hastily into a large handbag. "What are you doing here?"

"Investigator for the county attorney," he said. "Bohannon is my name. What's yours?"

"Where's Mrs. Donovan?" She came toward him, peering past his shoulder through the open door into the living quarters. She called out, "Alice? It's Margaret Weems." She looked at Bohannon. "We had an appointment." She read a tiny jewelled watch on a wrist strong enough to control an eight-horse hitch. "For twelve noon." She blinked. "Investigator?"

"Mrs. Donovan met with an accident," Bohannon said.

Margaret Weems went very still. Fashion wasn't doing her kind any favors. The exaggerated shoulders of the moment made her look like a linebacker in drag. Her tongue touched her lips. He couldn't read the look in her eyes. "Is she—all right? An automobile accident, you mean?"

Bohannon shook his head. "Assault. She's dead."

"My God." The woman's knees gave. Bohannon stepped out from behind the counter to catch her arm, but she didn't want that. She sat down, breathing hard, clutching the purse tight against her. She managed a pale, apologetic smile. "Excuse me. I'll just sit here a moment, if I may. It's such a shock."

"Get you anything?" he asked. "Water? Brandy?"

Eyes closed, she shook her head. "Assault. How dreadful." She opened her eyes. "She was so tiny."

"Were you a friend?" Bohannon said.

"Friend?" Her brief laugh had no humor in it. "No. Just a— customer." Her gaze caressed the jewelry, pottery, weaving. "She had such lovely things, didn't she?"

"You used her first name," Bohannon said. "If you were a friend, I thought maybe you could help me here."

Her look was guarded. "Help you how? With what?"

He shrugged. "If you talked together, maybe she said something—was she frightened of anything, anyone?"

Margaret Weems snorted. "Have you met her son?"

Bohannon grinned. "He once lifted me up over his head and threw me into the ocean. He and his high school friends got a little rowdy that night. Howard's a big, strong boy."

"I don't know how she could bear having him here."

"He's been locked up for the murder," Bohannon said. "I'm supposed to find evidence he didn't do it."

Margaret Weems gave a wry laugh. "I wish you luck," she said, and got off the chair, and walked out. Bohannon wanted to ask her what was in that envelope she'd stuffed so hurriedly into her handbag. But it would be smarter to wait. He watched her settle into a Mercedes that looked as if it got washed and waxed every day. He watched it roll off down the dusty trail, then went back to the kitchen to finish off his beer and nail shut the back door.

He found the box twenty minutes later, in a spring-operated compartment hidden behind a beautifully mitered drawer in a General Grant lowboy with a marble top. He sat on the fresh crimson velvet of a carved walnut chair, twanged the rubber bands from around the box, and lifted the lid. A sour smell came out. Inside lay a stack of small envelopes, note size, fastened by another rubber band. When he lifted them out, he saw a little packet of olive drab velvet, the same fabric that lined Alice Donovan's glass display cases.

He unfolded the velvet from around a piece of Navajo jewelry, a buckle. Not new like the stuff the Donovan woman was selling. Old. The stone was brown, not blue or green, and the heft of the piece, its time-worn smoothness, told him it was special. He rewrapped it and tucked it into his shirt pocket with the snapshots of the red-haired girl. Then he snapped the rubber band off the envelopes and shuffled through them. They were stained and gritty to the touch.

All were addressed in ballpoint pen to an Estella Hernandez

at a post office box in Guadalupe. There was no return address.
He pulled a letter out of its envelope. It was signed only G. He
read it and blinked. G seemed pretty worked up. He folded that
letter and put it back in its envelope and read the others, one
by one. G evidently thought he was in love. Starlight and
birdsong and the moon shining on a midnight ocean got into
the letters, but so did steamy sexual stuff. One of the letters,
the first one, was signed Galen. The postmarks were all Madrone. He rubber-banded the envelopes, stuffed them into a
pocket of his Levi jacket, put the empty box back into the
lowboy, closed the drawer, and left Alice Donovan's silent shop,
locking the door behind him.

Halfway down the path, he paused to squint up at the oak.
Crows were making a racket there, flapping around, diving at
something hidden in the leafage. It was an owl, a big Western
horned owl. He hunched on a branch, and looked like he meant
to stay there, like it was his tree, and the crows could do their
damnedest but he wasn't leaving. He glared up at them with
round yellow eyes and clacked his beak at them from time to
time, and now and then spread his wings and bounced up and
down as if on springs. Then he'd crouch again, screwing his
head around to face them, this way, that way, no matter from
what angle they came at him. Bohannon wished him luck and
climbed into his new pickup.

Deputy T. Hodges was seated at a little square table on the
screened porch of a luncheonette in Madrone. The table top
was Formica in a red gingham pattern. A red paper napkin lay
crumpled beside T. Hodges's plate. The remains of a hamburger
and a scattering of french fries lay on the plate. She was nursing
what Bohannon guessed was cold coffee. When he banged in at
the screen door, her shiny dark eyes lit up for a second in a
smile. She didn't often smile with her mouth. She had the
notion that her front teeth stuck out, which they did a little,
and this embarrassed her. By the time he pulled the empty
chair out at her table, she was frowning. She read her watch.

"I've only got ten minutes left," she said.

"Sorry." He sat down. "I was looking for something and I

wasn't too quick about finding it. You haven't had dessert. Shall we eat peach pie together?"

A fat girl in a sweatshirt stenciled RAIDERS came to the table and took a pencil from behind her ear. "Mr. Bohannon. Hi. How's my pal, Geranium?"

Geranium was a broad-backed, placid old buckskin mare who never put a big hoof wrong, and Cassie felt safe on her when she came up to the stables with one of her assorted boyfriends to ride the canyon trails on Mondays, when the cafe was closed.

"She missed you the other day," Bohannon said.

"I went swimming." She made a face. "Tony said we were going sailing in his boat, but he kept tipping it over. What will you have?"

"Peach pie for both of us," Bohannon said. "And Deputy Hodges needs a refill, and I'll have coffee, too, please."

"You got it," Cassie said, took T. Hodges's plate, and padded away.

"Looking for what?" T. Hodges said.

He told her. Then he laid the snapshots in front of her. "Ever see that girl before?"

"Howard had these?" Marveling, she shuffled them. "Yes, it's Andrea Norse." She gave an exaggerated sigh of envy and laid the photos down. "Stunning."

"College girl?" he said.

"She's past thirty, Hack, believe it or not. No, she's a psychological counselor for the county, family relations, that kind of thing. I suppose—" she touched the photos, lining them up "—that was how Howard met her, right?"

"Sounds logical." Bohannon scooped up the pictures and put them away. "Only what was she doing on a date with him? Letting him take her picture?"

"Maybe he didn't," she said. "Why not ask her?"

"I will." Bohannon laid the little packet of velvet on the table and unfolded it. "What does this suggest to you?" T. Hodges's eyes opened wide. She picked up the Navajo piece and studied it. "Stolen," she said.

"You're sure?"

She nodded. "From a private collection of old Indian jewelry in San Luis. The Kanter collection. By housebreakers six months ago. Every piece had been photographed, of course, for insurance company records. The San Luis police sent out fliers illustrated with the photos. I can dig ours out for you if you want."

"Valuable then," Bohannon said. Cassie came with the coffee pot and two slices of pie. She filled their mugs and admired the Navajo piece. "That's pretty." She looked enviously at T. Hodges. "He giving you that? What is it—your birthday or something?"

"It's stolen," T. Hodges said. "He's under arrest."

"I'll phone the TV news," Cassie said, and went away.

"In the neighborhood of a hundred thousand dollars." T. Hodges wrapped the piece up again. "For the whole collection, I mean." She held the little packet out, and Bohannon put it back into his shirt pocket. She cut into her pie. "What was Alice Donovan doing with something so valuable?"

"Why wasn't she the thief?" Bohannon said.

"Because the thief is in jail and the collection is back with the Kanters, all but this piece, which the thief insists he didn't sell. He didn't have time."

Bohannon ate pie, drank coffee, and thought. "Some kind of insurance scam on the part of the owners?"

"I think Mr. Kanter owns most of San Luis."

"Do you know exactly when Alice upgraded that shop?"

"About a year ago." T. Hodges said. "Mmm. This pie is heavenly."

"About a year ago a local man named Galen had an affair with a Guadalupe woman called Estella Hernandez."

"Ah—those letters you mentioned?"

"You know any man named Galen in Madrone?" Bohannon lit a cigarette and drank coffee. "It's not a common name."

"No Galens," she said. "You'll have to ask Estella Hernandez, won't you?"

"If I can find her. From the letters, I take it she lived in a trailer, mobile home. She could be long gone by now." He gave his head a shake. "What do you think? Was Alice Donovan into extortion? Freddy May says she didn't borrow the money to fix up the business. She couldn't have saved anything from the operation the way it was, nickels and dimes. And Howard must have cost a lot, smashing cars and having to be dried out in hospitals."

"So she blackmailed this Galen?" T. Hodges polished off her pie. "And Galen finally got fed up and stepped into the kitchen last night and bashed her head in with a skillet? Then why didn't he take the letters away with him?"

"I told you—they were hidden. No time to look for them. Howard got home very soon after she was killed. The killer would have had to hightail it not to be caught." Bohannon finished his coffee, took a long last drag from the cigarette, put it out. "Maybe it was Galen who came back early this morning and kicked in the back door, hoping to find the letters."

"And never found them," T. Hodges said.

"We better go." Bohannon got to his feet, slid bills from a worn wallet, laid them on the table for Cassie. He held open the screen door for T. Hodges. At the foot of the steps, on the crooked little trail, she read her watch again and looked woebegone.

"I'm really late," she said.

"I'll drive you back," he said.

He wanted to report to Fred May, but May was in court. So Bohannon drove down through the dunes, headed for Guadalupe. He didn't get there. He found a trailer park in a swale on the land side of the beach highway. The office had a temporary look to it, plywood and studs, but it had been there a while—the wood had darkened from rain, sun, wind, and salt spray. It had warped, too. When someone called, "Come in," from behind the door, he had to shoulder the door to get it open. It scraped the floor. The plywood counter had little bonsai trees on it, and a tiny Japanese woman in a wash-faded housedress was snipping at the branches of the trees, craftily, keeping them stunted, and perfect. Her face was like a withered apple. She smiled at him with crooked brown teeth and gave a little bow.

Bohannon touched his hat brim. "One of your tenants an Estella Hernandez?"

Her answer made him think of an owner's manual he'd got with a stereo he and Linda had bought some years back. It was in English, all right, but neither of them had been able to

understand it. But the little lady was used to this, it looked like.
She laughed at herself, came from behind the counter, took his
elbow, led him back outside, and pointed out the Hernandez
trailer to him.

It was like the rest of them there, halfhearted efforts at
looking like tract houses. Like the rest, it had been some time
since it had rolled down any highway on wheels. A tin awning
held up by spindly pipes sheltered the side of the place. A
skinny brown boy of maybe ten sat on the doorstep with a
scuba diver's mask in hand. When he heard the crunch of gravel
under Bohannon's boots, he looked at him, got off the steps,
and walked away, glum resignation in the slump of his shoulders, the way he scuffed the ground. Bohannon pulled open a
flimsy screen and knocked on the door.

From inside a woman's voice called to him in Spanish.

"It's Galen," he said. "Open up, Estella."

She opened the door, a dark, slim young woman, heavy
breasts in a flower print halter, a very tight pair of jeans, bare
feet with crimson toenails. She blinked long furry black lashes
at him, and gave a short, mocking laugh. "One thing I do know
is voices," she said. "Galen has a high voice." She tilted her
head and smiled while her glance ran up and down him. "If you
sang, you would sing bass." She frowned, puzzled. "Did Galen
send you?" She glanced up at the sun. "It is early in the day."

"Galen didn't send me," he said, and took out his wallet. "And
I'm not a client." He showed her his license. "I'm with the
county attorney. I need to find Galen."

"What for?" She waved a mocking hand at the wallet. "You
don't mean to tell me Galen has committed a crime." She
laughed. "He would not have the courage."

"What's his last name, Estella? Where does he live?"

"How do you know about him and me?"

Bohannon showed her the letters.

"I threw those in the garbage," she said.

"That's what they smell like," Bohannon said.

She made a bitter face. "That is what they are."

"You know Galen wouldn't have sent me or any other man
here. He was in love with you."

"He is a crazy fool. He nearly got both of us killed with his stupid jealousy."

"He didn't like your line of work?" Bohannon said.

She snorted. "A romantic teenager of fifty years of age. A married man. With a grandchild."

"His last name, please, Estella?"

She narrowed her eyes. "What is it worth to the county attorney's office?"

"Worth not getting busted for prostitution," Bohannon told her, "and for keeping a child on unfit premises."

She sighed grimly. "Why did I think you would be different? It don't matter how good-looking, a cop is a cop. His name is Worthy. Isn't that a joke?"

"And what's his line of work?" Bohannon said.

"He is a dentist." Her laugh was dry. "Galen, the first Galen in history, you know, was a famous Roman physician. He told me this. So his parents wanted him to be a doctor, but he failed medical school. You've got to have brains to be a doctor."

G.B. Worthy's offices were on the second floor of a brick business building in Madrone that didn't show its brick to the street any more. The front had been dressed in pecky cedar boards. The notion was to make the town look like the Wild West of 1880. Bohannon didn't much like that. The waiting room had bland framed prints on the walls, a pair of couches, a coffee table, a rack of magazines, a green tank of lazily swimming tropical fish. With a knuckle he touched the opaque glass of a service window. The woman who slid the glass back he pegged as Mrs. Worthy. She was stout, middle-aged, and fixed her hair around her head in bulky braids, yellow hair tinged with gray. She smiled with stunning teeth. "Have you an appointment?"

"I need some help from the doctor," Bohannon said, and showed her his license. "It's a law enforcement matter. It shouldn't take long."

She nodded knowingly, as if law enforcement matters were daily occurrences around there, as if the doctor were consulted by peace officers routinely, said, "One moment, please," closed the sliding glass. Voices murmured, then an inner door opened and a good-looking man, trim, slim, mustached, smiled and held out a hand. He said, "Whose dental charts do you want to see, Mr. Bohannon?"

Bohannon took the hand, gave Galen Worthy a conspiratorial look, and drew him out into the waiting room. He said softly, "Tell her we're going for coffee."

Worthy frowned and pulled his hand away. "What for? I don't understand. A police matter, my wife said."

Bohannon murmured. "The death of Alice Donovan. You want to discuss that here?"

"I—I don't know what you're talking about." Worthy's Adam's apple pumped. He turned a bad color. "Alice who?"

Bohannon pulled the smelly letters from his pocket and held them out so the dentist could get a good look. "Donovan. These were in her possession. You wrote them. Or so Estella Hernandez says."

The glass panel slid open. Mrs. Worthy said, "Galen, is everything all right?" She eyed Bohannon dubiously.

Her husband gave her a nervous smile. "It's all right, dear. But I have to go out for a few minutes."

"I won't keep him long," Bohannon told her.

He drove the dentist in his new pickup truck out of town, which didn't mean far in a little place like Madrone. They parked on a dusty foothill road. Worthy had been silent. Now he burst out:

"There are supposed to be two kinds of luck. Why do I always have the bad kind?"

"They say we make our own." Bohannon lit a cigarette.

"You'll kill yourself with those," Worthy snapped at him. "Worse than that, you'll kill those around you."

"I won't, but those letters could," Bohannon said. "How did the Donovan woman get hold of them, anyway?"

Worthy made a sour noise meant for a laugh. "Found them. You know how people dump their trash up in the canyons? Just drive along to a lonely spot and heave it out off the edge of the road. Disgusting."

"Go on," Bohannon said.

Worthy rolled down the window and waved a hand in front of his face to fend off the smoke. "Well, Alice had sent Howard on some errand, and he was hours late getting back. It was going to be dark soon. Knowing him, she figured he'd gotten drunk and passed out somewhere. So she borrowed a neighbor's car and went to find him. He'd driven off the road down a steep embankment. The car had come to a rest in a huge pile of plastic trash bags."

"From Estella's trailer camp, right?" Bohannon said.

Worthy's mouth twitched. "And bags had split open and spilled, hadn't they? And here were my letters strewn around for all the world to read. And the rest you know, don't you? How my money smartened up that shop for her?"

"To save your marriage?" Bohannon patted the letters in his side pocket. "I thought you loved Estella."

"Doris—Mrs. Worthy—put me through dental school after my own family gave up on me. I owe her everything."

"And it doesn't matter if you're a good dentist or not," Bohannon said, "she keeps you in style, right?"

"I didn't kill Alice Donovan," Worthy said.

"What size shoe do you wear, doctor?" Bohannon said.

Worthy blinked. "What kind of question is that?"

"Somebody heard on the early morning news that Alice was dead and hustled over to her shop and kicked in the back door with a size twelve shoe. Why wasn't it you, trying to get hold of these letters ahead of the sheriff?"

"It wasn't me." Worthy shook his head hard. "I drove straight to the office. You found the letters, not me."

"I didn't say you found them, only looked for them."

"I wasn't anywhere near there. I didn't know she was dead until you told me. We don't put the TV on in the mornings. Ask Doris."

Bohannon looked at him with his eyebrows raised.

"No. I don't mean that. She mustn't know."

"You and she go to work in the same car?" Bohannon said.

"She goes first to get things ready. I follow later."

"So you can't prove you didn't detour past Alice's."

Worthy said stubbornly, "And you can't prove I did." He read his watch. "I have to get back. I have appointments."

"What about last night?" Bohannon crushed out his cigarette

in the dashboard ashtray and pushed the little metal drawer shut. "Around midnight. You weren't at Alice's then, either?"

"I was in bed, asleep."

Bohannon twisted the key in the ignition and the new engine hummed to life. He couldn't get used to its quiet after the clatter of his old truck. It took him by surprise every time. Sometimes he didn't know the damned thing had started at all. He glanced at the dentist.

"You know, if you were there, either last night or this morning, chances are somebody saw you. Alice's place isn't the only one on that road. There are neighbors. It's not a dead end. It's on the way. People drive it. So if you'd like to change your story before it begins to fall apart, now is the time to do it."

Worthy stared straight ahead through the clean windshield. "It isn't a story," he said, "it's the truth."

"Then you've got nothing to be tense about." Bohannon reached over and touched the tight fist on the dentist's knee. Worthy jerked the hand away as if from an electric shock. "Relax," Bohannon said. "If anybody tells your wife, it won't be me."

"Give me back those letters," Worthy pleaded.

"Later," Bohannon said.

"What you have to know," he told Fred May, "is that somebody big got there before me this morning and broke the lock on the back door."

"And it wasn't Howard," the fat man smiled. "Good work, Hack. Who was it?" He touched the stained envelopes on his desk. "The dentist?"

"His feet are too small." Bohannon stared out the window, smoking, a can of beer in his hand. "And he claims he wasn't there. If he was, he didn't find the letters."

"It couldn't have been the Weems woman?" Fred May rocked back in his oak swivel chair and the spring twanged. "You say she's big."

"She still doesn't wear size twelve shoes." Bohannon took a swallow of beer, watched smoke from his cigarette drift out the window into the warm, late afternoon air. "And I don't think she knew Alice Donovan was dead."

"You really think she came to make a payment to her?" He poked with a fat finger at the Navajo buckle that lay on its ragged little square of velvet among the typed, blue-papered briefs and law books on the desk. "To keep Alice from revealing she was in possession of stolen property?"

Bohannon frowned and shook his head. "It doesn't make sense, Fred." He flicked the spent cigarette out the window into a flowerbed and dropped into an oak chair. "Why pay a black-mailer when you could easily explain to the San Luis police that you'd bought it innocently? It would be cheaper to take the loss on what she'd paid for it than to keep shelling out to Alice for the rest of her life."

"Then there's something Alice had around the place you didn't find." May drank diet soda from a can. "Or did the early riser who kicked in the door find it?"

"There wasn't any sign anybody had done any searching for anything." Bohannon finished his beer and tossed the empty can into the brown metal wastebasket beside May's desk, and made a face. "If bigfoot even came inside, he found what he wanted right there in the kitchen, or what he thought was there wasn't."

"What would it be?" May's forehead wrinkled.

"When I find him, I'll ask him." With a sigh, Bohannon got to his feet. It had been a long day. He was tired. "Meantime, I need the key to Alice's cash register."

May said, "Right here," opened a drawer, and took out a little flat key. Bohannon held his hand out, and May put the key into it. "What do you expect to find?"

Bohannon grinned and tossed the key in his hand. "Photographs of a very large, middle-aged lady," he said, "doing something she shouldn't."

The house was an expensive one on the beach, stone and beams and gloomy smoked glass on the road side. From the road where he left the pickup, he looked down on the flat roof of the house, which was covered in rocks white as chalk. He went down sandy stone steps into a cavelike entryway and put his thumb on a bell push. He stood listening to the silky rush and retreat of waves on the beach, and then the door opened. It wasn't the Weems woman. It was a young man, dressed in next to nothing. He was smooth and tan. His lean musculature looked carved. His hair was curly and black and he wore it long. Bohannon wondered on what beach Margaret Weems had found him.

Bohannon wasn't a type he'd encountered before. He looked puzzled, but he didn't say anything.

"Mrs. Weems here?" Bohannon gave his name. "We met this morning. Tell her. She'll remember me."

The young man blinked. Something was happening under all that theatrical hair. Maybe he was thinking. At last, with a small shrug, he turned and went down a long room whose far end had a wall of glass that showed the beach and the sea. The sun was lowering and the light on the water was turning flame-colored. The young man stepped outside, Bohannon stepped inside, shut the door behind him, went down the long room. The young man was back in the open panel of the glass wall in no time.

"What do you want?" he said in a French accent.

"I have something for Mrs. Weems from Alice Donovan's shop." He raised his voice, in case Margaret Weems was within earshot. "She'll want to see it."

The young man stepped toward him. "You must telephone and make the appointment." He reached for Bohannon's arm. Bohannon didn't want to knock him down, but he wasn't about to leave. He shook the hand off. The youth tried again, and a voice reached them both. Margaret Weems stood in the open glass panel. Her white terry cloth robe made her look like a polar bear.

"Oh, Mr. Bohannon." Her smile was nervous, and she lied. "I misunderstood. Jean-Marie's accent puzzles me sometimes." She tried for a laugh and missed. She came to them, gently but firmly pried the youth away from Bohannon, and aimed him at an inner doorway. "Dear Jean, be a darling and find us all some bubbly, will you?"

"Beer," Bohannon said, "thanks."

Jean-Marie scowled like a six-year-old, but after a second's pause, he grumbled away, glancing back menacingly at the pair of them. A jealous lover in the authentic Gallic mode, out of a silent movie. Funny.

Margaret Weems put a finger to her lips and led Bohannon out onto the deck, across the deck, down to the sand. She took his arm and hustled him along the sand. "You've got the pictures. That's what you found at Alice's shop, isn't it? Those dreadful pictures. Give them to me."

"You were paying Alice to keep quiet about them."

"I'll pay you. The money's in the house. Only give them to me. And the negatives? She said I could have the negatives this time."

"I don't think so," Bohannon said.

Her face fell. She let him go. "What?"

"I don't think she'd give you those." He gestured at the house. "You're well fixed, it appears to me. No. I think she'd bleed you with those pictures forever."

She sighed. "Of course. You're right. Awful woman."

"Where were you at midnight last night?" he said.

"We had a party," she said. "It was very lively. Young people. Music. Jean-Marie is a singer, you know. And a song writer. Guitar. Piano. He has a wonderful future. Everyone says so."

"Good," Bohannon said. "How late did this party run?"

"Until almost sunrise," she said.

"And you stayed until the last guest left?"

She gave him a rueful laugh. "Those were the days, weren't they? No, I was in bed by one-thirty, two. You can ask any of them—and you will, won't you?"

"When you give me the guest list," he said.

"Right away," she said.

Jean-Marie came along the sand, carrying a tray on which glasses glittered. All by his lonesome he turned this stretch of beach into the Côte d'Azure. There should have been a bevy of bikini-clad nymphets in his wake. Bohannon looked at Margaret Weems. She was watching the French lad as if she'd never seen anything so delicious in her life—and maybe she hadn't.

"Is it him Alice Donovan was threatening to show those photos to?" The photos had been taken in supermarkets and department stores. Alice must have followed her around for weeks with that camera hidden in a shopping bag. Margaret

Weems was a shoplifter. Not the first person-who-had-every-
thing Bohannon had run into who couldn't keep from stealing.
It was some kind of emotional short circuit. A bid for attention?
Maybe once Jean-Marie came along, she'd given it up. "Would
he leave you?"

She flushed. "Of course not. No, she'd have shown them to
my husband. He'd divorce me. I'd lose everything."

"He doesn't object to Jean-Marie?"

"I'm only helping Jean-Marie with his career."

"Where is Mr. Weems these days?" Bohannon said.

"In Hong Kong. He owns electronics parts firms there. Also
in Taiwan and South Korea. He's away much of the time."

"Too bad," Bohannon said.

Jean-Marie arrived with his tray. She beamed at him. "Dear
boy," she said, and took a tulip champagne glass from the tray.
While the French lad filled it, the Weems woman turned her
smile on Bohannon. "I miss Henry, of course, but I manage to
struggle along without him—somehow."

Bohannon took a glass and a bottle of Beck's from the tray. "I
see that you do," he said, and poured his beer.

They sat down on the sand. Mrs. Weems rubbed a big terry
cloth shoulder against the boy's naked one. She said, "Mr.
Bohannon works for the—uh—county attorney, and for reasons
I can't hope to understand, he needs a list of our guests last
night. Will you find it, please?"

The boy didn't turn to her. He watched leggy little shore
birds getting in their last long-beaked probings of the glassy
sand before nightfall. Maybe he was making up a song. He
certainly wasn't worried. "Oui," he said.

Bohannon got in and out of his truck often in the next three
hours. Each time he was behind the steering wheel again, he
unfolded the list Jean-Marie had given him, and at the end the
paper was coming apart. He sighed and tucked it away. He was
on a twisty road with few street lamps in Settlers Cove, a
section of houses hidden among pines on hills beside the sea.
Because they were farthest off, he had first checked on the
partygoers in Morro Bay and Los Osos. So far as any of them
remembered—a skinny girl painter, a fortyish male dancer who

wore mascara, a squat bald screenwriter in flowered knee-length surfer shorts—Margaret Weems had not only been highly visible in the house and on the beach at her place until the wee hours, but had been the life of the party. They all liked good old Margaret. Oysters chilled on the half shell, duck paté, lobster, and all the champagne you could drink. Really, Margaret was something else. And the story had been the same among the sighing night pines of Settlers Cove. He'd heard it here from a reed player with spiky blue hair, from a music video producer with one leg in a cast, from Mitch Russell, the big, bushy-bearded man who ran the little theater in Madrone. No point bothering anyone else. Bohannon started the truck and headed for home, food, a shower, and bed.

When Bohannon stopped the truck at the far end of the long, white, green-trimmed stable building, pulled the parking brake, and killed the engine, George Stubbs came out of his sleeping quarters next to the tackroom. He was an ex-rodeo rider, a fat old man now, who hobbled, his bones and joints remembering long-ago breaks and sprains. Bohannon climbed wearily down out of the truck and slammed the door in the night silence. Horses stirred in their dark box stalls behind closed doors and nickered softly. Mountains loomed above the place, dark and shaggy. The air was cool.

Stubbs limped up, looking a little peeved. His thick fingers, with their arthritis-swollen joints, were smudged with charcoal. Likely he'd been drawing in his room. He loved to draw—most commonly horses—and did it well and took pride in it. "Where you been all day and half the night? Couldn't you find a phone?"

"A crisis, was there?" Bohannon started for the house. "Anybody dead?"

Stubbs followed him. "Pretty dead supper in the oven, but I reckon that's my own fault, bothering about you."

"I'm sorry I didn't phone, George. I won't let it happen again." A long covered plank walk fronted the ranch house. Bohannon went along it to the kitchen, pulled the screen door, walked over to the big stove rearing up in a corner. He pulled open the door to the warming oven and squinted inside. Stubbs put a quilted mitten in his hand. Bohannon peeled foil off a beef, green pepper, noodle casserole, set it on a counter, shoveled it onto a plate. "This will be fine." He threw the skeptical-looking Stubbs a smile and carried the plate with a fork to the table. He sat down, began to eat—he was hungry— and a sheet of paper lying just outside the circle of light from the lamp in the center of the table caught his eye. "What's this?"

"T. Hodges was here tonight." Stubbs brought a mug of coffee to the table, sat down with a suppressed groan. "She stayed almost an hour, hoping you'd show up." He pried a bent cigarette from a crumpled pack, lit it with a kitchen match. "Finally says she had to go, and wrote you that."

The handwriting was just what he'd have expected of the deputy—firm and without flourishes, straight up and down, easy to read. It said a woman's dog had been struck and its leg broken on Pleasant Trail this morning early. Pleasant Trail was where Alice Donovan's shop was. And the woman lived across and just down the road from there. She said the car that hit the dog was a new red Suzuki Samurai but she didn't get the license number. It came out of the driveway at Ye Olde Oak Tree hell-for-leather, and caromed down the dusty little road. The driver was a tall, young-looking man with a deep tan and a trim little beard. The woman, Gladys Tyndall, didn't know him, never saw him before. But she would like to get her hands on him. Her dog was going to be okay, but he could as easily be dead for all that driver cared.

Bohannon scraped the fork around on the plate for the last taste of his supper. "That was good," he said. "Hardly dried out at all. Thank you, George."

Stubbs grunted. "You want some coffee now?"

"Any of that blueberry cobbler of yours left?"

Stubbs brought the cold cobbler and a mug of hot coffee. Bohannon got up and trudged to the sideboard for a whisky bottle, came back with it, added a jolt of whisky to his coffee, and sat down. He picked up T. Hodges's note and rattled it at Stubbs. "You know any young man with a trimmed beard, a suntan, who drives one of those new little Japanese jeeps?"

"I thought you'd never ask," Stubbs said. He twisted out his smoked-down cigarette in the big glass ashtray that lived on the table. "Him and that red-haired tall girl been up here a couple times to ride the trails."

"Her name—" Bohannon had a mouthful of cobbler; he swallowed, gulped some coffee "—is Andrea Norse. What's his?"

"Beats me," Stubbs said. "It was her that signed in."

"So her address is in our records," Bohannon said.

"If it ain't," Stubbs said, "I'm slipping, and I better start thinking about the old folks' home."

Bohannon got to his feet and went into the shadows for the scuffed gray cardboard box of file cards.

The Samurai stood high on its wheels under drooping blue wisteria beside a rickety white frame cottage among a lot of others like it. This was one of the earliest spots built up in Settlers Cove. Bohannon got down from his truck, ducked under the wisteria that showered him with dew. He pulled open an aluminum screen door and rapped at a brightly varnished wooden door. It was just past seven in the morning. So quiet he could hear the surf breaking, many streets away. Nobody stirred inside the house. He lit a cigarette and knuckled the door again, harder this time. After a ten-second pause, he heard the thump of footfalls, and the tall, redheaded girl opened the door, tugging down a big, loose sweater, shaking back her hair. She had on tight jeans and was barefoot. She winced in the morning light.

"What is it?"

"You know the owner of this vehicle?" Bohannon had his wallet out and open to show his license. He closed the wallet and pushed it away. "It struck a dog yesterday morning about this time, over on Pleasant Trail."

She looked wary. "Who are you, exactly?"

He told her. "Working for the public defender. On the Alice Donovan case? Did you know her, Miss Norse?"

She paled. "I—yes, I counseled her son, Howard." Her smile was thin and didn't last. "He had problems."

"You didn't counsel his mother?" Bohannon said. "Wasn't she behind those problems?"

Her tone hardened. "She didn't see it that way."

"That's how I see it." Bohannon gave her his best smile.
"Don't you agree with me?"

"It's very early in the morning, Mr. Bohannon. I have to get
ready for work. If you'll excuse me—"

"The Samurai is not your car, is it?" he said.

A bearded young man, naked to the waist, buttoning brown
walking shorts, came to the door. His dark hair was tousled
from sleep. He blinked and yawned. He was tall enough to reach
over Andrea Norse's head and take hold of the door she was
holding open. "What's this all about?" he said.

Bohannon told him about the dog. "What's your name?"

"Wolfe. I'm sorry about the dog. I didn't know I'd hit anything.
I'll pay the woman."

"You didn't know you hit anything because you came tearing
out of Alice Donovan's driveway in a sweat. Why? What were
you doing there? Why did you kick in her back door? What was
it you were after?"

Wolfe squinted. "Who's Alice Donovan?"

Looking mournful, Andrea Norse touched his chest. "It's no
use, Zach. He knows we know her." She turned to face Bohannon. "We heard on the early morning radio news that Alice had
been murdered. I was over there the night before, to plead with
her to change her tactics with Howard. I'd tried before. Howard
used to come to me in tears."

"Drunken tears?" Bohannon said.

"Not always, but always heartbroken. That sunny little
woman. She was a monster, you know. Sex-starved, smothering,
seductive—as mixed up and dangerous as they come."

"Should I quote you on that?" Bohannon twitched her a half
smile. "It doesn't sound exactly clinical."

"No." She looked ashamed of herself. "But I couldn't stand by
and not try to change the situation. She was destroying her own
son. He was very disturbed when he came to this door night
before last."

"So disturbed he killed her," Wolfe said, and swung away. "I
need coffee."

"I don't think so," Bohannon said. And to the Norse woman,
"So you went over to try to talk to her? When?"

"Howard stayed here spilling out his woes to me for hours.

When I'd got him calmed down and he left, I drove over to Madrone. What time? Ten? A little past."

"And she was all right?" Bohannon said.

"Self-righteous, smug, superior. Did I think you learned about human nature from books? What was I—thirty years old? Had I raised children of my own? She tried to keep him straight. But he wasn't bright, and boys like that awful Beau Larkin kept getting him into trouble."

"You knew Howard. Could he have killed her?"

"She was his god. We don't kill our gods."

"She wasn't your god. You didn't use that skillet?"

"No, of course not. I'd taken Howard's case folder with me—his history. I wanted to go through it point by point, episode by episode, to show her just how she—"

"And she wouldn't listen, and you walked out," Bohannon said, "and in your anger you left the file behind, and the next morning you remembered, and sent Zach to get it before the sheriff could connect you to the killing."

"He got it," she said wryly, "but it seems it didn't help. What am I, now? Under arrest for murder?"

Bohannon shook his head. "I don't arrest people. I just ask questions. Can you prove you weren't there at midnight? What time did you get home? Was anyone here?"

"Zach and a friend, Sonny Snyder. When? Eleven? Zach put *Diva* on the VCR. He knows it always calms me down."

Bohannon turned away. "Tell him to stop in at the sheriff's about the dog before he goes to work." He ducked under the wisteria. In the road he dropped his cigarette and stepped on it. And a bullet slammed into his shoulder. He heard the report of the rifle as he fell. It echoed off the hills. A second shot kicked grit into his face but that was all. Then Zach Wolfe was kneeling beside him.

"It's all right," he said, "I'm a doctor."

Gerard said, "We'll handle it from now on. Okay?" He sat on a chrome and wicker chair in a hospital room. Clear noon sunlight fell on him from a window. It gleamed off his scalp. Gerard was developing a bald spot. Bohannon hadn't noticed that before. He sat up in the high bed, left arm in a sling, lunch on a tray in front of him. He laid the fork down. The food was tepid and tasteless.

"Did you let Howard go? Obviously, he didn't shoot me."

Gerard shrugged. "Alice was blackmailing people. You were tracking those people down. It made somebody nervous. It doesn't change Howard's status."

"More than nervous," Bohannon said. "Deadly."

"We found the shell casings up the hillside in a tangle of brush and ferns and trees. They could have come from a thousand rifles around here. Thirty-thirty. No dwellings up there. We can't find anybody who saw him."

Bohannon stuck with his thought. "If he was willing to kill me, he was willing to kill Alice Donovan."

"It wasn't Dr. Worthy." Gerard pushed back the crisp cuff of his tan uniform shirt to read his watch. "It wasn't Mrs. Weems." He stood up. "That was sharp of you, having Andrea Norse check on them right then by phone."

"Oh, I'm a hee-ro, I am. Lying there bleeding in the dust and gasping out orders with my dying breath."

"Don't let it go to your head." Gerard opened the door. From the hallway came the squeak of nurses' shoe soles, the jingle of medication trays, the clash of lunch dishes being collected. "Fred May wants us to give you a medal."

"He was here earlier," Bohannon said. "He feels worse than I do about it. He takes things hard."

"We'll find who did it," Gerard said.

"Unless I find him first," Bohannon said.

Gerard turned back. "You stay where you are, dammit. It's the only way we can protect you." He spoke to the young deputy, posted on a chair outside Bohannon's door. "Don't let him trick you, Vern. He's sneaky."

Vern poked his yellow-haired head around the door frame and grinned at Bohannon. "I'll watch him, sir," he said.

Looking half amused, half grim, Gerard went away.

The phone by the bed was almost as good as freedom. He rang T. Hodges to confirm a suspicion about the Kanter case. He rang Andrea Norse to bring the new truck down to the hospital. And Manuel Rivera, at the stables, to bring him clothes without bloodstains and a packet of little firecrackers that had lain in a drawer of the kitchen sideboard for years.

Rivera appeared in his soutane. He was preparing for the priesthood and had supported himself while he studied at the seminary up on the ridge by working part time for Bohannon. Bohannon was going to be sorry to lose him. He was a good worker and an even better friend.

"Close the door," Bohannon told him. "Help me get dressed." It was tricky. There was the arm in the sling to work around, and he was slow from the painkillers they'd given him. But they managed it. "Okay," he said. "Now, you open the door, say good-bye to me, go on down the hall and around the corner, then light the firecrackers, drop them, and walk out as if you had nothing to do with it."

Rivera regarded him with doubtful brown eyes.

"It will work," Bohannon said. "Who's going to suspect a priest?"

"No one will be harmed?" Rivera asked.

"It will just make a racket."

"I don't feel good about it," Rivera said.

"Do it anyway," Bohannon said. "A postulant should learn what it's like to sin. Manuel, go on. It's important."

The slim lad sighed, shook his head, but he went.

Bohannon's only worry was that the firecrackers were so old they wouldn't go off. But they did. A few of them, and made sufficient noise to send Vern racing down the hall and out of sight. Bohannon went the other direction. He found the truck with the keys in it in the parking lot. By the time he was rolling down the street, his shoulder had begun to throb. But he was under way. He laughed to himself.

He could hear the music a block off when he halted the truck at a stop sign. The neighborhood was one of ranch style houses on comfortable lots with well-grown trees. How were they taking that clamor—the thud of drums, the snarl of electric guitars? And the crowd noises that went with it, shouts, raucous laughter, four-letter words? The street was parked up, too. How did the neighbors like that? He turned a corner, found an alley,

parked there, and entered the uproar through a back gate. The
rock music hit him like an eighteen wheeler.

The crowd he could see was all male, teenage, college age,
town boys, ranch boys, jeans, surfer trunks, workshoes, jogging
shoes, baseball caps, straw hats, and crazily shaved heads with
no hats at all. They stamped their feet to the roaring music,
howled and whooped, pushed and tripped each other. At a
brick outdoor barbecue a fat boy scorched hamburger patties.
Beside the grill a plastic tub held beer cans on ice. Empty cans
kicked around underfoot. Everybody had a can in his hand
except three boys who lay passed out on the grass. The smell
of mesquite smoke was strong in the windless air of the hot
afternoon. But so was the smell of marijuana.

Nobody noticed Bohannon. He looked around for the kid
hosting this shindig. He would stand out. He was almost as big
as Howard Donovan. Then Bohannon saw him. He came out the
back door of the house, surrounded by squealing girls, carrying
hamburger buns, ketchup, mustard, barbecue sauce. Drunken
cheers went up as they pushed through the crowd toward the
red-faced fat boy in the smoke. Bohannon followed, and waited
until the girls scattered. He poked the big boy's ribs. Beau
Larkin swung around and stared at him. The color drained from
his face. He licked his lips. He stammered.

"Hey, where did you come from?"

"Come on." Bohannon caught his arm and hauled him out
the back gate into the alley.

"You can't touch me, my father's a police officer."

"And he was on the Kanter robbery case, that collection of
Navajo Indian jewelry. And one piece disappeared from the
collection. I know your father. He's an honest cop. He didn't
take it. I think you took it. And tried to sell it to Alice Donovan,
only she recognized it for what it was, and she's been blackmailing you with it ever since. Making you pay her not to tell
your father."

Larkin reeked of beer. He peered glassily down at Bohannon.
He swayed. His speech was slurred. "Howard said she'd buy it
off me. I didn't know where else to go."

"Why did you kill her, Beau?"

"Because I was behind on my payments. My old man got sore

and cut off my cash flow. I couldn't pay her. But she didn't care. She was going to tell him. I had to kill her. I thought I was out of trouble. But then you got the thing from where she had it hid. Cassie at the cafe told Tony about this stolen Indian buckle you had, and he told me. And I heard how smart you are, and I knew you'd be after me soon. So I had to kill you, too. And now I have to do it again." He lunged. His big hands grabbed Bohannon's throat.

Bohannon struggled. His shoulder screamed pain. He put an open hand against the boy's face and pushed. He kicked. He kneed. Nothing helped. The boy's thumbs were cutting off his air. The light was going out. His ears rang. Then a shout sliced through the back yard noise. A gun went off. Larkin let him go, and Bohannon staggered a few steps, gasping, choking, until his legs wouldn't hold him. He slumped against a fence, and blurrily saw Larkin lying face down in weeds and cinders, and Vern bending over, snapping handcuffs on the boy's thick wrists.

"Hack, were you crazy?" T. Hodges made the rocker in Bohannon's pine plank bedroom creak angrily. "Going after a giant like that—with only one good arm, just out of surgery? How did you expect to even get there?"

He lay in his own bed. That was the good part. The bad part was how sore his throat was. He couldn't swallow food. It even hurt to talk. The sound that came out was hoarse, no more than a whisper. "It's over now. Calm down."

"You were lucky Vern got there when he did."

Vern gave his toothy kid grin. "Lieutenant Gerard warned me he was tricky." He stood gangly at the foot of the poster bed. "Soon as I saw those firecrackers, I knew it was Mr. Bohannon back of it. He didn't get much of a start on me. Broke a lot of speed laws, though. With that old patrol car I had, I almost lost him a couple of times."

"I was drugged," Bohannon whispered, "didn't know what I was doing." He heard voices in the hallway and looked at the door. Fred May came in, wearing a pup-tent-size pink sweatshirt that had once been red. He did his best to smile, but worry for how Bohannon felt spoiled the attempt. As if Bohannon were hovering near death, he looked for advice to the two young deputies.

"Is it okay?" he said. "I brought somebody."

"Fred, I'm all right." Bohannon hoped he was more successful with his try at smiling than May had been. "Who is it?"

Who it was filled the doorway. Howard Donovan. He held there, shy as a five-year-old, trying to find the words to thank Bohannon for getting him out of jail. "They all thought I killed my mother." Tears brimmed in his eyes, and he used big fists to knuckle the tears away. "You knew I didn't do that. You knew I wouldn't."

"I was betting on it."

Howard grinned unexpectedly. "Even if I did pick you up that night and throw you in the water."

"It's not the same," Bohannon said.

"That was only funning, wasn't it?" Howard said. He looked grave again. "She made me very mad sometimes, but I wouldn't hurt her. I never did hurt her. Even when she hit me. Not once." He frowned to himself. "It wouldn't be right. She was too little." He paused, and abruptly the small boy that lived in his head changed the subject. Excited. Eyes shining. "There's a big old owl up in our tree. Did you know that? And the crows been pestering him."

"Yes," Bohannon said, "I knew that."

"Well, guess what? When I came home from jail, there's black feathers all over the yard. Crow feathers. Guess that old owl showed them who's boss, didn't he?"

"It's his tree," Bohannon said. "We both knew that."

"And it's my house," Howard said. "Isn't it?"

# DONALD E. WESTLAKE
## DOMESTIC INTRIGUE

"**M**rs. Carroll," said the nasty man, "I happen to know that your husband is insanely jealous."

I happened to know the same thing myself, and so there was nothing to do but agree. Robert *was* insanely jealous. "However," I added, "I fail to see where that is any of your business."

The nasty man smiled at me, nastily. "I'll come to that," he said.

"You entered this house," I reminded him, "under the guise of taking some sort of survey. Yet you ask me no questions at all about my television viewing habits. On the contrary, you promptly begin to make comments about my personal life. I think it more than likely that you are a fraud."

"Ah, madam," he said, with that nasty smile of his, under that nasty little mustache, "of course I'm a fraud. Aren't we all frauds, each in his—or *her*—own way?"

"I think," I said as icily as possible, "it would be best if you were to leave. At once."

He made no move to get up from the sofa. In fact, he even spread out a bit more, acting as though at any instant he might kick off his shoes and take a nap. "If your husband," he said lazily, "were to discover another man making love to you, there's no doubt in my mind that Mr. Carroll would shoot the other man on the spot."

Once again I had no choice but to agree, since Robert had more than once said the same thing to me, waving that great big pistol of his around and shouting, "If I ever see another man so much as *kiss* you, I'll blow his brains out, I swear I will."

Still, that was my cross to bear, and hardly a subject for idle chatter with perfect strangers who had sailed into my living room under false colors, and I said as much. "I don't know where you got your information," I went on, "and I don't care. Nor do I care to discuss my private life with you. If you do not leave, I shall telephone the police at once."

The nasty man smiled his nasty smile and said, "I don't think you'll call the police, Mrs. Carroll. You aren't a stupid woman. I think you realize by now I'm here for a reason, and I think you'd like to know what that reason is. Am I right?"

He was right to an extent, to the extent that I had the uneasy feeling he knew even more about my private life than he'd already mentioned, possibly even more than Robert knew, but I was hardly anxious to hear him say the words that would confirm my suspicions, so I told him, "I find it unlikely that you could have anything to say to me that would interest me in the slightest."

"I haven't bored you so far," he said, with a sudden crispness in his tone, and I saw that the indolent way he had of lounging on my sofa was pure pretense, that underneath he was sharp and hard and very self-aware. But this glimpse of his interior was as brief as it was startling; he slouched at once back into that infuriating pose of idleness and said, "Your husband carries that revolver of his everywhere, doesn't he? A Colt Cobra, isn't it? Thirty-eight caliber. Quite a fierce little gun."

"My husband is in the jewelry business," I said. "He very frequently carries on his person valuable gems or large amounts of money. He has a permit for the gun, because of the business he's in."

"Yes, indeed, I know all that." He looked around admiringly and said, "And he does very well at it too, doesn't he?"

"You *are* beginning to bore me," I said. I half turned away, saying, "I believe I'll call the police now."

Quietly, the nasty man said, "Poor William."

I stopped. I turned around. I said, "What was that?"

"No longer bored?" Under the miserable mustache, he smiled once again his nasty smile.

I said, "Explain yourself!"

"You mean why did I say, 'Poor William'? I was merely thinking about what would happen to William if a Colt Cobra were pointed at him, and the trigger pulled, and a thirty-eight-caliber special bullet were to smash its way through his body."

I suddenly felt faint. I took three steps to the left, and rested my hands on the back of a chair. "What's his last name?" I demanded, though the demand was somewhat nullified by the tremor in my voice. "William who?"

He looked at me, and again he gave me a glimpse of the steel within. He said, "Shall I really say the name, Mrs. Carroll? Is there more than one William in your life?"

"There are no Williams in my life," I said, but despairingly, knowing now that this nasty man knew everything. But how? How?

"Then I must say the name," he said. "William Bar—"

"Stop!"

He smiled. His teeth were very even and very white and very sparkly. I hated them. He said, softly, "Won't you sit down, Mrs. Carroll? You seem a bit pale."

I moved around the chair I'd been holding for support, and settled into it, rather heavily and gracelessly. I said, "I don't know when my husband will be home, he could be—"

"I do," he said briskly. "Not before one-fifteen. He has appointments till one, and it's at least a fifteen-minute drive here from his last appointment." He flickered back to indolence, saying lazily, "I come well prepared, you see, Mrs. Carroll."

"So I see."

"You are beginning," he said, "to wonder what on earth it is that I want. I seem to know so very much about you, and so far I have shown no interest in doing anything but talk. Isn't that odd?"

From the alert and mocking expression on his face, I knew he required an answer of me, and so I said, "I suppose you can do what you want. It's your party."

"So it is. Mrs. Carroll, would you like to see your good friend William dead? Murdered? Shot down in cold blood?"

My own blood ran cold at the thought of it. William! My love! In all this bleak and brutal world, only one touch of tenderness, of beauty, of hope do I see, and that is William. If it weren't for those stolen moments with William, how could I go on another minute with Robert?

If only it were William who was rich, rather than Robert. But William was poor, pitifully poor, and as he was a poet it was unlikely he would ever be anything but poor. And as for me, I admit that I was spoiled, that the thought of giving up the

comforts and luxuries which Robert's money could bring me
made me blanch just as much as the thought of giving up
William. I needed them both in equal urgency. William's love
and Robert's money.

The nasty man, having waited in vain for me to answer his
rhetorical question, at last said, "I can see you would not like it.
William is important to you."

"Yes," I said, or whispered, unable to keep from confessing it.
"Oh, yes, he is."

Until William, I had thought that all men were beasts. My
mother—bless her soul—had said constantly that all men were
beasts, all through my adolescence, after my father disappeared,
and I had come to maturity firmly believing that she was right.
I had married Robert even though I'd known he was a beast,
but simply because I had believed there was no choice in the
matter, that one married a beast or one didn't marry at all. And
Robert did have the advantage of being rich.

But now I had found William, and I had found true love, and
I had learned what my mother never knew; that not *all* men
are beasts. Almost all, yes, but not entirely all. Here and there
one can find the beautiful exception. Like William.

But not, obviously, like this nasty man in front of me. I would
have needed none of my mother's training to know that *this*
man was a beast. Perhaps, in his own cunning way, an even
worse beast than brutal and blustering Robert. Perhaps, in his
own way, even more dangerous.

I said, "What is it you want from me?"

"Oh, my dear lady," he protested, *"I* want from *you?* Not a
thing, I assure you. It is what *you* want from *me."*

I stared at him. I said, "I don't understand. What could I
possibly want from you?"

As quickly as a striking snake, his hand slid within his jacket,
slid out again with a long blank white envelope, and flipped it
through the air to land in my lap. "These," he said. "Take a look
at them."

I opened the envelope. I took out the pictures. I looked at
them, and I began to feel my face go flaming red.

I recognized the room in the pictures, remembered that
motel.

The faces were clear in every one of the photographs. "What you'll want," said the nasty man, smiling triumphantly, "is the negatives."

I whispered, "You mean, you'll show these to my husband?"

"Oh, I would much rather not. Wouldn't you like to have them for yourself? The prints *and* the negatives?"

"How much?"

"Well, I really hadn't thought," he said, smiling and smiling. "I'd rather leave that up to you? How much would you say they were worth to *you*, Mrs. Carroll?"

I looked at the photos again, and something seemed to go click in my mind. I said, "I believe I'm going to faint." Then my eyes closed, and I fell off the chair onto the floor.

He had a great deal of difficulty awaking me, patting my cheeks and chafing my hands, and when at last I opened my eyes I saw that he was no longer smiling, but was looking very worried. "Mrs. Carroll," he said. "Are you all right?"

"My heart," I whispered. "I have a weak heart." It was untrue, but it seemed a lie that might prove useful.

It did already. He looked more worried than ever, and backed away from me, looking down at me lying on the floor and saying, "Don't excite yourself, Mrs. Carroll. Don't get yourself all upset. We can work this out."

"Not now," I whispered. "Please." I passed a hand across my eyes. "I must rest. Call me. Telephone me. I'll meet you somewhere."

"Yes, of course. Of course."

"Call me this evening. At six."

"Yes."

"Say your name is Boris."

"Boris," he repeated. "Yes, I will." Hastily he retrieved the fallen photos. "Call at six," he said, and dashed out of the house.

I got to my feet, brushed off my toreadors, and went to phone William. "Darling," I said.

"Darling!" he cried.

"My love."

"Oh, my heart, my sweet, my rapture!"

"Darling, I must—"

"Darling! Darling! Darling!"

"Yes, sweetheart, thank you, that's all very—"

"My life, my love, my all!"

*"William!"*

There was a stunned silence, and then his voice said, faintly, "Yes, Mona?"

There were advantages to having a poet for a lover, but there were also disadvantages, such as a certain difficulty in attracting his attention sometimes.

But I had his attention now. I said, "William, I won't be able to see you tonight."

"Oh, *sweet*heart!"

"I'm sorry, William, believe me I am, but something just came up."

"Is it—" his voice lowered to a whisper "—is it *him?"*

He meant Robert. I said. "No, dear, not exactly. I'll tell you all about it tomorrow."

"Shall I see you tomorrow?"

"Of course. At the museum. At noon."

"Ah, my love, the hours shall have broken wings."

"Yes, dear."

With some difficulty I managed to end the conversation. I then took the other car, the Thunderbird, and drove to the shopping center. In the drugstore there I purchased a large and foul-looking cigar, and in the Mister-Master Men's-Wear Shoppe I bought a rather loud and crude necktie. I returned to the house, lit the cigar, and found that it tasted even worse than I had anticipated. Still, it was all in a good cause. I went upstairs, puffing away at the cigar, and draped the necktie over the doorknob of the closet door in my bedroom. I then went back to the first floor, left a conspicuous gray cone of cigar ash in the ashtray beside Robert's favorite chair, puffed away until the room was full of cigar smoke and I felt my flesh beginning to turn green, and then tottered out to the kitchen. I doused the cigar under the cold water at the kitchen sink, stuffed it down out of sight in the rubbish bag, and went away to take two Alka-Seltzers and lie down.

By one-fifteen, when Robert came bounding home, I was recovered and was in the kitchen thawing lunch. *"My* love!" roared Robert, and crushed me in his arms.

That was the difference right there. William would have put the accent on the other word.

I suffered his attentions, as I always did, and then he went away to read the morning paper in the living room while I finished preparing lunch.

When he came to the table he seemed somewhat more subdued than usual. He ate lunch in silence, with the exception of one question, asked with an apparent attempt at casualness:

"Umm, darling, did you have any visitors today?"

I dropped my spoon into my soup. "Oh! Wasn't that clumsy! What did you say, dear?"

His eyes narrowed. "I asked you, did you have any visitors today?"

"Visitors? Why—why, no dear." I gave a guilty sort of little laugh. "What makes you ask, sweetheart?"

"Nothing," he said, and ate his soup.

After lunch he said, "I have time for a nap today. Wake me at three, will you?"

"Of course, dear."

I woke him at three. He said he'd be home by five-thirty, and left. I checked, and the crude necktie was no longer hanging on the doorknob in my bedroom.

When Robert came home at five-thirty he was even quieter than before. I caught him watching me several times, and each time I gave a nervous start and a guilty little laugh and went into some other room.

I was in the kitchen at six o'clock, when the phone rang. "I'll get it dear!" I shouted. "It's all right, dear! I'll get it! I'll get it!"

I picked up the phone and said hello and the nasty man's voice said, "This is Boris."

"Yes, of course," I said, keeping my voice low.

"Can we talk?"

"Yes."

"Isn't your husband home?"

"It's all right, he's in the living room, he can't hear me. I want to meet you tonight, to *discuss* things." I gave a heavy emphasis to that word, and put just a touch of throatiness into my voice.

He gave his nasty laugh and said, "Whenever you say, dear lady. I take it you're recovered from this afternoon?"

"Oh, yes. It was just—tremors. But listen, here's how we'll meet. You take a room at the Flyaway Motel, under the name of Clark. I'll—"

"Take a room?"

"We'll have a lot to—*talk* about. Don't worry. I'll pay for the room."

"Well," he said, "in that case . . ."

"I'll try to be there," I said, "as soon after nine as possible. Wait for me."

"All right, M—"

"I must hang up," I said hastily, before he could call me Mrs. Carroll. I broke the connection, went into the living room, and found Robert standing near the extension phone in there. I said, "Dinner will be ready soon, dear."

"Any time, darling," he said. His voice seemed somewhat strangled. He seemed to be under something of a strain.

Dinner was a silent affair, though I tried to make small talk without much success. Afterward, Robert sat in the living room and read the evening paper.

I walked into the living room at five minutes to nine, wearing my suede jacket. "I have to go out for a while, dear," I said.

He seemed to control himself with difficulty. "Where to, dear?" he asked me.

"The drugstore. I need nailpolish remover."

"Oh, yes," he said.

I went out and got into the Thunderbird. As I drove away I saw the lights go on in my bedroom. If it was nailpolish remover Robert was looking for, he'd have little trouble finding it. There was a nearly full bottle with my other cosmetics on the vanity table.

I drove at moderate speeds, arriving at the Flyaway Motel at ten minutes past nine. "I'm Mrs. Clark," I told the man at the desk. "Could you tell me which unit my husband is in?"

"Yes, ma'am." He checked his register and said, "Six."

"Thank you."

Walking across the gravel toward Unit 6, I thought it all out again, as it had come to me in a flash of inspiration this afternoon just before I had had my "faint." The idea that I could have Robert's money without necessarily having to have Robert along with it had never occurred to me before. But now it had, and I liked it. To have Robert's money without having Robert meant I could have William!

What a combination! William *and* Robert's money!

My step was light as I approached Unit 6.

The nasty man opened the door to my knock. He seemed somewhat nervous. "Come on in, Mrs. Carroll."

As I went in, I glanced back and saw an automobile just turning into the motel driveway. Was that a Lincoln? A *blue* Lincoln?

The nasty man shut and locked the door, but I said, "None of that. Unlock that door."

"Don't worry about me, lady," he said, grinning nastily. "All I want from you is your money." Nevertheless, he unlocked the door again.

"Fine," I said. I took off my suede jacket.

"Now," he said, coming across the room, rubbing his hands together, "to get to business."

"Of course," I said. I took off my blouse.

He blinked at me. He said, "Hey! What are you doing?"

"Don't worry about a thing," I told him, and unzipped my toreadors.

His eyes widened and he waved his hands at me, shouting, "Don't *do* that! You got it all wrong, don't *do* that!"

"I don't believe I have it wrong," I said, and stepped out of the toreadors.

With utter panic and bewilderment, the nasty man said, "But William said you'd—" And stopped.

We both stopped. I stared at the nasty man in sudden comprehension. All at once I understood how it was he had known so much about me, how it had been possible for him to take those pictures.

So William couldn't live on the amount I gave him willingly.

Mother was right, all men *are* beasts.

As I stood there, trying to get used to this new realization, the door burst open and Robert came bellowing in, waving that huge and ugly pistol of his.

I still wasn't recovered from my shock. To think, to think I'd been trying to save William from being killed, to think I'd been willing to sacrifice both Robert and the nasty man for William's sake! And all the time, all the time, William had betrayed me!

But then I *did* recover from the shock, and fast, because I saw that Robert had stopped his enraged bellowing and was glaring at me. At *me*. And pointing that filthy pistol at me.

At *me*.

"Not me!" I cried, and pointed at the nasty man. "Him! *Him!*"

The first shot buzzed past my ear and smashed the glass over the woodland painting above the bed.

I ran left, I ran right. The nasty man cowered behind the dresser. Robert's second shot chunked into the wall behind me.

"You lied!" I screamed. "You *lied.*"

All men are bea

# JOHN F. SUTER

# THE STONE MAN

**P**ete Bender never thought of the phrase "living rock" as a literal one, although he had heard it and understood it. It was the medium in which his father had made his life's work, as had other ancestors. Pete, himself, had planned his life to carry on the tradition.

Four other men worked for him, but for Pete the tradition and his line were about to end. With one of the tools of his trade, Bender had slain his wife, who had never presented him with a child of either sex.

Bender, a spare man with a lean face, intense blue eyes, and jet black hair, did not fit the image of Hercules as a stonemason. Perhaps his wife Marie, a hoydenish type only one generation away from France—as Bender was from his own native soil—had thought this herself.

"You build fine houses for the rich," she was fond of saying. "But do you bid on the fancy buildings for the city government? The exclusive clubhouses? The bridges in the city parks? No. What's wrong with you?"

Pete sipped his wine and bestowed a faint smile. "Aren't you living comfortably?"

"Comfortably, yes. Excitingly, no!"

Anyone could have written the script from then on. It ended on the day when Marie and Pete arrived home late within minutes of each other. Pete was sorting his tools at the back of his truck when the red Ferrari stopped to let Marie out. It roared off as she teetered in Pete's direction.

Bender eyed her with disgust. "What is it?" he said, biting off the words. "You're not worth enough for him to see you to the door? Or can't he look me in the face?"

She tried to toss back her hair, but the effort of lifting her chin was too much.

"Not afraid of you," she muttered. "You wouldn't make two bites for him."

Pete was holding his favorite knapping hammer. He hefted it. "That one, he wouldn't have any teeth to bite with."

Marie tried to focus her eyes on the tool. "You know somethin'? Long time ago, you cut yourself a hunk of granite and stuck it in your chest. Where most men have a heart. No blood in you, either. Just water 'n' a sludge of granite dust."

"A home," Pete growled, "what kind of home have you ever made for me?"

"Who could make a home outta . . . maus—mausoleum?" She swayed, spilling words. "I need to be warmed."

Once Pete had wanted to create for her something beyond anything a man had ever made. He remembered this now and mentally saw it washed away like a sand castle by the sea. Warmth he had provided, to excess. Suddenly, it was all too much.

His arm came up, almost unbidden, and he hit her with the flat of the hammer. Four times, each blow on a different side, her head turned with the force of every stroke.

When he stood over what was left, he passed his right hand over his face and groaned. Then he went into the house to the telephone.

To his surprise, his call was answered.

Gathering his will, he said, "This is Bender. You'd better call the police. I've just killed your whore."

"May I fill your glass again, judge?" Arthur Price asked, gesturing in the direction of his visitor's right hand.

Judge Whiteman stirred in the depths of the leather chair. "I'd like that, Art."

Price, a successful lawyer still some years away from becoming an Institution, walked across the family room to his bar. "Have I told you we're thinking of a new house?" he said casually.

Judge Whiteman, a John Doe sort who donned distinction with his black robe, looked about him. "Hunting a place to spend it, is that it? I'd be satisfied with this, myself."

Price added water and ice to the scotch. "It's been quite comfortable, but frame has always bothered Anne. New paint job every few years, this and that. She'd like for us to go to stone."

"Lower upkeep, I'll agree," the judge said, accepting the glass. "Initial outlay—you can afford it, I'd say. Who would do your stonework?"

"That's the problem," Price said, sitting in the companion chair opposite. He smoothed his graying hair. "You're about to sentence the man I'd hoped to get. I'll probably have to hire somebody from out of town. There's nobody else any more."

Judge Whiteman sipped. "Bender? He didn't operate all by himself. Get his crew. They might come up with somebody to head it."

"I thought of that, but they feel that they'd need someone with Bender's business sense and eye for the finished product."

The judge mused. "A pity that his father had to die twelve years ago. That old Italian—" He paused. "Or was he Austrian? He changed his name before he came here. Could it have been Benda? Or Bendt? No matter."

"As you say, no matter," the lawyer said impatiently. "What sentence are you going to give Bender?"

Judge Whiteman stared into his glass. "I haven't made up my mind yet."

Price consulted his own drink. "It's a pity to make a talented person's services unavailable to the public. Under the circumstances, I might have done just what he did."

The judge looked up. "I have never explored what I think you're hinting. But why not? Other judges have done it."

"It might not be too popular."

"With whom?" the judge asked. "Oh, with Jules Vernet, the wife's brother—of course. And maybe with that hunk of sleaze who precipitated it all. I wonder why Bender didn't split *his* skull? Can you think of anyone else?"

"Some of the unpredictable public. Those who've seen Marie Bender's picture but who never knew her."

Judge Whiteman thought it over. "I try never to let the public influence me. Still, careful thought seems to be indicated."

Judge Whiteman had called two persons into chambers before he sentenced Pete Bender for the second degree murder of his wife, Marie. One was Bender himself; the other was Jules Vernet, a wide-shouldered, barrel-chested worker of wrought iron. Where Bender's darkness ended at his hair, Vernet was black of eyes and beard, as was his scowl.

The judge, now robed, was, to his visitors, the unquestioned embodiment of the law. He looked first at Vernet, seated on his left.

"I have requested both of you to be here," he said, "because what I intend to say in court will be unusual. Mr. Vernet, I don't want you in there unprepared because I don't want you upsetting the dignity of my court."

Vernet's milk-white skin flushed. "I respect the law, Your Honor."

The judge rubbed his chin. "I'm sure you do. All the same—"

He turned to Bender. "What sentence are you expecting?"

Bender shrugged, expressionless. "Not for me to say. You're the judge."

"Mr. Vernet. Any opinions?"

The red was fading on Vernet's cheekbones. "I'd throw the book at him."

Judge Whiteman nodded. "Understandable. She was your sister."

He clasped his hands and looked down at them. "The evidence would indicate that Mr. Bender acted in a moment of blind rage, after some provocation. He should, of course, have checked himself. He is not known to be a violent man, according to those familiar with him. He is also recognized as being especially talented in his work. Unfortunately, the penal system in this state has no outlet for his talent, even in hard labor.

"On the other hand, when Mr. Bender is sent to prison, this community will lose the services of a very skilled person. True, he has been well paid for those services. And one way of looking at his incarceration is that the citizens of this state will be paying handsomely to keep him locked up, his talents no longer available for anything constructive.

"In recent years," he continued, looking up, "the courts have taken a careful look at certain criminals: hit and run killers, embezzlers, perpetrators of various types of involuntary manslaughter, and others. They have decided that justice is better served by allowing them to remain outside prison, dividing their time between continuing with their normal lives and devoting their energies to a public service. This permits their families to survive and society to benefit."

The judge looked directly at Bender. "I have decided that this is what I shall require of you, Mr. Bender."

The stone contractor's voice was husky. "Thank you, Your Honor. It's better than I deserve."

"And *that's* an understatement!" Vernet roared. He leaped from his chair and started for Bender. "I'll kill him now and take my chances!"

Judge Whiteman had anticipated this and had already pushed a buzzer. The rear door burst open, and two husky guards rushed in. Vernet had barely reached Bender before they seized him and dragged him aside.

"Mr. Vernet!" the judge snapped. "Now you see why I wanted this private session. Set him in that chair again," he directed.

When things had quieted, Judge Whiteman addressed the room in general. "I'll now finish this discussion. Mr. Bender will be permitted to take up his business again. But, there are two things he is required to do, and others might be added later.

"First, the county wants to build a small nondenominational chapel in memory of its citizens who died in the Korean and Vietnamese wars. They prefer that the material be stone. You will undertake this contract. Your men will be paid. You will not. Your efforts will be a public service. When this is finished, there might be more.

"Second, you are to build a memorial obelisk for the woman you murdered."

"She's already buried, with a good headstone over the grave," Vernet interrupted.

"The column will be set in one of the divider islands in one of the cemetery drives," the judge said. "It will be an honor, sir."

He turned back to Bender. "You will be given a sketch of the obelisk. You will be furnished with the materials you specify. You are to do the entire erection of the column yourself. There are certain rules you must follow."

"Anything you say," Bender agreed.

The judge continued. "You will be permitted to lay the pavement around the base at your own pace. However, you are to construct this column with stones no larger than ten inches long by six inches in each of the other dimensions. These stones can be irregular. You may lay only one stone a month. The last act will be to fix a simple bronze plaque to the face of the column. It will read 'Marie Vernet Bender, February 17, 1943—June 6, 1973.'

"When you complete the column, your sentence will be served."

Bender had listened attentively and with growing interest to the conditions of his sentence. From the moment of his arrest until an hour ago, something had been dying within him. Not to be shaping stone would reduce him to zombie status. Now he would be at least almost whole again. He truly mourned for Marie—the Marie of the day they married. He privately felt that the Marie he had killed had enough memorial already.

"I have some questions, Your Honor," he said.

"Go ahead."

"For this column—what kind of stone?"

"Sandstone, limestone, granite—it makes no difference."

"I should have said 'which style.' "

The judge frowned. "Dressed, quarried stone." He studied the stonemason. "Are you trying something, Bender?"

Bender shook his head. "I'd have preferred rubblestone, but I'll follow directions, Your Honor."

"Rubblestone!" Vernet snorted. "Plain old fieldstone. Even now, he hasn't any respect for her!"

"I'll make it so that even you will be proud of it," Bender said.

"That's another point," Judge Whiteman interrupted. "Mr. Vernet will be one of three inspectors of your handiwork. He will be critical, but fair. We shall see to it that he is."

Bender whistled between his teeth. Then he said, "Is the column to be hollow or solid?"

"Solid."

Bender's eyebrows raised.

"Are these requirements unsatisfactory?" the judge asked. "If so, I have an alternate sentence ready. It's the customary type."

"Quite satisfactory, Your Honor," Bender said, avoiding looking at Vernet. "At least, to me."

After Judge Whiteman had pronounced sentence in open court, Pete took steps to adjust his life to the new pattern imposed upon it. He cleared the house completely of any influence Marie had ever imposed upon it. This done, he found himself living in austere surroundings. He coped with them temporarily by closing rooms he did not immediately need and generated cash by selling discards. Vernet attempted to claim some of these things, but Bender ignored him.

In quiet moments, he made calculations about the column. It was directed to be no less than three feet square at the base, tapering to a point no fewer than six feet above ground. He was allowed to extend the square at the base or to increase the height if he wished.

When he had finished his estimates, he understood the judge's stipulations. He mentally bowed to the jurist or to his advisor, if one had been involved.

The construction, at one stone a month, would last twelve years.

He grinned. Unless—

There was no specification about the mortar.

He could use as many or as few stones as he wished, provided the workmanship was sound and pleasing to the eye.

His feeling of elation diminished. He knew that his pride of workmanship would not let him take absurd shortcuts.

He decided to count on eleven years, at least.

The adjustment to a changed life was not easy. Bender found himself unwelcome in places where Marie had been favored, many of them not in the least cheap or tawdry. In the large, the congregation of his church shunned him, preferring to forget one of the teachings of their Leader. In the end Pete found religious acceptance by a mission doing no-questions-asked work in the lower stratum of society.

He did not look for friendship and companionship. His workers had not changed loyalties, and there were enough friends and acquaintances who remembered with disapproval Marie in her later years.

He had intended to begin on the memorial, both as a start to freedom and as a renewal of his personal bond with stone. Before he could do more than order a supply of sandstone from local quarries, Arthur Price had approached him about his new house.

Bender studied the plans before him on his work table.

"A well-designed house," he said. "It will be a pleasure to work for you, Mr. Price."

"You don't see any problems?" the lawyer asked, running a long finger down the edge of the table.

"Oh, no. You'll find us very adaptable. One thing: you don't need us to lay up the block for your foundation or inner wall. After all, the stone is the facing on the block. It might cost you less to have somebody like Miller Brothers do the block. We can do it all, of course, but we get along with the Millers. It's your money."

Price stood absorbed in thought.

Bender smiled. "Take your time, Mr. Price. Give me an answer later. We have plenty of other work, I assure you."

"I'm thinking of Zimmerman as the main contractor. Any ideas?"

"Good man. I don't know his feelings about me. We'll see."

Price rapped the edge of the table with his knuckle. "Well, if it's all right with you, I'll see about Miller Brothers."

"Sure." And good public relations for you, thought Bender. You'll be running for something someday. Spread it in lots of places.

The mistaken thought also came to him that Judge Whiteman was directing work toward him, to help him remain a useful citizen.

He frowned. In his mind's ledger, there was enough debit already.

The county was stalling on the memorial chapel, still arguing about small points in the design.

As soon as he realized this, Bender went to the cemetery, located the spot intended for the memorial, and measured it off. He arranged with the superintendent for removal of the sod for the base of the column. Then, when the grass was gone, he returned, dug and smoothed the ground, and poured footers. The next day, he came back with boards he had sawn for the frame and installed them. Then he took the cornerstone he had already cut and dressed and carefully laid it, wiping away the small amount of excess mortar when he had finished.

It looked small and inconsequential, a token beginning of something a trifler would never complete. In Pete's mind it was different. Each stone would remind him of what he had done.

The base of the monument took him eighteen months. His first thought was to fill the center with concrete, without stone, but he feared the effects of expansion. A faulty job would tie him to this project for too long a time.

Price's house was long since finished, to his and Judge White-man's satisfaction. The memorial chapel construction was into its second month.

The nineteenth month of the obelisk had come, and Bender had laid the first stone of the second course, tapering the edges of the outer face.

The day after it was laid, he received word from Judge Whiteman's secretary that the three-man inspection team would be looking at his work. Bender was asked to be present.

The request was a surprise. Bender knew that previous inspections had been made, but he had never attended and no comments had ever been made to him.

He arrived at the cemetery at ten in the morning. His ex-brother-in-law and two other men were already there.

Vernet looked at him when he walked up, then at the other men. "I guess we can start now," he said. He addressed Sheets, a weatherbeaten general contractor. "Why don't you look at it first, Bill?"

Sheets glanced apologetically at Bender. He clearly viewed inspecting one stone as a waste of time. He walked to the monument and bent over, peering at it.

"Looks like a good job of layin' to me," he said.

"Not lopsided? Is it good and firm? Go on, Bill, shake it," Vernet prodded.

The older man, looking even more sheepish, leaned over and began a halfhearted push at the stone. As mild as his effort was, it was too much.

The mortar crumbled, and the stone fell to the ground.

"Well, would you look at that!" Vernet bellowed. "Bill—you saw that. So did you, George. That's shoddy workmanship if I ever laid eyes on it. Did you think you could get away with this, Bender?"

Bender's mouth was set in a thin line. "It's been tampered with. Never in my life have I set a joint that didn't hold."

"Would you listen to him," his ex-brother-in-law hooted. "That was the story of my sister's marriage: cheap, skimpy, tenth-rate . . ."

"I'll reset it this afternoon," Bender said. "If it's not like the Rock of Gibraltar tomorrow, I'll quit my business."

"You won't quit until the whole job's done," Vernet roared, shaking a big finger. "And you won't put it back until next month. It counts as another stone."

"But—"

"Another stone. Ask the judge."

Bender glanced at the other two men. "Hey, you guys, you know me. You know my work. Ever know me to do anything like this?"

Both of them avoided his eye. Sheets muttered that anyone could have an off day. "You'd have caught it next month, I'm sure, Pete," he finished.

Bender said nothing. He picked up the stone and drove off with it, thinking hard all the way.

When he reached his supply shed, he went to the materials that had been specifically furnished for the construction of the column. He ignored the stone pile but headed for the bags of sand, lime, and cement. He put samples from each into separate small bottles.

An hour later, he was at Vernet's place of business. He found the man in the workroom where he shaped the wrought iron. A hanging lamp in the last stages of construction was getting attention.

"What do you want?" the heavy man demanded. "You come here whinin', wantin' me to get you off the hook?"

"Not me," Bender replied. "I just took samples of some of my materials over to Elementals Labs for analysis. It wouldn't be too hard for some switching to have been done. And I think it happened."

"You lookin' at me?"

"Not necessarily, Jules. But you have to admit, I might think I should."

Vernet picked up a hammer and hefted it. Bender wondered if he was going to work with it or was making a threat. "Yeah, I can understand. To me, you'll always be a bastard. Marie was my kid sister, and you could have done a lot of things other than killin' her."

Bender looked about him. Several large charts illustrating different styles of calligraphy were taped to the walls. "What are those? You taking up fancy writing on the side?"

The change of subject surprised Vernet. "No. I got a contract for puttin' rails on fancy balconies on a house for Dave Grinstead. They want alternate initials worked into 'em, his and hers, to match their handwriting. I got these for study and practice."

"All right," Bender said. "I'll put it this way: I don't think you'll use spot welds when you put initials into Grinstead's rails. Do you think I'd do cheap work on Marie's monument?"

Vernet gave him a long look. "No, Bender, I don't think you would, believe it or not. I don't know what the lab will tell you, but I've not touched your stuff. But that doesn't let others out."

He turned to lay the hammer down, then he glanced back at Bender. "Or maybe somebody had it done."

Later, Bender learned that powdered chalk had been substituted for his lime and a mixture of barytes, carbon black, and a trace of cement (for odor) for his cement. He got rid of the bags and put his own materials in their place. The problem never recurred although once, two years later, the entire upper surface of the older construction was soaked with an oily substance that prevented new, water-based mortar from adhering. Bender restored the surface with paint thinner and a wire brush, then laid the next stone successfully.

No incidents ever occurred on his private jobs or with the chapel.

The years passed without any other bother. Once a fresh bag of cement set up a month after being received. Since Bender still used his own supplies on the monument, this was no problem. He did suspect that water had been injected into the bag with needles, but he returned the bag without comment and got a fresh bag.

Four years after Marie's death, Bender met an attractive blonde, Louisa Trubar. She was twenty-eight, born in Slovenia, Yugoslavia, but a resident of Maryland since early childhood. She and Bender met at a beach in Virginia, found they were decidedly compatible, and married. The union was happy, and their first son arrived fourteen months after the wedding.

Not long after the wedding, Bender met Sheets, the contractor, on the street.

"Hey, Pete," the older man said, thumping him on the shoulder, "I hear you got something nice at home now. Congratulations."

Bender thanked him, and they made small talk.

"How's your ex-brother-in-law taking it?" Sheets asked.

"Hasn't said a word," Bender replied. "Hardly his business, is it?"

"Well, no," Sheets admitted. "He's of Corsican descent, isn't he? Aren't they supposed to harbor grudges?"

"I don't know. Are they? Louisa's people had a hard time in World War II, but she's not about to cut down on any Germans."

Sheets spat into the gutter. "I never could figure out if he was madder at you or Judge Whiteman over your sentence. He had his back up with the judge even before that, I guess you know."

"No, I hadn't heard."

"I guess it came to a head while you were waitin' for a trial. Jules's father had bought a nice piece of land out in Overbrook, before Jules was born. About five acres. He kept it up, but he never did anything with it. When he died, Jules inherited it. He had his own place, so he figured it for an investment. So it would have been, if any new industry would be wanting to move a small unit here.

"At the same time, the school board was starting to think about a new grade school, but they were unaware of this land. Judge Whiteman knew what they wanted, and the Vernet land was well situated, so he talked them into considering it. They ended up getting it."

"But didn't Jules get a fair deal?" Bender asked.

"Oh, yes, but you know the board can use eminent domain. They did. Jules didn't get anything like he might have otherwise. He couldn't dicker. He's pretty bitter about it."

Sheets added an afterthought. "I heard rumors about a commission."

Bender grimaced. "I don't even want to guess who got it."

Eleven years and seven months passed, and the memorial was all finished except for setting the paving and fixing the plaque.

Bender, now the father of two boys and a girl, worked harder on the last day's stonework than he had on any of it. This was the pavement around the base, where he was permitted to work at his own pace, ignoring the number of stones. He worked with a steady rhythm, truly enjoying it and realizing that it had been worth the doing.

I destroyed a person, he thought. Not a nice person. But I had no right to make that judgment. Maybe this was the way to make me realize it. God, forgive me. Then this other thought: Marie, forgive me.

The pavement completed, he went home. Next week, the plaque would be installed.

The next day, he drove by the site to have a look, to see if any final changes should be made.

As he wound his way among the headstones, the columns, and the occasional small tombs, something seemed odd. The general panorama was changed somehow. Bender could not explain the feeling.

Then he rounded the last turn before the three-sided island where the monument stood.

Had stood.

Nothing was there except a barren square spot surrounded by a larger area bare of everything except sand. A shower of stone chips and chunks of mortar covered the grass and part of the cemetery drive.

One of the cemetery workmen was shoving the debris of the paving into piles with a pushbroom.

Bender, shaken and unbelieving, climbed from his car and walked over to him.

"What in God's name happened here?" he asked.

The workman, a short, sinewy man in navy jeans and khaki work shirt, slowed his effort without stopping completely.

"City. Couple fellows come by with a big pickup and some sledgehammers. Busted 'er up but good, flung it all in the truck, and hauled it away."

Bender knew the man was not involved, but he had difficulty restraining himself from physical assault.

He finally calmed. "But why?" he said.

"You better go see Keller," the man answered. "They showed him some paper. I never saw it."

Bender wasted no more time but went to the superintendent's office. To his relief Keller, who was in charge, was in.

The superintendent was an average-sized man with a long face. He wore striped coveralls and a railroader's cap, from which gray hair straggled. He was sorting work slips when Bender came in.

"Hello, Pete," he said. "Guess I don't have to guess why you're here. Sit down?"

"No, thanks," Bender said. "How come, Sam? You know how many years' work have gone down the drain?"

Keller leaned back. "I do. Can't tell you how sorry I am. But they came here with a fistful of papers, and there was no way to argue."

"Papers? What kind?"

"An order from Judge Whiteman that the monument was to be torn down. It had been inspected and found in a deteriorating condition."

"Deteriorating?" Bender shouted. "That shaft would have stood up to a nuclear bomb!"

"Woulda said so, myself," agreed Keller. "But they had a copy of an inspection report, and deteriorating's what it said. Signed by Bill Sheets, Jules—"

"I know who signed it," grated Bender. "And the shaft's gone, so I can't stuff the lie down their throats."

He stood cursing under his breath. "Not that it matters, but what did they do with the stone?"

Keller rubbed his chin. "Probably took it to use in the base for the cut-through between First and Clark."

"No good to me, anyway," Bender said. "I'll have to start all over."

"Maybe they won't ask that of you," Keller remarked.

"But they will," Bender growled. "You can count on it, they will. I should have seen this coming, years ago. I heard a legend when I was a kid. A guy in hell, rolling a rock up a hill. Just as he got it to the top, it always rolled back down. That's what they set up."

When he left, he went home. His chest felt as though it contained the stone that Marie had said it did years ago.

When he entered, his house was empty. That suited him because he wanted to be alone for the moment.

He began by calling Sheets.

"Bill. Pete Bender. What's this about a bad inspection report on my monument?"

Silence met his question. Finally Sheets spoke. "Pete, I'm not sure I heard you right. Inspection report? What inspection report?"

"The one that made Judge Whiteman order them to tear down Marie's column. The one you three clowns signed. And don't give me any innocent crap. A guy saw a Xerox of the thing."

"Pete, I swear by anything you want to name that I don't know what you're talking about. I never even saw such a thing, let alone signed it."

"You swear?"

"I swear."

He hung up, his hands shaking and his thoughts racing. The actual work on a new column was small, measured by time consumed and labor done. Its weight on his spirit was as of the Earth itself.

His memory went back to the time he had seen Vernet about

the earlier bad inspection. He replayed the scene—the business with the hammer, the calligraphy charts—

Forgery would not be too difficult for a man with a good eye. Signatures—easier on paper than in iron?

A rage began to build in him, the sort of thing that had not happened for nearly twelve years.

Bender went to his home workshop, looking for his knapping hammer. He was unable to find it.

He left the house and went to his business storage and tool shed. He searched for the hammer, but it failed to turn up even there.

"The bastard's own tool," he growled. "Better yet, I'll use that."

Before he left he picked up a pair of heavy rubber gloves, worn when smoothing large areas of mortar. He threw them into his car and drove to Vernet's house.

There was no answer when he rang the bell of the sprawling ranch-style dwelling. He was not surprised. Vernet was childless, and his wife spent much time on community projects.

He walked to the rear, to the neat aluminum shed where Vernet worked. The door was locked, but Bender was surprised to find no deadbolt or guard. On a chance he took from his pocket a multifunction tool that contained key chain, pocket knife, and other useful implements. He opened out a sturdy nail file and applied its point to the lock. In seconds he had it open.

Vernet's workroom was a collection of articles in various stages of construction. Bender went through them, looking for a hammer. He found a small sledge, considered picking it up but decided to wait until he had determined to confront Vernet.

As his attention wandered, a new thought began to build in his mind. It had not been Vernet who had conceived his punishment in the first place. In fact, his ex-brother-in-law had been antagonistic to the judge, as Sheets had said. And Vernet had made vague hints when the poorly laid stone had been found.

Bender noticed that he stood by a telephone extension, with a directory beneath it. He picked up the directory, found a number, and punched it in.

After one ring, a woman's voice answered. "Judge Whiteman's office."

"Is Judge Whiteman in?"

"I'm sorry," the woman said. "Judge Whiteman will not be here during the next three days."

"Is he in town? I'd like to reach him."

"You might try his residence. I don't believe he's away."

Bender thanked her and hung up. This was better than he had hoped. Whiteman was a confirmed bachelor, living in his family's spacious old house. If he was there, he might be in a relaxed mood, less alert to possible trouble.

Bender put on the gloves and carefully edged the hammer onto an old newspaper, then wrapped the tool in the paper. He did not want anyone aware of what he carried, least of all the judge.

It took only twelve minutes to drive to the judge's house, a large, red brick, ten room two story on a hillside overlooking the city. A five-acre lot surrounded it, well maintained by a crew that came once a week. A cleaning woman gave the inside minute attention biweekly, but the judge employed nobody else. He dined out.

Bender walked to the steps leading up to the wide porch spanning the front of the house, the wrapped hammer tucked awkwardly under his left arm. He mounted the steps and crossed the porch, trying to organize his approach. It might be well, he finally concluded, to come to no decision until he saw a lead.

He rang the bell and waited. There was no response. He heard the chimes reverberating in the hallway.

His mind came alert. The sound was not muffled. The door—

He looked closely at the door. It was open about an inch.

But no one had responded. Perhaps the judge was in the yard.

Bender walked around the house and looked as closely as he could among the numerous trees and bushes. No person was visible.

He returned to the porch. The door had not moved. He decided to go in.

He pushed the door open and stepped into a deep hall carpeted with a long red Oriental runner.

"Judge Whiteman," he called.

No answer came, and no sound of movement was heard.

He explored several of the rooms leading off the hall without encountering anyone. Then, in the last room on the right, he found him.

In his book-lined study, Judge Whiteman was sprawled across his blood-spattered mahogany desk, his head beaten in, the floor beneath him a red horror. He was unquestionably dead.

Bender's first instinct was to turn and run as fast as he could. Then an inner compulsion caused him to look closer at the scene. It was because of that that he found it.

Behind the desk, its head drenched in blood, was his own hammer.

A grim smile crossed his face. "Trying for two for the price of one, eh, Jules? Well, I don't think so."

He unwrapped the other hammer and carefully exchanged it for his own. He then smeared Vernet's hammer equally and dropped it behind the desk.

He was pondering how to draw attention to Vernet as he climbed back into his car. Suddenly he lost interest in that for the moment.

"My God!" he said, his hand arrested in the act of inserting the ignition key. "I almost made it *first* degree this time."

Lowering his head, he vowed to restore Marie's monument, no matter what time limits were required.

# PATRICIA MOYES

## A YOUNG MAN CALLED SMITH

Of course, the whole thing was my fault. I admit that. All the same, even though my husband Tom says that I'm the daffiest, most scatterbrained woman that ever walked, I maintain that it was the sort of mistake anybody might have made.

It happened last summer, when Tom decided that since he was going to Paris for the International Plastics Exhibition, he might as well take a quick flip around his clients in Zurich, Vienna, Milan, and Lisbon while he was about it. That's one of the disadvantages of being married to a tycoon. Half the time you see him only before breakfast and after dinner, and the rest of the time you don't see him at all. However, there are compensations, like a flat in town and a rambling country house near the Sussex coast and a well-stocked wardrobe and a bank manager who sees you personally to the door, bowing all the way. I wouldn't like you to think I was complaining, especially as I happen to have the best and sweetest husband in the world thrown in as a sort of bonus.

Tom's quite a bit older than I am, and I think maybe that's why he's so considerate, and why he worries about having to leave me alone when he goes off on these trips. This time, I must admit that I was really quite upset when he broke the bad news. You see, we were all set to go down to Meadowcroft—that's the Sussex house—for a couple of weeks' peace and quiet.

"Never mind, Margie love," he said. "You go on down to Meadowcroft, and I'll join you when I can."

"I don't like being there alone," I objected. We don't have any help living in at Meadowcroft, just a woman who comes in two mornings a week.

Then Tom had an inspiration. "I know. Why don't you take Sister Susie down there with you? She's on holiday, isn't she?

She'd probably enjoy it, and she'll be company for you. You can take it in turns to guard my stamps."

This last was a bit of a family joke. Tom's passion in life, next to the plastics business, is stamp collecting. He's been at it ever since he was a schoolboy, and by now—with money to spend and plenty of know-how—he's accumulated a collection worth several thousand pounds. As he keeps on pointing out to me, stamps are just about the easiest things for a thief to smuggle out of the country, and he's so scared of his collection's being burgled that it travels everywhere with us, in a sort of tin trunk. There are only two keys, one on Tom's key ring and the other in a special drawer in whichever house we're in: Tom says he wouldn't trust it to my handbag, and I dare say he's right. Mind you, it's not that he couldn't afford to replace the whole collection over and over again: it's the time and trouble he's put into those stamps that make them so precious to him.

Well, my young sister Sue jumped at the idea of coming to Meadowcroft with me. She was teaching at a primary school in South London at the time, and, having blued all her available cash on a skiing holiday in January, she was faced with the prospect of spending the long summer vacation either doing a temporary job, or moping in her dismal bedsitter in Clapham. As we drove down to Sussex, Sue confided to me that my invitation had been especially welcome because she had just parted forever from the latest of a long line of boyfriends.

"Not that I'm moping for him, Margie, don't think that. He turned out to be a complete birdbrain. But I'd sort of got used to having him around."

This seemed to give me an opportunity of bringing up a subject that I'd had on my mind for some time.

"I do think, Sue," I said, "that you ought to think seriously about your future." I tried to sound as mature and parental as I could, which wasn't very, considering that Sue's twenty-three and I'm only five years older: but since our parents died ten years ago, I've had to do quite a bit of mothering vis à vis young Sue, and she generally took it very well when I lectured her.

This time, however, she seemed to sense what was coming, and shut up like a clam. "I don't know what you mean," she said. She closed her mouth very tight and looked out of the car window.

"Look, honey," I said. "Let's face it. You and I have only one asset in this world—our looks. There's no getting away from it."

"I happen to think that other things matter," said Sue, stubbornly.

"Of course they do," I said. "It's just that we don't happen to be well endowed with the other things. I admit you're ten times as clever as I am, but that still doesn't put you in the Einstein class, does it? You may like to think of yourself as a great intellect, but in fact you're an overworked, badly paid schoolteacher, and likely to remain so, if you don't get a grip on yourself."

"And do what?"

"Now where looks are concerned," I went on, ignoring her interruption, "you're in the number one, A level, super first class. You begin where Helen of Troy left off."

This wasn't such an exaggeration, either. As I've hinted, we're both quite personable, but whereas I tend to be the small, fluffy blond type, Sue is sort of statuesque. I don't mean in her measurements. I mean in the sort of dignity and elegance she has. She's got corn-colored hair and green eyes the size of gobstoppers and a honey and peaches skin, and when she smiles it's as though some goddess or archangel had dropped in to make sure that all's well with the world. My objection was that she insisted on wasting these riches on penniless art students and would-be poets—the whole tribe of washouts that Tom had christened "Sue's bearded weirdies." I put this point of view to her now.

"I'm not suggesting," I said, "that you should sell yourself for filthy lucre, so stop looking at me like that. I'm just saying that if you'd only take the trouble to meet a few people who are . . . well . . . getting on in the world, as it were . . . then it's almost a dead cert that you'll fall in love with one of them. Look at Tom and me. You don't think I married him for his money, do you?"

"Of course not, Margie." Sue sounded shocked by the idea. "You were just terribly lucky."

"Lucky *and* sensible," I pointed out. "I found Tom simply

because I decided to exclude from my circle of acquaintances any man whose income fell below a certain level. And sure enough, after a bit, along came Tom. Set your sights in the upper brackets, my girl—there are some nice fellows up there, you know."

Sue sighed. "I *do* get a bit bored with being broke," she admitted. "The trouble is, all the rich men I've ever met are so stupid. They're shallow, ill-informed, and fatuous."

"That's because you haven't explored far enough," I said. I could tell I was making headway because Sue fell into a thoughtful meditation, quite unlike her earlier hostile silence.

At last she said, "All right. I'll give it a try. You introduce me to all the rich men you can find while we're at Meadowcroft, and I'll be prepared to consider them."

"That's my girl," I said.

As it turned out, the laugh was on me because when we got to Sussex I found that any of our neighbors who fell into the right category were away sunning themselves in Elba or Sardinia. In England, the weather was idyllic. The sun shone, and Sue and I had tea in the garden: but we had it alone. She never said a word about our conversation in the car, but I couldn't help feeling that she was laughing at me, just a little.

After a week, I began to get worried in case she was bored, and fretting for the banished boyfriend. So I was pleased when, around teatime on the second Tuesday, I looked up from my gardening to see a battered red sports car making its way noisily up the drive. It looked and sounded as though it had been constructed out of a do-it-yourself kit with several vital parts missing, but as it roared to a shuddering halt outside the front door, I saw that it contained a young man. Rather a good-looking young man. I stepped out of the herbaceous border, beaming welcome.

"Good afternoon," I said.

The young man jumped out of the car and came towards me. "Oh," he said. "You must be . . . I mean . . . are you Mrs. Westlake?"

"I am."

"My name's Smith. Bobby Smith. I work for Amalgamated Plastics. I met your husband at the Paris Exhibition last week,

Mrs. Westlake, and when he heard I was planning to holiday in Shinglesea, he suggested I should look you up. I hope you don't mind."

"Not at all," I said. I didn't try to make it sound too convincing. A closer look at Mr. Smith had decided me that Sue and I could well do without him. He was wearing a dirty duffel coat and crumpled grey flannels, and his brown hair looked as though it hadn't been combed for a week. In fact, he looked too much like a bearded weirdie for comfort, and I hoped that he would take the hint from my chilly tone, and leave.

But not a bit of it. "So I thought I'd—" he began. And then suddenly his eyes seemed to grow larger, and to protrude as though pushed from within, and his face turned a dull puce. He emitted a sound which can best be transcribed as "glug." What had happened, of course, was that Sue had come out of the house.

"This is my sister, Sue Davidson," I said. "Sue, meet Bobby Smith, a friend of Tom's."

"How do you do?" gurgled Smith. "Delighted to meet you. Not really a friend of Mr. Westlake's, you know . . . just met at the Paris show . . ."

He had got hold of Sue's hand by this time, and was pumping it up and down as though he expected thereby to induce water to gush from her mouth. Sue looked at him with, I was pleased to note, no enthusiasm at all.

"How are you?" she said distantly, like a goddess making conversation with some of the less desirable elements of the underworld. There was an awkward pause.

I was aware of mixed emotions. Much as I wanted to be rid of the young man, he had been invited by Tom to call on us, and hospitality is hospitality. I didn't feel I could send him packing without the elementary courtesy of a cup of tea. This I offered, and he accepted with alacrity. I left him in the drawing room with Sue while I went to boil the kettle.

When I came back, Sue was sitting on the sofa, with Bobby Smith as close beside her as it was possible for him to be without actually constituting the basis for a complaint. Every time Sue edged away from him, he shifted towards her to close the gap, and by now he had her pretty well pinioned in the corner. He was talking about the insides of racing cars. He continued to talk while we had our tea, and afterwards asked to be shown Tom's stamp collection, about which he had heard so much. Reluctantly, I unlocked it, and, by making him walk over to the display case to see it, succeeded momentarily in relieving the pressure on Sue.

As soon as the stamps had been inspected, admired, and locked up again, Bobby reverted to the subject of cars, and began to press Sue to come for what he called "a spin in my old bus." Now, Sue is a gently nurtured girl and finds it difficult to dish out a plain, discourteous refusal. Having made it obvious in at least six different ways that she did not want to go, she eventually agreed to a short ride, but only on condition that I came, too.

It was purgatory. There was, strictly speaking, no back seat— just a sort of bench covered with a filthy, moth-eaten rug. We scorched and snarled our way to the nearest village where Bobby stopped at the inn and bought us each a disgusting bottle of livid-green fizzy lemonade and a petrified sausage roll. We eventually arrived home at half-past six; I was aching in every muscle and bone, and it was with horror that I realized that Bobby had no intention of departing. He settled himself comfortably in the drawing room with the drink which I had felt in duty bound to offer him.

When I went out to the kitchen to fetch more ice, Sue followed me. As soon as the door was shut behind her, she let fly. "Margie, it's too *awful!* You *must* get rid of him! He'll be here all night at this rate, and he keeps trying to *paw* me . . . it's *disgusting.* Can't you *do* something?"

"Don't worry, honey," I said. "Leave him to me."

I went back to the drawing room and said, with a cold smile, "Well, Mr. Smith, I'm so sorry I can't ask you to stay any longer, but my sister and I are due at a cocktail party at seven, and we have to change. So—"

"Oh, that's all right," replied the wretched youth airily. "I'll wait for you down here, and drive you over to your party."

"And how," inquired Sue icily, "do we get back again?"

"I'll wait for you," he said, cheerfully. "I'd be glad to come in with you, but I'm not really dressed for a social evening, and these country houses are so hideously bourgeois. It'll be up to you to slip away pretty smartly, and we'll all go out to dinner together."

Sue shot me a look of utter despair, but I was able to take this one in my stride. "I'm sorry, Mr. Smith," I said, "this isn't the sort of party that we want to slip away from, and we're invited to stay on for dinner afterwards."

"Oh, I say," he said. "What frightfully bad luck." You could tell he was really sorry for us, missing the treat of dining with him. "Anyhow, I'll wait till you leave, and speed you on your way."

There was nothing for it. Sue and I had to go upstairs and solemnly change into cocktail rig, and get the car out. Even then I didn't think we'd get rid of him. He insisted on writing down for Sue the address of the third-rate boardinghouse in Shinglesea which had the bad luck to have drawn his custom, and he assured us that he'd be calling again very soon. Our spirits lifted a little when he said that he was breaking his holiday the following day to visit an aunt in Norfolk, but they sank again when he urged us not to worry, as he'd be back by the weekend.

When we finally got into the car and drove off, he followed us for several miles until I finally shook him off by superior local knowledge. It was then, speeding recklessly up a leafy lane, that Sue and I both began to laugh hysterically. By the time we got home, however, our mood had hardened: and the last straw came when I found, on the drawing room sofa, the gold propelling pencil which Bobby had produced from his pocket to write his address for Sue. It bore the engraved initials *R.S.*

"He did it on purpose!" exploded Sue. "He deliberately left it behind so that he'd have an excuse to come back. Well, he's got another think coming. We've got his address, so you can send it back to him, Margie, with a note telling him to go and jump off the cliff."

"I can't very well do that," I said, "but I can write and tell him that you've had to go back to London. He won't come here for the pleasure of *my* company."

"Good idea," said Sue. "And the next time an unidentified car

comes up this drive, Margie, you and I are going to dive into
the nearest haystack and stay there until the all-clear sounds."

She was wrong, of course. It was just after four next afternoon, and I was in the pantry arranging some flowers that I'd
cut from the garden, when I heard the gentle purring of an
expensive motor car in the drive. For a moment, I had a panicky
fear that it might be the unspeakable Smith returned unexpectedly from Norfolk—but the well-bred murmur of the engine
reassured me. I went to the drawing room window and looked
out.

In the drive stood a grey E-type Jaguar, and beside it stood a
young man who might have stepped straight into a women's
magazine illustration, no questions asked. He was tall and slim,
with straight, shining fair hair, and he wore a beautifully cut
sports jacket and a crisp white shirt with a silk scarf in the neck
of it. You could tell at a glance that he didn't suffer from
halitosis, B.O., or dandruff. He was sunburnt, and even from the
drawing room I could see that his hands were as lean and
sensitive a couple as ever caressed a steering wheel. Then he
turned his head toward me, and I saw that his eyes were dark
cornflower blue, thus giving him a score of ten out of ten. The
reason he had turned was that Sue had seen him from her swing
chair on the lawn, and was walking over to investigate.

By the time I got there, Sue was standing beside the Jaguar,
gazing at its proprietor with a sort of stunned expression. She
did not actually say "glug," but it was implicit in her whole
demeanor.

"Margie," she said, in a faint voice, "this is Robin Smith. He's
a friend of Tom's. Mr. Smith, this is my sister, Mrs. Westlake."

"How very nice to meet you." The apparition turned to me,
giving me the full benefit of the dark blue eyes, together with a
smile which made even my matronly heart beat a little faster.
"I ran into your husband in Paris, and he suggested I might look
you up. I'm holidaying in Shinglesea for a week or two."

"You will come in and have some tea, won't you?" Sue asked
anxiously, with half an eye on me. I think she was afraid that I
might not have grasped that this was the exception that proved
the rule.

"If you're sure I'm not disturbing you," said Robin. "I only meant to stay a moment . . ." We fairly hustled him indoors.

I went off to get tea. When I came back, Sue was sitting—if that's the right word—on the sofa, displaying a length of exquisite leg, like a goddess who has heard that Apollo will be along at any moment and is anxious not to miss him. Robin was sitting on a small and rather uncomfortable chair on the far side of the room, talking about the implications of pop art. This seemed almost too good to be true. When, over the cucumber sandwiches and thin bread and butter, he went on to discuss twelfth century stained glass and the influence of Ezra Pound on modern poetry and the correct method of preparing *coq au vin*, I could barely contain myself for delight.

The effect on Sue was apparent. By the time we got to Ezra Pound, she had stopped draping herself over the sofa, and was taking a lively part in the conversation—which is more than I was, but that didn't matter. The important thing was that the two of them were striking sparks off each other.

Eventually, we got round to the subject of cars, and Sue dropped a couple of mammoth hints about how she'd always wondered what it would be like to ride in a *really* fast car. Robin simply said that he'd wondered the same thing himself, and hoped that a friend of his might let him try a couple of laps at Silverstone in a Lotus one of these days. Then he looked down at his watch, and said that he really must be going.

Sue was looking at me in a dumb, pleading sort of way, but I couldn't detain the man by force. I did my best to prolong the conversation by asking where in Shinglesea he was staying.

"Just outside the town," he said. "The Shinglesea Towers. Do you know it?"

"I do indeed," I said. It was one of the most exclusive and expensive seaside hotels in Britain.

"It's not bad," he said. "Quite reasonable food, taken all in all, and of course everything tastes better when eaten on a terrace on a warm, moonlit night."

"Like tonight," said Sue, brazenly. (I felt quite ashamed of her.)

After that the poor man could hardly fail to invite us to dine with him. He did it beautifully, though—exactly as though it was a brilliant idea which had just occurred to him.

I tried to keep some semblance of dignity, but the way Sue said, "Oh, yes, *please,*" ruined any effect it might have had. We both went up to change, and I lent her my coffee-colored Balmain chiffon, my mutation mink stole, and some diamond clips and a bracelet. I must say she looked good enough to eat.

It was arranged that Sue and Robin should go ahead in the Jaguar, and that I should follow on in the little runabout we keep in the country. The two of them were in the lounge when I arrived, and Robin provided us with cocktails and then went off to change. One doesn't dine in a sports jacket at the Shinglesea Towers. A few minutes later he came back in a dark suit, looking more like an advertisement for gracious living than ever, and we made our way through the dining room and out onto the terrace.

Though I say it myself, we were quite a sensational-looking trio, and we caused a stir. Waiters were fairly tripping over each other for the privilege of showing us to our table, and I was aware of knives and forks freezing into immobility all over the room as a hundred heads turned to watch our progress. I sneaked a quick look at Sue, and was delighted to see that she was carrying it off superbly. A goddess moving graciously among her humble, earthly devotees. (I felt proud of her.)

It was an enchanted evening. We ate *fois gras* and *homard a l'américaine* and fresh peaches, and we drank champagne. Sue and Robin danced together with as much ease and expertise as if they'd been rehearsing for weeks, and in the intervals of dancing, they talked about every subject under the sun. Most of the conversation was miles above my head, but I was perfectly happy just to sit and listen. It seemed to me that I was seeing my sister in her natural element for the first time. She was never meant to live in a bedsitter and teach English to pudding-faced kids, and it pleased me to think that Sue was obviously coming to the same conclusion herself.

It seemed no time at all before the witching hour arrived. The band played the last waltz, the dancers and diners dispersed, and Sue and I found ourselves on the front steps of the hotel, shaking hands with Robin and thanking him for a marvel-

ous evening. Then we got into the car, and I waved a last good-
bye to Robin and drove off. At once, Sue burst into tears.

"Take it easy, honey," I said. "I know you're excited and—"

"I've . . . I've n-never had such a b-b-beautiful evening in all
my life . . ." sobbed Sue.

"I know," I said, soothingly. "But you'll have plenty more."

This produced a despairing wail. "I w-won't! I'll never see
him again!"

"That's just nonsense," I said. "He's obviously crazy about
you."

"Then why d-didn't he say a s-single word about meeting
again?" sniffed Sue. "He's only here till next week, and he didn't
even ask for my address in London, or give me his. I may as
well face it, Margie," she went on, in a fresh burst of misery, "I
b-bore him stiff. I'm not pretty enough or clever enough or—"

"My dear young idiot," I said firmly, "pull yourself together.
Robin Smith is a very correct and well-mannered young man.
When you come to think of it, he thrust his company on us this
evening—"

"He didn't!"

"I'm looking at it from his point of view. He turned up
uninvited. Then he asked us to dinner, and we accepted—but
for all he knows, it may have been just politeness on our part.
What I'm driving at is that the next move is up to us. Up to me,
to be precise."

"Is it?" Sue still sounded doubtful.

"Of course it is. I shall write to Robin tomorrow, and ask him
to . . . to . . . I know! To spend the weekend at Meadowcroft."

"Margie, you're an angel!" squeaked Sue, and nearly put us
into the ditch by flinging her arms round my neck just as I was
taking a tricky bend. She sang happily to herself the rest of the
way home.

The next morning, when I went to my desk to write to Robin,
I found myself face to face with that horrible gold propelling
pencil, and decided to write both letters while I was about it. It
was even more important, now, to keep the unspeakable Bobby
away from the house.

I spent some time composing the letters, and when I had

finished I felt quite pleased with them. I took them to Sue for
her to read.

The first one went as follows:

*Dear Mr. Smith,*

*After your visit, I found the enclosed pencil, which I
think belongs to you. I am sending it back to save you
the trouble of calling here for it.*

*My sister has asked me to tell you that she has had to
return to London unexpectedly. I do not expect to see her
again for some time.*

*Yours sincerely,*
*Margaret Westlake*

"Pretty chilling, I think you'll agree," I said to Sue, with
satisfaction. She was for making it even ruder, but I protested
that only a rhinoceros would fail to get the message. I then
showed her the second letter.

*Dear Mr. Smith,*

*Neither Sue nor I feel that we thanked you enough for
entertaining us so regally. It was a splendid evening, with
superb food, drink, and company—and Sue is still talking about her ride in your fabulous car.*

*It occurred to me that, if you feel you have had enough
of hotel life for the time being, you might like to spend
this coming weekend with us here at Meadowcroft. It
would give us such pleasure—do say you'll come, and
make it Friday evening if you can.*

*Very sincerely,*
*Margie Westlake*

I had to drive into Shinglesea to do some shopping, so I
decided to drop the letters in by hand, to avoid delay. The two
envelopes were lying on my desk—one addressed to "R. Smith,
Esq., Shinglesea Towers Hotel," and the other to "R. Smith, Esq.,
Ocean View, Pebble Road, Shinglesea." I wrapped the appropri-
ate letter round the propelling pencil, and then slipped both
letters into the envelopes and sealed them. One I delivered to

the immaculate receptionist at the Shinglesea Towers, and the other to the sleazy landlady of Ocean View. I expect you'll have guessed by now what happened, and I still maintain that anybody might have made the same mistake.

Disaster struck with the arrival of the post on Friday morning. At first, I was pleased to see a letter with the monogram of Shinglesea Towers embossed on the envelope, but when I picked it up and felt the long, thin, solid object inside, my heart did an unpleasant somersault. I tore open the envelope. Out fell the propelling pencil. Trembling, I opened the letter, which was written in a handsome Italian hand.

*Dear Mrs. Westlake,*

*I am returning the pencil, as I am afraid that, despite the similarity of initials, it is not mine.*

*I am sorry to hear that your sister has had to leave so suddenly.*

*Yours sincerely,*
*Robin Smith*

Of course, I had to confess to Sue. She began to wail like a banshee, declaring that her life had been ruined and that she might as well sign on for the nearest convent straight away. This brought me to my senses.

"There's no point just sitting there snivelling," I said. "Fortunately, no great harm has been done. I shall ring Robin straight away and explain that there's been a mistake."

I contacted Robin at the Shinglesea Towers without any difficulty, and although he sounded a bit standoffish at first—and no wonder, after that letter—he soon melted, and said that he was delighted to hear that Sue hadn't had to go to London after all, and that nothing would please him more than to spend the weekend with us. In fact, he said, he'd been on the point of going back to London because he found hotels desperately boring after a few days. Such was our rejoicing at this, and so pressing was the planning of menus, and the shopping, and the deciding of what clothes to wear, that the darker side of the picture remained completely forgotten until after lunch.

It was only then, when Sue was up in my room trying on

everything in my wardrobe to see what suited her best, that the awful truth hit me. If Robin had received the chilly letter, then the unspeakable Bobby had received a gushing invitation to spend the weekend with us. An ordinary person, I reflected, reading that letter with its references to superb food and drink and a fabulous car, would realize immediately that there'd been a mistake, but Bobby Smith was perfectly capable of construing it as a legitimate description of our hellish jaunt to the local pub. I fairly ran to the telephone.

"Ocean View," said the flat, unpleasant voice that I recognized as belonging to the landlady.

"I want to speak to Mr. Robert Smith."

"He's left."

"Yes, I know. But he's back again, isn't he? I mean, he said he was coming back today."

"He's left and come back and left again. Not half an hour ago. No consideration, some people haven't."

"You mean—he's gone for good?"

"That's what he said. Without so much as by-your-leave. The room was reserved till Sunday." The voice took on a menacing note.

"Do you know where he went?"

"I do not. To stay with friends in the neighborhood, he said. A likely story, I don't think. Hadn't got the money to pay till Sunday, more like."

"You don't happen to know if he . . . I mean, I left a note for him this morning and I wondered whether he'd received it . . ."

"If it was left in, it'll have been handed to him," said the voice huffily.

"Thank you," I said, and rang off.

As I came out into the hall, I met Sue careering down the stairs. She was still wearing the gold lamé evening dress that she'd been trying on when I went to telephone. She clutched my arm.

"Margie! Coming up the drive! He's here!"

"I thought as much," I said, gloomily.

"You've got to get rid of him!"

"My dear Sue, I'll do my best, but I can't work miracles. You'd better go up and change into something more suitable. And for heaven's sake, behave yourself."

It was plain that Sue would have liked to express herself at some length, doubtless on the ruined-life motif, but the angry snarl of the homemade red car put an end to further conversation. Sue gave me a look into which she managed to pack a couple of tirades, a tragic renunciation of all future happiness, and a raspberry. She then gathered up the gold lamé and scudded up the stairs like a goddess surprised by a satyr, just as Bobby Smith walked in through the front door. He did not even bother to ring.

"Ah, Margie! Here I am," he announced unnecessarily. "Good idea of yours, having me here for the weekend. Shinglesea was becoming tedious."

"As a matter of fact—" I began, feebly.

"Shan't be a moment. Just get my things out of the car."

I followed him to the front door. The red menace was standing steaming in the drive, and from its noisome interior Bobby began producing an assortment of articles, as a conjuror will from a top hat. First came three battered suitcases, and a kind of wickerwork basket tied up with a string. Then a tennis racket, a snorkel mask, a pair of ice skates, binoculars, a bagful of golf clubs, an inflatable air bed, and a string bag full of paperback thrillers.

"Never know how the holiday's going to turn out, do you?" remarked Bobby, as he assembled this collection in the porch. "If you'll just show me my room, I'll take this lot up, and then come back for the rest."

"The rest?"

"Oh, just my cameras and transistor radio and tape recorder. I don't like leaving valuable equipment in an open car. You never know who's skulking in the shrubbery, do you?" He laughed loudly.

"No," I said. "You don't."

"Well . . ." He was festooned with baggage by this time. "Lead on, MacDuff. I'm right behind you. But quick, woman, before I drop the lot."

It was all too much for me. Meekly, I led the way to the smaller of the two spare rooms.

When the last load of gear had been safely stowed away, Bobby strolled into the drawing room, flopped onto the sofa and put his feet up, and remarked, "Where's young Sue?"

"She's changing," I said. I knew that Sue, from behind her bedroom door, must have observed what had happened, and I knew she wouldn't appear until she had to.

"Changing?" Bobby smiled, with repellent smugness. "She needn't have bothered to dress up just for me."

"She isn't," I assured him.

"What do you mean?"

"Just that we're expecting another house guest. He should be here any moment."

Bobby looked really annoyed. "Oh, lord," he said. "Couldn't you have put him off? We don't want anybody else."

There was a pretty solid statuette of the Goddess of Plenty in pink jade on a small table near my right hand, and I came within an ace of grabbing it and beaning the wretched youth. My hand was stayed, however, by the whisper of tires in the drive: through the window, I saw the Jaguar pulling up.

"There he is now," I said, and hurried out.

Robin had only one suitcase ("No point in getting the rest of the stuff out of the car," he said). I took him up to the best spare room, where Sue had lovingly arranged a big bowl of red roses. I showed him the guest bathroom, and told him that drinks would be ready downstairs whenever he was. When I came into the drawing room with the tray of glasses, Bobby and Robin were both sitting there, eyeing each other with mutual suspicion.

"Have you two introduced yourselves?" I asked, with a ghastly attempt at gaiety. "Mr. Smith, meet Mr. Smith. Robin, this is Bobby. Bobby—Robin."

They smirked halfheartedly at each other, in the manner of small boys forced to shake hands politely but only waiting for the schoolmaster's back to be turned for the rough stuff to begin.

"I thought perhaps you might know each other already," I went on, "since you both met Tom at the Plastics Exhibition in Paris." This produced no reaction. I blundered on. "Bobby's in plastics, I know—Amalgamated, isn't it?" Bobby nodded. "I suppose you're in the same line of country, Robin."

"In a way," said Robin. There was another endless pause.

"Well," I said, "what about a drink?"

I poured the drinks, and we sat there in clammy silence. I offered a tour of the garden, which both young men declined. Their attention was fixed unswervingly on the door through which Sue might be expected to appear.

At last I stood up and said, "Well, if I don't get things going in the kitchen, we'll have no supper. Do help yourselves to drinks. I'll see if I can find that sister of mine to entertain you."

I ran upstairs and into Sue's room. She had changed into a simple brown linen dress and was lying on her bed, reading a detective story.

"Sue!" I said. I wanted to shout, but I had to make do with a sort of stage whisper. "For heaven's sake! You've got to come down and help me!"

"I won't come down while that man's in the house."

"Don't be childish! You simply can't leave me to cope by myself."

"It was all your fault in the first place," Sue pointed out. "And anyway, I don't know what you're complaining about. You're not being pursued by that . . . that gargoyle."

"But—"

"Get him out of the house, and I'll come down. Otherwise, I stay here."

"I can't simply throw him out! He's got about fifty suitcases, and he's just unpacked."

Sue was sensible enough to see the logic of this. She relented a little. "All right. Get him out of the place for an hour or so, to give me a chance of seeing Robin alone . . . please, Margie . . . I promise I'll behave if I can have just an hour . . ."

Well, there was only one way to do it. I went downstairs again and begged Bobby to take me for another ride in his gorgeous motor car.

I was gratified to see that I had judged him correctly. Nothing else would have gotten him out of the house. As it was, I could see the inner struggle that was going on, and I quickly tipped the balance by enthusing in a nauseating way over the vile

machine, and asking endless questions. We were all three out in
the drive by then, admiring the scarlet brute. The gray Jaguar
stood quietly aloof, looking aristocratic and unamused. Bobby
had already dismissed it with a quick glance and a scathing, "I
see you've got one of those reliable old ladies. Too run-of-the-
mill for my taste, I'm afraid." This had done nothing to endear
him to Robin.

At last we set out, bumping and roaring across the country-
side, with Bobby humming tunelessly to himself, and me clutching the solider portions of the vehicle and praying for a quick
release. After about two hundred years, we stopped at the same
pub, and this time I insisted on a double gin. After all, I wasn't
driving, and the mere sight of that green lemonade made me
feel sick.

To my surprise, Bobby started talking about Robin. Wanted to
know how long I'd known him, where I'd met him, and so on.
Most impertinent, I considered, but it's difficult to refuse out-
right to answer a question. By the time the catechism was over,
I was uncomfortably aware that I had revealed that I knew
nothing whatsoever about Robin. "Any more than I do about
you," I added, pointedly. "If you knew my husband better,
you'd understand. He's a tremendously friendly soul, and he's
continually issuing invitations to total strangers. I'm quite used
to it."

What I didn't add was that, while it's true that Tom does
scatter invitations, his scattering is usually very selective. He
sums people up in a flash, and has a way of finding out their
entire life history in the time that it takes most people to shake
hands and comment on the weather. Robin was just the sort of
person who would appeal to Tom, but I couldn't understand
how he had come to fraternize with a character like Bobby
Smith. I'd never known Tom to pick a dud before, and it
bothered me.

We got home eventually, to find that Sue and Robin had gone
off in the Jaguar. This made me very cross, and since Bobby
obviously felt the same way, a bond of a kind was created
between us. I must say that he was very useful in the kitchen,
too. When, between us, we'd prepared a delicious mixed grill
and green salad and there was still no sign of the others, we

decided to go ahead and eat. I opened a bottle of Tom's Volnay, and by the time it was half empty, I had decided that Bobby Smith might be almost tolerable if only he'd get the engine oil out of his fingernails and try not to be so conceited.

Robin and Sue came back at half-past eight, sparkling and laughing and hoping that we hadn't waited dinner for them. I'm afraid I was pretty terse with them both. Apart from anything else, Bobby had succeeded in planting nasty little wisps of suspicion in my mind. I became increasingly aware that I knew nothing whatsoever about either of these two young men. I should never have invited one, let alone both, to stay in the house. Sue and I were quite defenseless, several miles from the nearest village, and with Tom's stamp collection—let alone my jewelry—simply asking to be burgled. Later on in the evening, when Sue actually suggested getting the stamps out to show them to Robin, I could have screamed. Since by now both our visitors knew where the key was normally kept, I decided to slip it into my handbag and take it up to my room for the night.

I slept hardly at all. I lay awake for hours, wishing that Tom were at home or that I could contact him. As it was, I didn't even know what country he was in. Next morning I was up and about by seven, making myself a cup of tea. And when the postman dropped a letter in Tom's handwriting through the letter box, it seemed like a direct answer to prayer. I rushed to open it.

Tom's not much of a letter writer. This was a typical scrawl, written in the middle of a busy day from a hotel in Milan. All was going well, he said. He was just off to Lisbon, and couldn't possibly say when he'd be home, but I could be sure it would be as soon as ever he could make it. Paris had been magic, business-wise, and he'd bought me a little present. The letter ended with his reassurances that I was the only girl in the world as far as he was concerned, and sketched out a rough program of what he planned to do the moment he got home. That was all. Then I noticed the small letters P.T.O. at the bottom. I turned the page over and read—

*P.S. You may get a visit from a young man called Smith. Met him in Paris. A very bright lad, and could be impor-*

*tant, so be specially nice to him, will you, angel? Thought
he might be amusing company for Sister Sue.*

I read the P.S. three times, and each time it made me feel
sicker. Of course. What an idiot I'd been. It was too much even
for the long arm of coincidence that Tom should have met *two*
young men in Paris, both called Smith, both in plastics, and
should have invited them both to visit us. The letter clinched
it. *A* young man, it said. Not two young men. No, I had to face
it. One of them was an impostor—an adventurer, probably a
criminal, who had overheard Tom's invitation to the genuine
Smith, and taken a chance on cashing in on it. The question
was—which was the real Smith, and which was the phony?
There seemed no way of finding out.

I was sitting miserably in the kitchen, reading Tom's P.S. for
the tenth time, when the door began to edge open slowly. My
nerves were so taut by then that I wouldn't have been surprised
to see a Thing from Outer Space creeping round the door. I let
out a small scream. What did, in fact, creep round the door was
Bobby Smith. He was wearing an ancient camel-hair dressing
gown, and he looked like a Thing from Outer Space that has left
its comb and razor on a neighboring planet.

He appeared as surprised to see me as I was to see him. For a
moment, we goggled at each other. Then he gave a sort of gulp,
and said, "Oh. Good morning, Mrs. Westlake."

"Good morning," I said.

"I see you're up."

"Yes."

"I . . . er . . . I woke early, and I thought I . . . that is . . . a cup
of tea, you know . . ."

"Help yourself," I said. "I've just made it."

"Oh. Thanks very much."

He sat down at the table opposite me and poured himself a
beaker. Then he said, "As a matter of fact, I'm glad to have an
opportunity of talking to you, Mrs. Westlake."

"Really?"

"Yes. It's about . . . well . . . it's rather awkward, really. It's
about Smith."

"Robin Smith?"

"That's right. It's been worrying me ever since yesterday. You see, I was positive I'd seen him before somewhere. And this morning, lying in bed, it suddenly came to me."

"What did?"

"Where I'd seen him. It was last week in Paris, at the Exhibition."

"Well, of course it was." I was in no mood for banalities, and I suppose I must have spoken sharply because Bobby looked at me in a surprised way. Then he said, in a patronizing drawl, "I'm afraid you don't quite understand, Mrs. Westlake. Events like the Plastics Show . . . well, they attract the best people in the business from all over the world . . . people like your husband, for example . . ."

"I know that."

He leant forward, and took another gulp of tea. "They also attract a crowd of hangers-on. The nastiest sort, who skulk around in the bars on the off-chance of getting an introduction to somebody important. All of them are shady characters, and some are downright crooks." He paused impressively. "And your Robin Smith was one of them!"

"How can you be so sure?" I felt cold with fear, thinking of Sue.

"I remember now. It was the day I met Mr. Westlake. I noticed this crowd of suspicious-looking shysters hanging round the bar where we lunched. Robin Smith was one of them."

"How curious," I said, "that it's taken you so long to recognize him."

This did not disconcert Bobby. "It's the clothes, you see. And the beard."

"The what?"

"The clothes, the car, the whole setup . . . he had me fooled for a bit, I admit that. You see, when I saw him in Paris, he was as scruffy as the rest of them. And he wore a beard. A disguise, I presume."

"Bobby," I said, faintly, "I think you must be making a mistake."

"I hope I am, for your sake," said the young wretch. "I suppose it just might be one of those cases of doubles or identical twins that one reads about, but I doubt it. I doubt it very much. So if you've got any valuables in the house, I'd advise you to keep them under lock and key."

"I shall go and have a bath," I said.

By the time I had bathed and dressed and come downstairs again, Bobby had gone. My dear, comforting Mrs. Waters had arrived and was clucking round the kitchen like a plump Sussex hen. Coffee was brewing, and a clutch of boiled eggs nestled under a tea cosy, beside a rackful of toast. In the dining room, Robin—devastating as ever in a silk dressing gown—was reading the morning paper. He jumped up as I came in.

"Good morning, Mrs. Westlake. What can I get you? Coffee, tea, eggs?"

"I'll serve myself, thank you, Robin," I said.

He sat down again. When I had helped myself, he took a quick glance round, as though to make sure we were alone, and then said, "I'm afraid I owe you an apology for yesterday evening."

"Oh, for heaven's sake, it doesn't matter," I said. "If you and Sue wanted to—"

"No, no. You don't understand." Again the furtive look round. "You see, the reason we were so long over our drive was that Sue was telling me about . . ." He hesitated. "About the *other* Mr. Smith."

"Bobby, you mean?"

"Yes. Now, I don't want to alarm you, Mrs. Westlake, but just how long have you known him? Have you checked up on his background and his credentials? I was in Paris myself last week, and I know the sort of undesirables who hang around international shows in the hope of meeting a big man like your husband. Sue is distinctly worried about Smith, and I don't blame her."

"Sue has taken a personal dislike to him," I said. "That doesn't make him a criminal."

"Of course it doesn't. I'm not accusing anybody of anything," said Robin, rather hastily. "But I understand that he has shown a suspicious interest in your husband's stamp collection. Not to mention Sue's diamonds."

"Sue's—?" I began, astonished, and then I remembered our

dinner in Shinglesea. Of course Robin thought the jewels were hers. "He asked to see Tom's stamps, that's all," I said.

"Exactly. Now, what I'm going to suggest is that you'd be easier in your mind if you turned the keys of the stamp collection and the jewel cases over to me. It's a man's responsibility to look after valuables like that. Sue absolutely agrees with me."

"Certainly not!" I had blurted out the words before I could stop myself. I gulped a bit, and then went on, more calmly, "I do appreciate your offer, Robin, but I'm quite used to standing on my own feet, you know."

"Well, at least tell me where the keys are, so that I can keep an eye on them. I noticed you didn't put the stamp collection key back in its usual place last night."

"The keys are quite safe, thank you," I said, hoping I sounded more confident than I felt. "I think it's better for all of us that nobody but myself should know where they are." Actually, they were in my sponge bag.

"If you really feel like that . . ." said Robin, shaking his head regretfully. And at that moment Sue appeared, looking ravishing in the orange silk trousers and lilac shirt that I brought back from Italy in the spring.

"Margie, darling," she cried, "has Robin told you what I—"

Fortunately, before she could get any further, Bobby came in, rubbing his hands and enthusing about the weather. We all had breakfast.

While I was eating, I was also making a plan. I know I'm a constitutional dimwit, so I dare say my strategy wasn't up to much. Napoleon or Alexander the Great would have done better. However, after intensive brooding over two boiled eggs, I came to these conclusions:

1. One of the Smiths was an impostor.
2. I could see no way of ascertaining which.
3. The object of the impostor was robbery.
4. The object of the robbery was in the house, viz. Tom's stamps or my diamonds or both.
5. Nobody can steal a thing while separated from it by several miles of Sussex.

6. We would therefore spend the day picnicking on the beach.

"I have decided," I said, "that we will spend the day picnicking on the beach."

I didn't exactly expect the others to fall over themselves with delight at the idea, but I did think they might have shown a little more polite enthusiasm. However, my determination to keep both Smiths away from Meadowcroft for as long as possible far outweighed any sensitive feelings I might have had. I went ahead with my preparations regardless, and by eleven o'clock we were rolling towards the coast—Sue and Robin in the Jaguar, Bobby and myself in the runabout. I couldn't have faced the scarlet horror again to save my life. In the car Bobby made an attempt to bring up the subject of Robin and his unreliability, but I was firm.

"I want to hear no more of that," I said. "We've come out for a jolly picnic, and a jolly picnic we're jolly well going to have. So shut up."

Well, it wasn't all that jolly, but it might have been worse. The sun shone, and the sea was smooth and blue, and the seagulls fooled about catching crumbs in a distinctly diverting manner. We all swam and sunbathed, and then I opened the vacuum flask and dished out ice-cold martinis, and the atmosphere grew a little more relaxed.

Not for long, alas. Young Sue, in a euphorious state of mind and a minuscule black bikini, had rashly decided to include even Bobby in the sunshine of her smile. This, of course, revived all the miserable young man's ardor, with the result that he immediately tried to muscle in between Robin and Sue. The effect of my carefully prepared picnic lunch was quite spoiled by the fact that the two men were sniping at each other verbally the whole time, as well as physically jockeying for position, which made the whole party a bit restless. Afterwards, I managed to persuade them both to go off for another swim while Sue and I took a nap. At least that was the proposed program, but in fact I started pouring my heart out to Sue the moment the men were out of earshot.

I told her about Tom's letter, with its sinister P.S.; I told her about Bobby's suspicions and Robin's sinister offer to look after the keys. I appealed to her to help me. Useless, of course. She was absolutely furious.

"If anybody's an impostor, it's that frightful Bobby!" she said. "How exactly like him, trying to blacken Robin's character behind his back! Of all the filthy, snide, low-down tricks . . . You wait. By the time I've finished with that young man, he'll wish he'd gone to Devil's Island for his holiday!"

"Do be reasonable, Sue," I begged—but it was no good. However, by pretty rigorous questioning, I was able to elicit some interesting information—not from her replies, but from her stubborn silences. It appeared that, in spite of all the time they had spent together, she knew as little about Robin as when she first met him. He had not told her where he worked, or what his job was. She did not know his address, or even where he lived, although she had gathered that it was somewhere in London. He had made no mention of parents, sisters, or brothers. The only thing she had learned was that he did a lot of traveling, both in England and on the continent—and this fact brought me no comfort.

By the time we got home, we were all fairly exhausted, what with the fresh air, the hot sunshine, and the highly charged emotional atmosphere. So it was not surprising that we all voted to call it a day quite soon after supper and departed to our respective bedrooms.

I strung the keys of the stamp cabinet and my jewel case on a ribbon round my neck, climbed into bed, and fell asleep almost at once. But a couple of hours later I was awake again, tossing and turning and brooding. I wasn't really worried about the diamonds. I could see the outline of the jewel case on my dressing table, faintly silhouetted against the uncurtained window. Anyway, the diamonds were mine, and they were well insured. Tom's stamps, on the other hand, were quite a different matter. A competent burglar could very easily pick the lock, and some of the rarer specimens were virtually irreplaceable. I heard the hall clock strike midnight, and then the half hour, and I could bear it no longer. After all, I was responsible. I'd told Tom I would look after his stamps, and I didn't mean to let him down. I decided to go downstairs, taking the jewel case with me, and sleep on the sofa beside the precious collection.

The house was dark and sleeping as I tiptoed out of my room. I slipped down the back stairs so as not to disturb the others, and for the same reason I did not switch on any lights. I made my way through the kitchen to the drawing room, groped my way to the sofa, stowed the jewel box on the floor, and was about to settle down when a small, insistent noise made me sit bolt upright, frozen with fright. I listened again. There was no doubt about it. Someone was coming slowly and stealthily down the main staircase and across the hall.

It was very dark in the drawing room, for the heavy damask curtains were closely drawn. My eyes had become somewhat accustomed to the gloom, but even so I could distinguish no more than the anonymous figure of a man as he came slipping silently through the half-open doorway. I sat rigid, not breathing. The man moved rather clumsily across the room towards me, groping among the chairs and tables.

And then something else happened. More footsteps—louder this time—and a second figure creeping in through the half-open door. A moment of darkness and stillness. Then a step, a sudden crash as a table overturned, and a man's voice shouted, "Got you!"

All bedlam broke loose then. The dark room seemed full of flailing arms and legs, snorts and grunts and shouts, the thud of falling furniture and the tinkle of breaking ornaments. There was nothing for it but swift action.

With my superior local knowledge, it was quite easy for me to make my way to the door that led to the main hall, and neither of the combatants was in any state to notice my movement. Once at the door, I flung it open and switched on the light, as though I had just arrived from upstairs. At the same moment, Sue came flying down the stairs like a fugitive naiad in her pale green chiffon negligée. We stood together in the doorway, watching with interest and apprehension as our two Mr. Smiths rolled about on the floor, evidently bent on mutual destruction.

It was all over quite quickly. Robin was the stronger and fitter of the two, and soon he had his rival securely pinioned, arms behind him, and was sitting astride Bobby's angrily writhing body.

"Well, Mrs. Westlake," said Robin, only slightly out of breath, "what did I tell you? I don't think he'll give you any more trouble. I suggest that you ring the police at once."

"Oh, Robin, you are wonderful," said Sue.

"Mrs. Westlake," came an indignant mutter from the floor. Bobby was finding some difficulty in speaking through a mouthful of carpet. "Mrs. Westlake! It's all a mistake! I can explain—"

"Now, you two," I said with as much authority as I could muster, "will you kindly get up off the floor and sit down like reasonable human beings and tell me what happened."

Robin looked doubtful. "Is it safe to let him go?" he asked.

"I'll take the responsibility," I said. "Get up."

The two of them climbed to their feet and dusted themselves off. Fortunately Bobby was none the worse for his trouncing, and soon we were all sitting round in armchairs, like a ghastly travesty of an ordinary late-night party.

"Now," I said, "I want both your stories. You first, Robin."

"Very simple," said Robin. "I was lying awake in bed when I heard somebody moving about down here, and so I came down to investigate. The room was pitch dark, but I could hear somebody breathing, and I hadn't been in here more than a few seconds before he attacked me. Smith—*if* that is his name, which I doubt—obviously decided that attack was the best form of defense."

"A pack of lies!" shouted Bobby. "I've told you my suspicions already, Mrs. Westlake, and I thought it probable that Smith—*if* that is his name, which I doubt—would make an attempt at burglary tonight. So instead of going to bed, I put out my light and kept watch from my room. My door was very slightly ajar, and I could see his door. Sure enough, soon after half-past twelve I saw him come out and sneak downstairs. So I followed him, and caught him in here, red-handed. The police should be informed at once."

It was at that moment that Robin spotted the jewel case on the floor.

"That settles it," he shouted. "Do you see? He'd already taken the jewel case from upstairs!"

"I hadn't! It was you—!"

"How could Robin have taken the jewel case," Sue chimed in, "if you watched him come out of his room and go downstairs?"

"Exactly!" said Robin, triumphantly. "Mrs. Westlake, I really advise you to call the police."

"So do I," said Sue.

"And so do I," said Bobby.

They were all looking at me. There was a terrible silence—and then it was broken by the loveliest sound I've ever heard in my life. The banging of the front door, heavy steps in the hall, and Tom's voice calling, "Hey, Margie! Are you still up?"

I was out into the hall like a rocketing pheasant, and the next moment my arms were round Tom's neck and my nose firmly embedded in his shirt front. He seemed surprised.

"Here, I say, no need to overdo it, old girl," he said, laughing. "Yes, I got through in Lisbon by five o'clock, grabbed a plane at eight, picked up my car at London Airport, and here I am."

I didn't say a word. I just propelled him into the drawing room. The two young men were both on their feet, and I couldn't help noticing that Robin had gone very pale. Sue must have noticed it, too, because she had edged over and was standing beside him in a protective sort of way, like a tigress with a brood of cubs.

"Hello, young Sue," said Tom, cheerfully. "Having a good holiday?" He turned to Bobby. "Ah, my young friend from Amalgamated Plastics. So you found your way here. I hope Margie's been looking after you."

"Mrs. Westlake has been very kind," said Bobby, with a nasty emphasis.

Tom turned to me. "Young Bobby Smith," he said, "is a future captain of the plastics industry, and I'd say the same even if his father weren't the chairman and owner of Amalgamated Plastics. The boy's starting at the bottom and working up, and a very good thing, too. Your father tells me you're living on your salary," he added, to Bobby.

"That's right, sir."

"Most creditable," said Tom, "for a young fellow who must be a millionaire in his own right already, eh?"

I closed my eyes. I heard Sue give a sort of strangled gasp. And then I opened my eyes again, and saw that Tom had turned to look at Robin. That young man was standing very upright and swaying slightly, as though facing a firing squad.

"Well," said Tom, cheerfully, "and who's this? Margie, aren't you going to introduce me—?" Then, suddenly, he stopped dead. And began to laugh. "Good lord," he said. "If it isn't Robin." He slapped Robin affectionately on the back. "Why the fancy dress, eh? Come into money, or something?" Robin went from white to pink and back again, but said nothing. Tom said to me, "Didn't recognize the young scamp for a moment. Last time I saw him, in Paris, he was wearing dirty jeans, a shirt covered in paint, and a rather offensive beard. His usual rig."

"So . . . you do know him . . . ?" I began.

"Certainly I do. Known him for years. Son of one of my oldest friends. You remember Valentine Smith."

"The artist!" gasped Sue.

"That's right. Could have been a big businessman, old Val, but chucked it all to go beachcombing and painting. And Robin's followed in his footsteps. How's the old man, Robin? Still stony broke and enjoying it?"

"Yes, sir," said Robin, in a small voice.

"Well," Tom went on, "I'll be frank with you, old lad, I'm glad to see you smartening yourself up a bit. Life in a garret on bread and cheese is all very well, but . . . So you've got yourself a steady job at last, have you?"

"Of course he has," said Sue. She was almost shouting. "He's got an E-type Jag and he stays in the best hotels and—"

"Please, Sue," said Robin. He sounded as though he had a fishbone stuck in his throat. "I think . . . I'd better explain . . ."

"Explain what?"

"I haven't got a job. I haven't got any money. The Jag isn't mine—I borrowed it. You see, last week I won five hundred pounds with a Premium Bond, and—"

"A Premium Bond?" said Sue, as if she'd never heard of the things.

"That's right. And a pal of mine bet me I couldn't carry it off for a week—staying in a snob hotel, and everything. So I

borrowed the car, bought some clothes, and came down
here—"

"Why down here?" Sue was ominously quiet.

"Well, I knew my father's old friend Tom Westlake had his
country house here—"

I could keep silent no longer. "I see," I said. "I see it all very
clearly. You met Tom in Paris, and he told you that I would be
here with my sister. You reckoned that Tom's sister-in-law
would be a good catch. You came here deliberately fortune-
hunting—"

"Don't say that," pleaded Robin. "It sounds so terrible. It was
just a joke. I'd never met a rich, beautiful, spoilt girl, dripping
in diamonds, and I thought it would be a bit of fun to find one,
and lead her on, and then tell her I was only a penniless artist
after all. I never reckoned that she'd be a person like Sue—"

"Well," I said, with triumph, "your plan misfired, didn't it?
Because it may interest you to know that the diamonds and the
mink and everything else are mine. Sue teaches English in a
primary school in Clapham, and lives in a bedsitter, and—"

There didn't seem much point in going on because I had lost
my audience. Sue and Robin were looking at each other in a
starry-eyed sort of way, and the next thing I knew they were
locked in the sort of embrace that was obviously going to go
on for a very long time. There didn't seem anything for it but
to melt tactfully into the kitchen and prepare drinks all round.

I'd hustled Tom and Bobby out of the room, and was just
leaving myself, when Sue looked at me over Robin's shoulder.
"You see, Margie darling," she said, "I *knew* he was too nice to
be rich!"

# RALPH McINERNY
## IN THE BAG

**I** changed planes in Cleveland and continued westward in a puddle jumper that touched down in Jackson and Kalamazoo before it got to South Bend. Such flights seem always to begin just short of midnight and to grope into darkness. The cabin lights are turned off, the flight attendants are stingy with the coffee and soft drinks, smokers ignore any restrictions on their activities. When we landed at Jackson I was groggy, more bored than tired. We would be on the ground fifteen minutes. I made sure my safety belt was buckled, tipped back my seat, and fell asleep.

"You'll have to straighten your seat for takeoff, sir."

The stewardess was smiling down at me. I did not smile back. I had managed to fall asleep, but now I was wide-awake for the daring fifteen-minute flight to Kalamazoo. I should have spent the night in Cleveland. What was the point of getting home at such an ungodly hour? Tomorrow I'd be all out of sorts, unable to work efficiently.

This time I fell asleep with my seat in the upright position. The landing in Kalamazoo brought me almost to the surface of consciousness, but then I dropped once more into sleep. When I awoke, we were still on the ground, or so I thought. A sleepy look out the window snapped me awake. This was South Bend.

I attempted to stand but was held in place by my belt. I unbuckled it, grabbed my briefcase, and stumbled up the aisle. The stewardess was chatting with the pilot through the open door of the front cabin and she did not turn while I unhooked my garment bag.

"This is South Bend," I said accusingly.

She glanced at me and nodded. "That's right."

"I was asleep."

"Lucky you."

She didn't seem to realize—or care—that I might have missed

151

my destination. I might have flown on to Chicago. I hoisted the garment bag over one shoulder and went down the steps and across the windy apron to the terminal.

The sight of Connie waiting for me in the brightly lit waiting room drove the grouchiness from me. As much as anything else, my return from Cleveland had been prompted by a desire to erase the memory of the quarrel we had had before my going. We seemed always to be quarreling lately. Yet here she was, bright-eyed and welcoming in the wee hours of the morning.

She took my briefcase, I got an arm around her waist, and we headed out of the terminal, bumping hips. The advantage of traveling light is that you don't have to wait for luggage to be unloaded. I had found that I could carry all I needed in the briefcase and garment bag, both of which I could take aboard. At that moment, saving time seemed all the more desirable. In the car, Connie started the motor and then turned to me for a kiss. Thank God I hadn't stayed in Cleveland.

It was nearly three o'clock in the morning when the phone beside the bed rang. Reaching for it, not wanting to turn on the light, I knocked it on the floor and had to reach around for the fallen receiver. A muffled voice was audible in the dark. Beside me Connie groaned and turned away.

I found the phone and put it to my ear.

"Is this Martin Quimby?"

"Who's this?" I demanded. The voice was unfamiliar. It was certainly no voice I felt I must defer to, nor was it the voice of a relative bearing bad news.

"Were you on United Flight 667 from Cleveland tonight?"

"Yes."

"I have your garment bag, Mr. Quimby. I assume you have mine."

"I have my own," I protested.

"Yours looks very much like mine. Look, I'm calling from Chicago. Could you check and see if you have my garment bag?"

The garment bag was hooked to the doorknob across the room. I had put it there, anxious to get to bed.

"Just a minute," I said, and put the phone down.

Connie moaned in protest when I threw back the covers. I crossed the room, took the garment bag into the bathroom, and turned on the light. As soon as my eyes got used to the glare I could see the garment bag wasn't mine. There was an identification flap. It read "Cedric Adams."

I went back to the phone. "What's your name?"

"Adams. Cedric Adams. My name's on the bag. Do you have it?"

"Yes. I'm sorry. I was asleep when we landed and—"

"I need that bag," Adams said urgently. It occurred to me that I needed mine, too. For one thing, it contained a new suit that had cost me three hundred dollars.

"How can we exchange them?"

"It's simple. I've checked with the airline. You put my bag on their eight o'clock flight to Chicago this morning, and I'll send yours down on the plane that leaves here at ten."

"Chicago time?" It was a stupid question, prompted by the dismal thought that I would have to get out of bed within hours and take Adams's bag to the airport. But then, he would have to go to some trouble to return mine to me. And, after all, the fault was mine. I had taken his bag. I agreed to do as he suggested and said again that I was sorry.

"Just put that bag on the eight o'clock plane," he said in a voice of command. He added in a softer tone, "I have to have it tomorrow."

I hung up, got back under the covers, and screwed my head into the pillow. But if I was ready for sleep, sleep did not return. Realizing one has been a damned fool is not conducive to sleep. If I hadn't been annoyed by the stewardess, if I had paid attention to what I was doing, I wouldn't have taken Adams's bag when I left the plane. I had no one to blame but myself. Adams had every right to be angry with me. I had sensed he would have liked to speak more bluntly than he had.

I lay sleepless, listening to the steady sound of Connie's breathing, the sleep of the just, a faintly accusing sound. If I had stayed in Cleveland, this mixup wouldn't have happened. Adams's phone call had left me with the same depression I felt after a quarrel with Connie. Why had I taken that milk run from Cleveland?

This suggested warm milk as a soporific. I slipped out of bed cautiously so as not to wake Connie—her temper was at its shortest when she first woke up—and took Adams's bag downstairs with me.

It was while I was waiting for the milk to warm that I unzipped Adams's garment bag.

I could plead weariness, the fact that while I couldn't fall asleep I wasn't really awake either. I could draw attention to the fact that it was after three in the morning, a time of day when the moral code seems in suspension anyway. The truth is I wasn't thinking much of anything when I laid the garment bag flat on the kitchen table and drew the zipper down diagonally across the bag. Perhaps anyone would have done the same in my place. I imagined Adams opening my garment bag in his motel room near O'Hare, thinking it was his own.

How shocked he must have been to find only clothes, my clothes. The contents of his bag certainly shocked me.

Actually it was the contents of the pockets of his sport jackets that shocked me. The four manila envelopes sticking out of them had the name of a Cleveland bank printed on them. In the envelopes were twenties, fifties, hundreds, and five hundreds.

Some realizations are quicker than a calculator. I knew at once that this was a great deal of money. There's something public and impersonal about money; it could belong to anyone. A man's clothes may be his own and bear his stamp, but money is either used and bears the mark of many hands or it's new and might be anyone's. The bills in the envelopes I had removed from the pockets of Cedric Adams's sport coats were new. Examining them in my kitchen, they seemed as much mine as anyone's. From the first glimpse I had of them, I was possessed by the impulse to confiscate the money. It was a small temptation at first—I thought of taking one bill from each envelope—but a six-hundred-seventy-dollar windfall seemed paltry when I thought of how much would remain.

The smell of burning milk shook me from my reverie. I snatched the pan from the stove and poured the milk into the sink. Opening a lower cupboard I took out a bottle of bourbon, poured three ounces neat into a glass, and pondered how I might with impunity become the possessor of all that money.

I arrived at a simple answer. I considered and reconsidered it, fearful that it was the bourbon or the hour or blindness induced by avarice that made it seem a plan without flaw. But I could discover nothing wrong with it.

Adams had lost his garment bag on a flight from Cleveland to Chicago, a flight that had made three intermediate stops. If someone had taken his bag, this could have happened in Jackson or Kalamazoo as well as in South Bend. But he had called me and I had admitted I had his bag. What proof did he have of that? He had no more proof that the person he had spoken to on the phone was Martin Quimby than I had that my caller was Cedric Adams. If I put his bag on the eight o'clock flight without the money, he would pick it up at the United luggage counter in O'Hare, and he would have no way of proving that the loss was due to my having taken his bag. And if he kept his end of the bargain, my garment bag would come in from Chicago, and what proof would there be that Adams had anything to do with its return?

Of course he had already spoken with airlines officials and would doubtless do so again in the morning. I myself would not do that at eight o'clock. The kitchen clock now read five past four, but I was more dismayed by how long I must wait to go to the airport than by the lateness of the hour.

And then I thought, why wait? If I took Adams's bag to the terminal now, the place would be all but deserted and I could drop it on the baggage belt and it would look like a forgotten or lost piece of luggage, having no connection with me at all. Perfect. I would do it. I put on a raincoat over my pajamas and went out to the garage, hugging Adams's garment bag to me. I eased open the garage door carefully, taking a full minute. The motor sounded like an artillery barrage before a battle when I turned the ignition key. I backed down the driveway with the lights out, huddled over the wheel, praying that I hadn't awakened Connie. I didn't want her privy to my crime.

Crime? But if I was guilty of theft, it was a thief I was robbing. Who but a thief would be traveling with that much money stashed in his luggage? To steal stolen money seemed almost innocent, as if I were rectifying a moral imbalance by appropriating those envelopes. Why then did I feel like an outlaw, speeding to the airport at this ungodly hour? I didn't really believe that I could just drop off Adams's bag and go.

I was wrong. It was as easy as I had imagined. The only other person in the terminal was an elderly woman swabbing the floor listlessly to the uncertain tempo of the Muzak. The belt that emerged from one opening carrying baggage past waiting travelers and disappeared into another opening was, of course, at rest. I shoved Adams's bag into one of those openings and hurried away, half expecting a shout to halt me. But I was leading a charmed life. I had left the car motor running. I slipped out of the No Parking zone and was on my way home only minutes after having arrived at the terminal. Before turning into my driveway, I flicked off the headlights. Dawn was already graying the sky, and I had sufficient visibility to put the car in the garage.

I crept upstairs, entered the bedroom, and stopped. Connie seemed still asleep. I went into the closet and put the envelopes on the shelf, pushing them back beneath a stack of my shirts. When I got into bed, Connie stirred. I lay quiet but in a moment she spoke.

"You've been drinking."

"I couldn't sleep."

I was tense. That exchange could have been a prelude to argument. My drinking had more than once provided the occasion for a quarrel. Connie sighed and turned away, pulling the covers over her shoulder. It might have been a rebuff. It might have summed up our marriage. But I was thinking of all that money on the closet shelf. You would have thought I had received it in exchange for Connie, that it represented a way out of the unhappiness that seemed to grip us both.

The windows grew bright with a new day before I fell asleep.

In the morning, I telephoned the airport and told the airline I had left a bag on the Cleveland-to-Chicago flight the night before. Would they put through an inquiry on it? I described the bag. I gave the girl my name. Yes, my name was on the bag.

When I hung up and turned smiling from the phone, Connie stood on the stairs looking quizzically at me.

"What was that all about?"

"I wanted to tell the airline about my garment bag."

"What about it?"

"I left it on the plane last night. It must have gone on to Chicago."

She tipped her head to one side and frowned at me. Was she remembering me coming toward her at the terminal with the garment bag slung over my shoulder? She said, "Who called last night?"

"It was a wrong number."

"Then why were you on the phone so long?"

"I wasn't. It must just have seemed that way at that hour."

This was worse than taking Adams's money. Adams was a stranger, but Connie was my wife; deceiving her was worse than theft. I told myself I was protecting her, that we would both enjoy the money, but in a deeper recess of my soul I knew I regarded that money as a ticket out of our humdrum life together. Has any crook ever considered himself a crook in his heart of hearts? I didn't. If I felt anything, it was righteousness. I had thwarted a thief.

In the kitchen, Connie put away the bottle of bourbon. She said, "Well, I didn't dream you came down here for a drink, did I? What did you need a drink for anyway?"

"That flight from Cleveland was awful," I said.

"How could you forget to pick up your bag?" Thelma, my secretary, asked when I told her I wanted her to go out to the airport and pick up my garment bag. She had just brought a cup of coffee and the mail into my office. I knew that the prospect of getting away from her typewriter and out of the office excited her.

"Call the airline and see if it's come in," I advised her. "No point in making the trip in vain."

I felt indifferent to the fate of my bag, in spite of the three-hundred-dollar suit it contained, but of course I couldn't just forget it. The vices of the nouveau riche suddenly had appeal—wastefulness, obsolescence, conspicuous consumption. "If they've lost it, I'll sue," I said, trying to impress myself as much as Thelma.

At ten o'clock she buzzed to say my bag had come in from Chicago and she was on her way to pick it up.

An hour later, when my phone rang, I answered it myself. Connie's voice spoke in my ear in a strangled, terrified tone. "Martin, there's a man—"

She stopped, as if a hand had been clapped over her mouth. Then a man's voice spoke.

"Quimby, you know what I want. I assume you'd prefer to have your wife alive. Where is it?"

It was Adams's voice. Listening to it, I thought of the bank envelopes on the closet shelf, pushed far back under the pile of shirts.

"I don't understand," I said. "Who's speaking?"

"Don't play around, Quimby." His voice was one of controlled rage. I could hear Connie whimpering in the background. "Where's the money?"

"So you're a thief. Listen. My wife is telling the truth. We don't keep money in the house. You must believe her." I paused. "I can go to the bank. How much—"

"I don't want *your* money; I want mine! The money that was in the garment bag you took from the plane last night."

"Plane? I wasn't on any plane last night."

"That isn't what your wife said." He grunted and Connie screamed.

I closed my eyes. "Stop it! If you touch her again, you'll get nothing from me."

"Do you have it with you?"

I thought.

"Yes," I said. "I have it with me."

"Bring it."

"No. You come here for it. I have it here in my office. That's the only way you'll get it."

"Not your office," he said with finality.

"Then where?"

"The airport."

Finally I agreed. I repeated my warning that he not touch Connie again. It seemed the least I could do for her.

It seemed a farewell gift.

Before I left the office, I called the police. I told them that a man named Cedric Adams had been making threatening phone calls to my house and that he was now at my house demanding that I give him a large sum of money. There was a possibility that he would harm my wife.

When I came out of the elevator on the ground floor, I ran into Thelma carrying my garment bag. I took it from her.

"I have to go home for a while. I'll drop it off there."

She shrugged, as if the day had stopped making sense to her hours ago.

It took me longer to get to my house than it would take him to get to the airport. The traffic was terrible. I cruised past the house, saw Connie's car in the driveway, went to the corner, turned, and entered the street behind and parallel with my own. I parked, got out of the car, and cut through a yard to my own back fence. Once over that, I stood under an apple tree and stared at my house. It looked as it always had. I regretted not having telephoned Connie that I was on my way. Had Adams really gone to the airport? There was only one way to find out.

I dashed across the yard, up onto the back porch, and grasped the knob of the back door. I turned it. Locked. While I fumbled for my keys, I pressed the button that set off the chimes within. That was a message to Connie: I was home, she was safe. But she didn't come to open the door for me. I had to use my key. I pushed open the door and hesitated before stepping inside. Closing the door behind me, slowly, quietly, I was struck by the silence of the house.

"Connie?" A dreadful thought crossed my mind. "Connie!"

I made a quick circuit of the downstairs, dashing from room to room, but there was no sign of her. When I came to the stairway, I stopped and looked up at the landing where a rubber tree stood. It suggested a jungle, atrocities, God knew what. I lifted one foot and put it carefully on the first step. I mounted the stairs as if I were wading through water.

When I reached the landing and the rubber plant, I turned; the upper floor was level with my eyes. Had I expected to see

Connie sprawled on that floor? I felt the slightest twinge of disappointment. The bathroom was visible, too, but what was visible of it was empty. I went and looked inside, in the bathtub. Nothing. Again that involuntary twinge of disappointment.

In our bedroom, which was also empty, I went to the closet and pushed my hand to the back of the shelf, under the shirts. When my hand didn't make contact with the envelopes I felt carefully to one side, then the other. I pulled the shirts from the shelf and felt around with both hands.

The envelopes weren't there.

Stunned, I came out of the closet and crossed the room to the bed. I sat on it and put my face in my hands. The enormity of my unspoken hope shocked me. I wished I had never seen that money. But why had Adams taken Connie as hostage after he'd found the money? Now that the money was gone, I found myself able to tremble at the thought of harm coming to her. She was my wife. I brought my hands together and prayed that no harm would come to her.

The ringing phone lifted me from the bed, I was so startled. I let it ring three times before answering.

"Mr. Quimby? Sergeant McIntyre of the South Bend police. We have Mr. Adams in custody."

"How is my wife?"

"Your wife?"

"He took her as a hostage. Isn't she there?"

"No, she isn't. He was alone. Mr. Quimby, we have a problem. The money Adams stole in Cleveland—it isn't on him."

"He stole some money?"

"That's why we acted on your call. Those phone calls you mentioned, we couldn't arrest him for those. Where's the proof? But the name rang a bell and, sure enough, they want him in Cleveland—"

I hung up on the efficient, plausible voice. I went to the window and looked down at the driveway. Connie's car wasn't there. If I had turned into the driveway instead of going past the house . . .

When I went to the closet again, I set the row of empty

hangers tinkling. I hadn't noticed before that Connie's side of the closet was empty. Her clothes were gone. The money was gone. Connie was gone.

Downstairs I mixed a drink and tried unsuccessfully to feel betrayed.

# LOREN D. ESTLEMAN
# GREEKTOWN

The restaurant was damp and dim and showed every indication of having been hollowed out of a massive stump, with floorboards scoured as white as wood grubs and tall booths separated from the stools at the counter by an aisle just wide enough for skinny waitresses like you never see in Greektown. It was Greektown, and the only waitress in sight looked like a garage door in a uniform. She caught me checking out the booths and trundled my way, turning stools with her left hip as she came.

"You are Amos Walker?" She had a husky accent and large, dark, pretty eyes set in the rye dough of her face. I said I was, and she told me Mr. Xanthes was delayed and sat me down in a booth halfway between the door and the narrow hallway leading to the restrooms in back. Somewhere a radio turned low was playing one of those frantic Mediterranean melodies that sound like hornets set loose in the string section.

The waitress was freshening my coffee when my host arrived, extending a small right hand and a smiling observation on downtown Detroit traffic. Constantine Xanthes was a wiry five feet and ninety pounds with deep laugh lines from his narrow eyes to his broad mouth and hair as black at fifty as mine was going gray at thirty-three. His light blue tailor-made suit fit him like a sheen of water. He smiled a lot, but so does every other restaurateur, and none of them means it either. When he found out I hadn't eaten he ordered egg lemon soup, bread, feta cheese, roast lamb, and a bottle of ouzo for us both. I passed on the ouzo.

"Greektown used to be more than just fine places to eat," he sighed, poking a fork at his lamb. "When my parents came it was a little Athens, with markets and pretty girls in red and white dresses at festival time and noise like I can't describe to you. It took in Macomb, Randolph, and Monroe Streets, not just one block of Monroe like now. Now those colorful old men you see drinking retsina on the stoops get up and go home to the suburbs at dark."

I washed down the last of the strong cheese with coffee. "I'm a good P.I., Mr. Xanthes, but I'm not good enough to track down and bring back the old days. What else can I do to make your life easier?"

He refilled his glass with ouzo and I watched his Adam's apple bob twice as the syrupy liquid slid down his throat. Afterwards he was still smiling, but the vertical line that had appeared between his brows when he was talking about what had happened to his neighborhood had deepened.

"I have a half-brother, Joseph," he began. "He's twenty-three years younger than I am; his mother was our father's second wife. She deserted him when he was six. When Father died, my wife and I took over the job of raising Joseph, but by then I was working sixty hours a week at General Motors and he was seventeen and too much for Grace to handle with two children of our own. He ran away. We didn't hear from him until last summer, when he walked into the house unannounced, all smiles and hugs, at least for me. He and Grace never got along. He congratulated me on my success in the restaurant business and said he'd been living in Iowa for the past nine years, where he'd married and divorced twice. His first wife left him without so much as a note and had a lawyer send him papers six weeks later. The second filed suit on grounds of brutality. It seems that during quarrels he took to beating her with the cord from an iron. He was proud of that.

"He's been here fourteen months, and in that time he's held more jobs than I can count. Some he quit, some he was fired from, always for the same reason. He can't work with or for a woman. I kept him on here as a busboy until he threw a stool at one of my waitresses. She'd asked him to get a can of coffee from the storeroom and forgot to say please. I had to let him go."

He paused, and I lit a Winston to keep from having to say anything. It was all beginning to sound familiar. I wondered why.

When he saw I wasn't going to comment he drew a folded

clipping from an inside breast pocket and spread it out on the table with the reluctant care of a father getting ready to punish his child. It was from that morning's *Free Press*, and it was headed PSYCHIATRIST PROFILES FIVE O'CLOCK STRANGLER.

That was the name the press had hung on the nut who had stalked and murdered four women on their way home from work on the city's northwest side on four separate evenings over the past two weeks. The women were found strangled to death in public places around quitting time, or reported missing by their families from that time and discovered later. Their ages ranged from twenty to forty-six, they had had no connection with each other in life, and they were all WASPs. One was a nurse, two were secretaries, the fourth had been something mysterious in city government. None was raped. The *Freep* had dug up a shrink who claimed the killer was between twenty-five and forty, a member of an ethnic or racial minority group, and a hater of professional women, a man who had had experiences with such women unpleasant enough to unhinge him. It was the kind of article you usually find in the science section after someone's made off with the sports and the comics, only today it had run on page one because there hadn't been any murders in a couple of days to keep the story alive. I'd read it at breakfast. I knew now what had nagged me about Xanthes' story.

"Your brother's the Five O'Clock Strangler?" I tipped half an inch of ash into the tin tray on the table.

"Half-brother," he corrected. "If I was sure of that, I wouldn't have called you. Joseph could have killed that waitress, Mr. Walker. As it was he nearly broke her arm with that stool, and I had to pay for X-rays and give her a bonus to keep her from pressing charges. This article says the strangler hates working women. Joseph hates *all* women, but working women especially. His mother was a licensed practical nurse and she abandoned him. His first wife was a legal secretary and *she* left him. He told me he started beating his second wife when she started talking about getting a job. The police say that because the killer strangles women with just his hands he has to be big and strong. That description fits my half-brother; he's built more like you than me, and he works out regularly."

"Does he have anything against white Anglo-Saxon Protestants?"

"I don't know. But his mother was one and so was his first wife. The waitress he hurt was of Greek descent."

I burned some more tobacco. "Does he have an alibi for any of the times the women were killed?"

"I asked him, in a way that wouldn't make him think I suspected him. He said he was home alone." He shifted his weight on the bench. "I didn't want to press it, but I called him one of those nights and he didn't answer. But it wasn't until I read this article that I really started to worry. It could have been written about Joseph. That's when I decided to call you. You once dug up an eyewitness to an auto accident whose testimony saved a friend of mine a bundle. He talks about you often."

"I have a license to stand in front of," I said. "If your half-brother is the strangler I'll have to send him over."

"I understand that. All I ask is that you call me before you call the police. It's this not knowing, you know? And don't let him know he's being investigated. There's no telling what he'll do if he finds out I suspect him."

We took care of finances—in cash; you'll look in vain for a checkbook in Greektown—and he slid over a wallet-sized photo of a darkly handsome man in his late twenties with glossy black hair like his half-brother's and big liquid eyes not at all like Xanthes' slits. "He goes by Joe Santine. You'll find him working part-time at Butsukitis's market on Brush." Joseph's home telephone number and an address on Gratiot were written on the back of the picture. That was a long way from the area where the bodies were found, but then the killer hardly ever lives in the neighborhood where he works. Not that that made any difference to the cops busy tossing every house and apartment on the northwest side.

He looked like his picture. After leaving the restaurant, I'd walked around the corner to a building with a fruit and vegetable stand out front and a faded canvas awning lettered BUTSUKITIS'S FINE PRODUCE. While a beefy bald man in his sixties with fat quilting his chest under a white apron was dropping some onions into a paper sack for me, a tall young man came out the front door lugging a crate full of cabbages. He hoisted the crate onto a bare spot on the stand, swept large shiny eyes over the milling crowd of tomato-squeezers and melon-huggers, and went back inside swinging his broad shoulders.

As the grocer was ringing up the sale, a blonde wearing a navy blue business suit asked for help loading two bags of apples and cherries into her car. "Santine!" he bellowed.

The young man returned. Told to help the lady, he hesitated, then slouched forward and snatched up the bags. He stashed them on the front seat of a green Olds parked half a block down the street and swung around and walked away while she was still rummaging in her handbag for a tip. His swagger going back into the store was pronounced. I paid for my onions and left.

Back at the office I called Iowa information and got two numbers. The first belonged to a private detective agency in Des Moines. I called them, fed them the dope I had on Santine and asked them to scrape up what they could. My next call was to the Des Moines *Express,* where a reporter held me up for fifty dollars for combing the morgue for stories about nonrape female assault and murder during the last two years Santine lived in the state. They both promised to wire the information to Barry Stackpole at the Detroit *News* and I hung up and dialed Barry's number and traded a case of scotch for his cooperation. The expenses on this one were going to eat up my fee. Finally I called John Alderdyce at police headquarters. "Who's working the Five O'Clock Strangler case?" I asked him.

"Why?"

I used the dead air counting how many times he'd asked me that and dividing it by how many times I'd answered.

"DeLong," he said then. "I could just hang up because I'm busy, but you'd probably just call again."

"Probably. Is he in?"

"He's in that lot off Lahser where they found the last body. With Michael Kurof."

"The psychic?"

"No, the plumber. They're stopping there on their way to fix DeLong's toilet." He broke the connection.

*  *  *

The last body had been found lying in a patch of weeds in a wooded lot off Lahser just south of West Grand River by a band student taking a shortcut home from practice. I parked next to the curb behind a blue-and-white and mingled with a group of uniforms and obvious plainclothesmen watching Kurof walk around, with Inspector DeLong nipping along at his side like a spaniel trying to keep up with a Great Dane. DeLong was a razor-faced twenty-year cop with horns of pink scalp retreating along a mouse-colored widow's peak. Kurof, a Russian-born bear of a man, bushy-haired and blue of chin even when it was still wet from shaving, bobbed his big head in time with DeLong's mile-a-minute patter for a few moments, then raised a palm, cutting him off. After that they wandered the lot in silence.

"What they looking for, rattlesnakes?" muttered a grizzled fatty in a baggy brown suit.

"Vibes," someone answered. "Emanations, the Russky calls 'em."

Lardbottom snorted. "We ran fortune-tellers in when I was in uniform."

I was nudged by a young black uniform, who winked gravely and stooped to lay a gold pencil he had taken from his shirt pocket on the ground, then backed away from it. Kurof's back was turned. Eventually he and DeLong made their way to the spot, where the psychic picked up the pencil, stroked it once between the first and second fingers of his right hand, and turned to the black cop with a broad smile, holding out the item. "You are having fun with me, officer," he announced in a deep burring voice. The uniform smiled stiffly back and accepted the pencil.

"Did you learn anything, Dr. Kurof?" DeLong wanted to know.

Kurof shook his great head slowly. "Nothing useful, I fear. Just a tangible hatred. The air is ugly everywhere here, but it is ugliest where we are standing. It crawls."

"We're standing precisely where the body was found." The inspector pushed aside a clump of thistles with his foot to expose a fresh yellow stake driven into the earth. He turned toward one of the watching uniforms. "Give our guest a lift home. Thank you, doctor. We'll be in touch when something else comes up." They shook hands and the Russian moved off slowly with his escort.

"Hatred," the fat detective growled. "Like we needed a gypsy to tell us that."

DeLong told him to shut up and go back to headquarters. As the knot of investigators loosened, I approached the inspector and introduced myself.

"Walker," he considered. "Sure, I've seen you jawing with Alderdyce. Who hired you, the family of one of the victims?"

"Just running an errand." Sometimes it's best to let a cop keep his notions. "What about what this psychiatrist said about the strangler in this morning's *Freep?* You agree with that?"

"Shrinks. Twenty years in school to tell us why some j.d. sapped an old lady and snatched her purse. I'll stick with guys like Kurof; at least he's not smug." He stuck a Tiparillo in his mouth and I lit it and a Winston for me. He sucked smoke. "My theory is the killer's unemployed and he sees all these women running out and getting themselves fulfilled by taking his job and something snaps. It isn't just coincidence that the statistics on crime against women have risen with their number in the work force."

"Is he a minority?"

"I hope so." He grinned quickly and without mirth. "No, I know what you mean. Maybe. Minorities outnumber the majority in this town in case you haven't noticed. Could be the victims are all WASPs because there are more women working who are WASPs. I'll ask him when we arrest him."

"Think you will?"

He glared at me, then he shrugged. "This is the third mass-murder case I've investigated. The one fear is that it'll just stop. I'm still hoping to wrap it up before famous criminologists start coming in from all over to give us a hand. I never liked circuses even when I was a kid."

"What are you holding back from the press on this one?"

"You expect me to answer that? Give up the one thing that'll help us differentiate between the original and all the copycats?"

"Call John Alderdyce. He'll tell you I sit on things till they hatch."

"Oh, hell." He dropped his little cigar half-smoked and crushed it out. "The guy clobbers his victims before he strangles them. One blow to the left cheek, probably with his right fist. Keeps 'em from struggling."

"Could he be a boxer?"

"Maybe. Someone used to using his dukes."

I thanked him for talking to me. He said, "I hope you are working for the family of a victim."

I got out of there without answering. Lying to a cop like DeLong can be like trying to smuggle a bicycle through customs.

It was coming up on two o'clock. If the killer was planning to strike that day, I had three hours. At the first telephone booth I came to, I excavated my notebook and called Constantine Xanthes' home number in Royal Oak. His wife answered. She had a mellow voice and no accent.

"Yes, Connie told me he was going to hire you. He's not home, though. Try the restaurant."

I explained she was the one I wanted to speak with and asked if I could come over. After a brief pause she agreed and gave me directions. I told her to expect me in half an hour.

It was a white frame house that would have been in the country when it was built, but now it was shouldered by two housing tracts with a third going up in the empty field across the street. The doorbell was answered by a tall woman on the far side of forty with black hair streaked blond to cover the gray and a handsome oval face, the flesh shiny around the eyes and mouth from recent remodeling. She wore a dark knit dress that accentuated the slim lines of her torso and a long colored scarf to make you forget she was big enough to look down at the top of her husband's head without trying. We exchanged greetings and she let me in and hung up my hat and we walked into a dim living room furnished heavily in oak and dark leather. We sat down facing each other in a pair of horsehair-stuffed chairs.

"You're not Greek," I said.

"I hardly ever am." Her voice was just as mellow in person.

"Your husband was mourning the old Greektown at lunch and now I find out he lives in the suburbs with a woman who isn't Greek."

"Connie's ethnic standards are very high for other people." She was smiling when she said it, but I didn't press the point. "He says you and Joseph have never been friendly. In what ways weren't you friendly when he was living here?"

"I don't suppose it's ever easy bringing up someone else's son. His having been deserted didn't help. Lord save me if I suggested taking out the garbage."

"Was he sullen, abusive, what?"

"Sullen was his best mood. 'Abusive' hardly describes his reaction to the simplest request. The children were beginning to repeat his foul language. I was relieved when he ran away."

"Did you call the police?"

"Connie did. They never found him. By that time he was eighteen and technically an adult. He couldn't have been brought back without his consent anyway."

"Did he ever hit you?"

"He wouldn't dare. He worshiped Connie."

"Did he ever box?"

"You mean fight? I think so. Sometimes he came home from school with his clothes torn or a black eye, but he wouldn't talk about it. That was before he quit. Fighting is normal. We had some of the same problems with our son; he grew out of it."

I was coming to the short end. "Any scrapes with the law? Joseph, I mean."

She shook her head. Her eyes were warm and tawny. "You know, you're quite good-looking. You have noble features."

"So does a German shepherd."

"I work in clay. I'd like to have you pose for me in my studio sometime." She waved long nails toward a door to the left. "I specialize in nudes."

"So do I. But not with clients' wives." I rose.

She lifted penciled eyebrows. "Was I that obvious?"

"Probably not, but I'm a detective." I thanked her and got my hat and let myself out.

*　*　*

Xanthes had told me his half-brother got off at four. At ten to, I
swung by the market and bought two quarts of strawberries.
The beefy bald man, whom I'd pegged as Butsukitis, the owner,
appeared glad to see me. Memories are long in Greektown. I
said, "I just had an operation and the doc says I shouldn't lift
any more than five pounds. Could your boy carry these to the
car?"

"I let my boy leave early. Slow day. I will carry them."

He did, and I drove away stuck with two quarts of strawberries. They give me hives. Had Santine been around I'd planned
to tail him after he punched out. Beating the steering wheel at
red lights, I bucked and squirmed my way through late afternoon traffic to Gratiot, where my man kept an apartment on
the second floor of a charred brick building that had housed a
recording studio in the gravy days of Motown. I ditched my hat,
jacket, and tie in the car and at Santine's door put on a pair of
aviator's glasses in case he remembered me from the market. If
he answered my knock, I was looking for another apartment.
There was no answer. I considered slipping the latch and taking
a look around inside, but it was too early in the round to play
catch with my license. I went back down and made myself
uncomfortable in my heap across the street from the entrance.

It was growing dark when a cab creaked its brakes in front of
the building and Santine got out, wearing a blue windbreaker
over the clothes I'd seen him in earlier. He paid the driver and
went inside. Since the window of his apartment looked out on
Gratiot I let the cab go, noting its number, hit the starter, and
wound my way to the company's headquarters on Woodward.

A puffy-faced black man in work clothes looked at me from
behind a steel desk in an office smelling of oil. The floor tingled
with the swallowed bellowing of engines in the garage below. I
gave him a hinge at my investigator's photostat, placing my
thumb over the "Private," and told him in an official voice I
wanted information on the cab in question.

He looked back down at the ruled pink sheet he was scrib-
bling on and said, "I been dispatcher here eleven years. You
think I don't know a plastic badge when I see one?"

I licked a ten-dollar bill across the sheet.

"That's Dillard," he said, watching the movement.

"He just dropped off a fare on Gratiot." I gave him the address. "I want to know where he picked him up and when."

He found the cab number on another ruled sheet attached to a clipboard on the wall and followed the line with his finger to some writing in another column. "Evergreen, between School-craft and Kendall. Dillard logged it in at six-twenty."

I handed him the bill without comment. The spot where Santine had entered the cab was an hour's easy walk from where the bodies of two of the murdered women had been found.

I swung past Joe Santine's apartment near Greektown on my way home. There was a light on. That night after supper I caught all the news reports on TV and looked for bulletins and wound up watching a succession of sitcoms full of single mothers shrieking at their kids about sex. There was nothing about any new stranglings. I went to bed. Eating breakfast next day I turned on the radio and read the *Free Press.* There was still nothing.

The name of the psychiatrist quoted in the last issue was Kornecki. I looked him up and called his office in the National Bank building. I expected a secretary, but I got him.

"I'd like to talk to you about someone I know," I said.

"Someone you know. I see." He spoke in cathedral tones.

"It's not me. I have an entirely different set of neuroses."

"My consultation fee is one hundred dollars for forty minutes."

"I'll take twenty-five dollars' worth," I said.

"No, that's for forty minutes or any fraction thereof. I have a cancellation at eleven. Shall I have my secretary pencil you in when she returns from her break?"

I told him to do so, gave him my name, and rang off before I could say anything about his working out of a bank. The hundred went onto the expense sheet.

Kornecki's reception room was larger than my office by half. A redhead at a kidney-shaped desk smiled tightly at me and found my name on her calendar, and buzzed me through. The inner sanctum, pastel green with a blue carpet, dark green Naugahyde couch, and a large glass-topped desk bare but for a telephone intercom, looked out on downtown through a window whose double panes swallowed the traffic noise. Behind the desk, a man about my age, wearing a blue pinstripe and steel-rimmed glasses, sat smiling at me with several thousand dollars' worth of dental work. He wore his sandy hair in bangs like Alfalfa.

We shook hands and I took charge of the customer's chair, a pedestal job upholstered in green vinyl to match the couch. I asked if I could smoke. He said whatever made me comfortable and indicated a smoking stand nearby. I lit up and laid out Santine's background without naming him. Kornecki listened.

"Is this guy capable of violence against strange women?" I finished.

He smiled again. "We all are, Mr. Walker. Every one of us men; it's our only advantage. You think your man is the strangler, is that it?"

"I guess I was absent the day they taught subtle."

"Oh, you were subtle. But you can't know how many people I've spoken with since that article appeared, wanting to be assured that their uncle or cousin or best friend isn't the killer. Hostility between the sexes is nothing new, but these last few confusing years have aggravated things. From what you've told me, though, I don't think you need to worry."

Those rich tones rumbling up from his slender chest made you want to look around to see who was talking. I waited, smoking.

"The powder is there," he went on. "But it needs a spark. If your man were to start murdering women, his second wife would have been his first victim. He wouldn't have stopped at beating her. My own theory is that the strangler suffered some real or imagined wrong at a woman's hand in his past, and that recently the wrong was repeated, either by a similar act committed by another woman, or by his coming into contact with the same woman."

"What sort of wrong?"

"It could be anything. Sexual domination is the worst because it means loss of self-esteem. Possibly she worked for a living, but it's just as likely that he equates women who work with her dominance. They would be a substitute; he would lack the courage to strike out at the actual source of his frustration."

"Suppose he ran into his mother or something like that."

He shook his head. "Too far back. I don't place as much importance on early childhood as many of my colleagues. Stale charges don't explode that easily."

"You've been a big help," I said, and we talked about sports and politics until my hundred dollars were up.

From there I went to the Detroit *News* and Barry Stackpole's cubicle, where he greeted me with the lopsided grin the silver plate in his head had left him with after some rough trade tried to blow him up in his car. He pointed to a stack of papers on his desk. I sat on one of the antique whisky crates he uses to file things in—there was a similar stack on the only other chair besides his—and went through the stuff. It had come over the wire that morning from the Des Moines agency and the *Express,* and none of it was for me. Santine had held six jobs in his last two years in Iowa, fetch-and-carry work, no brains need apply. His first wife had divorced him on grounds of marriage break-down and he hadn't contested the action. His second had filed for extreme cruelty. The transcripts of that one were ugly but not uncommon. There were enough articles from the newspaper on violent crimes against women to make you think twice about moving there, but if there was a pattern it was lost on me. The telephone rang while I was reshuffling the papers. Barry barked his name into the receiver, paused, and held it out to me.

"I gave my service this number," I explained, accepting it.

"You bastard, you promised to call me before you called the police."

The voice belonged to Constantine Xanthes. I straightened. "Start again."

"Joseph just called me from police headquarters. They've arrested him for the stranglings."

I met Xanthes in Homicide. He was wearing the same light blue suit or one just like it and his face was pale beneath the olive pigment. "He's being interrogated now," he said stiffly. "My lawyer's with him."

"I didn't call the cops." I made my voice low. The room was alive with uniforms and detectives in shirtsleeves droning into telephones and comparing criminal anecdotes at the water cooler.

"I know. When I got here, Inspector DeLong told me that Joseph walked into some kind of trap."

On cue, DeLong entered the squad room from the hallway leading to Interrogation. His jacket was off and his shirt clung, transparent, to his narrow chest. When he saw me his eyes flamed. "You said you were representing a *victim's* family."

"I didn't," I corrected. "You did. What's this trap?"

He grinned to his molars. "It's the kind of thing you do in these things when you did everything else. Sometimes it works. We had another strangling last night."

My stomach took a dive. "It wasn't on the news."

"We didn't release it. The body was jammed into a culvert on Schoolcraft. When we got the squeal we threw wraps over it, morgued the corpse—she was a teacher at Redford High—and stuck a department store dummy in its place. These nuts like publicity; when there isn't any they might check to see if the body is still there. So Santine climbs down the bank at half past noon and takes a look inside and three officers step out of the bushes and screw their service revolvers in his ears."

"Pretty thin," I said.

"How thick does it have to be with a full confession?"

Xanthes swayed. I grabbed his arm. I was still looking at DeLong.

"He's talking to a tape recorder now," he said, filling a Dixie cup at the cooler. "He knows the details on all five murders, including the blow to the cheek."

"I'd like to see him." Xanthes was still pale, but he wasn't needing me to hold him up now.

"It'll be a couple of hours."

"I'll wait."

The inspector shrugged, drained the cup, and headed back the way he'd come, side-arming the crumpled container at a steel wastebasket already bubbling over with them. Xanthes said, "He didn't do it."

"I think he probably did." I was somersaulting a Winston back and forth across the back of my hand. "Is your wife home?"

He started slightly. "Grace? She's shopping for art supplies in Southfield. I tried to reach her after the police called, but I couldn't."

"I wonder if I could have a look at her studio."

"Why?"

"I'll tell you in the car." When he hesitated, I said, "It beats hanging around here."

He nodded. In my crate I said, "Your father was proud of his Greek heritage, wasn't he?"

"Fiercely. He was a stonecutter in the old country and he was built like Hercules. He taught me the importance of being a man and the sanctity of womanhood. That's why I can't understand . . ." He shook his head, watching the scenery glide past his window.

"I can. When a man who's been told all his life that a man should be strong lets himself be manipulated by a woman, it does things to him. If he's smart, he'll put distance between himself and the woman. If he's weak, he'll come back and it'll start all over again. And if the woman happens to be married to his half-brother, whom he worships—"

I stopped, feeling the flinty chips of his eyes on me. "Who told you that?"

"Your wife, some of it. You, some more. The rest of it I got from a psychiatrist downtown. The women's movement has changed the lives of almost everyone but the women who have the most to lose by embracing it. Your wife's been cheating on you for years."

"Liar!" He lunged across the seat at me. I spun the wheel hard and we shrieked around a corner and he slammed back against the passenger's door. A big Mercury that had been close on our tail blatted its horn and sped past. Xanthes breathed heavily, glaring.

"She propositioned me like a pro yesterday." I corrected our course. We were entering his neighborhood now. "I think she's been doing that kind of thing a long time. I think that when he

was living at your place Joseph found out and threatened to tell
you. That would have meant divorce for a proud man like you,
and your wife would have had to go to work to support herself
and the children. So she bribed Joseph with the only thing she
had to bribe him with. She's still attractive, but in those days
she must have been a knockout; being weak, he took the bribe,
and then she had leverage. She hedged her bet by making up
those stories about his incorrigible behavior so that you
wouldn't believe him if he did tell you. So he got out from
under. But the experience had plundered him of his self-respect
and tainted his relationships with women from then on.

"Even then he might have grown out of it, but he made the
mistake of coming back. Seeing her again shook something
loose. He walked into your house Joe Santine and came out the
Five O'Clock Strangler, victimizing seemingly independent
WASP women like Grace. Who taught him how to use his fists?"

"Our father, probably. He taught me. It was part of a man's
training, he said, to know how to defend himself." His voice
was as dead as last year's leaves.

We pulled into his driveway and he got out, moving very
slowly. Inside the house we paused before the locked door to
his wife's studio. I asked him if he had a key.

"No. I've never been inside the room. She's never invited me
and I respect her privacy."

I didn't. I slipped the lock with the edge of my investigator's
photostat and we entered Grace Xanthes' trophy room.

It had been a bedroom, but she had erected steel utility
shelves and moved in a kiln and a long library table on which
stood a turning pedestal supporting a lump of red clay that was
starting to look like a naked man. The shelves were lined with
nude male figure studies twelve to eighteen inches high, posed
in various heroic attitudes. They were all of a type, athletically
muscled and wide at the shoulders, physically large, all the
things the artist's husband wasn't. He walked around the room
in a kind of daze, staring at each in turn. It was clear he
recognized some of them. I didn't know Joseph at first, but he
did. He had filled out since seventeen.

*　　*　　*

I returned two days' worth of Xanthes' three-day retainer, less expenses, despite his insistence that I'd earned it. A few weeks later court-appointed psychiatrists declared Joe Santine mentally unfit to stand trial and he was remanded for treatment to the State Forensics Center at Ypsilanti. And I haven't had a bowl of egg lemon soup or a slice of feta cheese in months.

# JOHN LUTZ

# WHAT YOU DON'T KNOW CAN HURT YOU

**"Y**ou are Nudger?"

"I am Nudger."

The bulky woman who had leaned over Nudger and confirmed his identity had a halo of dark frizzy hair, a round face, round cheeks, round rimless spectacles, and a small round pursed mouth. She reminded Nudger of one of those dolls made with dried whole apples, whose faces eerily resemble those of aged humans. But the apple dolls' usually are benign; the face looming over Nudger came equipped with tiny dark eyes that danced with malice.

Behind the round-faced woman had stood two silent male companions. She and the two men hadn't spoken when they'd entered Nudger's office without having sounded the buzzer and in workmanlike fashion had begun beating him up.

"Who? What? Why?" a frightened Nudger had asked, wrapping his arms around his head and trying to think of who other than his former wife would want to do this to him. He couldn't divine an answer. "I don't need this!" he implored. "Stop it, please!"

And they had stopped. Extent of damage: sore ribs, cut forehead, but no damaged pride. Nudger was still alive; that was the object of his game.

But there was more to it. He'd felt his shirtsleeve being unbuttoned, shoved roughly up his forearm. And the abrupt bite of a dull hypodermic needle as it was inserted just below his elbow.

Sodium pentothal, he deduced, before floating away on a private, agreeable cloud. His mouth seemed to become completely disassociated from his brain. He was vaguely aware that he was answering questions posed by the round-faced woman, that he was rambling uncontrollably. Yet he couldn't remember the questions or his answers a few seconds after they were uttered.

Then an emptiness, a breathtaking slippage of light and time.

Nudger opened his eyes and wondered where he'd been dropped. It didn't seem proper that he should be slowly revolving. Then the sensation of motion ceased, and with relief he realized he was lying on his back on his office floor. He felt remarkably heavy and comfortable.

Moving only his eyes, he gazed around and took in the open desk drawers and file cabinets, the papers and yellow file folders strewn about the floor. He remembered the hulking round-faced woman and her greedy pig's eyes and her two silent masculine helpers. He tried to recall the round-faced woman's questions but he couldn't.

Nudger struggled to a sitting position and a headache fell on him like a slab from the ceiling. When he'd become somewhat accustomed to the idea of enduring throbbing pain for the rest of his life, he stood, dizzily staggered to his desk, and sat down. The squeal of his swivel chair penetrated his brain like a hot stiletto.

What was it all about? What could he know that the round-faced woman wanted to know? All he was working on now was a divorce case, like dozens of other divorce cases he'd handled as a private investigator. The husband was sleeping with his secretary, the wife had a compensatory affair going with her hairdresser, the husband had hired Nudger to get the goods on the wife. That would be easy; she was flaunting the affair. All of these people were suburbanites who wouldn't know a round-faced woman who shot up people with sodium pentothal; they were mostly concerned about who was going to come away with the TV and the blender.

Nudger made his way over to where the coffee pot sat on the floor by the plug in the corner. He tried to pour a cupful but found that the round-faced woman and friends had emptied the pot and spread the grounds around on the floor. Maybe it was diamonds they were looking for.

Sloshing through a shallow sea of papers and file folders,

Nudger got his tan overcoat from its brass hook, wriggled into it, put on his crushproof hat, and went out, not locking the door behind him. He took the steep steps down the narrow stairwell to the door to the street, feeling the temperature drop as he descended. He shoved open the outer door and braced himself as the winter air stiffened the hairs in his nostrils. The sudden rush of cold made his headache go away. He almost smiled as he stepped out onto the treacherous pavement and walked quickly but gingerly in a neat loop through the door of Danny's Donuts, directly above which his office was located.

Nobody was in the place but Danny. That was the usual state of the business. Nudger breathed in deeply the sudden warmth and cloying sweetness of the doughnuts and unbuttoned his coat. He sat on a stool at the end of the stainless steel counter. Without being asked, Danny set a large plastic-coated paper cup of steaming black coffee before him. Danny was Danny Evers, a fortyish guy like Nudger, and, some might say, a loser like Nudger. Even Danny might say that, aware as he was that he made doughnuts like sash weights.

But what he said was, "You cut yourself shaving?" as he pointed at the cut on Nudger's forehead.

Nudger had forgotten about the injury. He raised tentative fingers, felt ridges of blood coagulated by the cold. "I had a visit from some friends," he said.

"Some friends!" Danny said, changing the emphasis. He put some iced cake doughnuts and a couple of glazed into a grease-spotted carry-out box. He was a sad-featured man who seemed to do everything with apprehensive intensity, a concerned basset hound.

"Actually I never met them before this morning," Nudger said, sipping the coffee and burning his tongue. "So naturally we were curious about each other, but they asked all the questions."

"Yeah? What kinda questions?"

"That's the odd thing," Nudger said. "I can't remember."

Danny laughed, then cocked his head of thick graying hair and squinted again at the cut on Nudger's forehead. "You serious about not remembering?"

"It's not the knock on the head," Nudger assured him. "They

shot me up with a drug that made me a regular mindless talking machine. It's called truth serum. It works even better than cheap scotch."

"Maybe you oughta see a doctor, Nudge."

"Find me one that doesn't charge twenty dollars a stitch."

"I mean about the memory."

"That kind of a doctor charges twenty dollars a question."

Both men were silent while a blond secretary from the office building across the street came in, paid for the carry-out order, and left. Nudger smiled at her but she ignored him. It took a while for the doughnut shop to warm up again.

"I could drive you," Danny offered. "Emil is coming in to take over here in about fifteen minutes." Emil was Danny's hired help, a sometime college student working odd jobs. He made better doughnuts than his boss's.

"I've got my car here," Nudger said.

"But maybe you shouldn't drive."

"I won't drive anywhere for a while," Nudger said. "What I'll do is go back upstairs and straighten up my office. If you'll give me another cup of coffee and a jelly doughnut, and put them on my tab."

"Straighten up why?" Danny asked, reaching into the display case.

"It's always a mess after friends drop by unexpectedly," Nudger told him.

"Some friends, those boys and girls," Danny reiterated, dropping the doughnut into a small white bag. It hit bottom with a solid smack.

As he trudged back up the unheated stairwell to his office, Nudger tried again, with each painful step, to surmise some reason for his interrogation. He could think of none. Business had been slow ever since summer, and he had been a good boy. Danny's horrendous coffee had started his stomach roiling. He'd take a few antacid tablets before drinking a second cup.

He stopped at his office door and stood holding the sack. It was a morning for surprises. In the chair by the desk sat a slender man wearing a camel hair topcoat with a fur collar. On his lap were expensive brown suede gloves. On his gloves rested pale, still, well-manicured hands. The man's bony face was as calm as his hands were.

"There's no need to introduce myself, Mr. Nudger," he said in a smoothly modulated voice. "On your desk is a sealed envelope. In the envelope is five thousand dollars. You've proved yourself a clever man, so you can't be bought cheap." A thin smile did nothing for him. "But, like all men, you can be bought. I know your present financial status, so five thousand should suffice."

The man stood up, unfolding in sections until he was at least four inches taller than Nudger's six feet. But he was thin, very thin, not a big man. He gazed down his narrow nose at Nudger with the remote interest of a scientist observing familiar bacteria.

"The problem is," Nudger told him, "I don't know who you are or what you're buying."

"I'll make myself clear, Mr. Nudger: stay away from Chaser Heights, or next time you'll be paid a visit of an altogether more unpleasant nature."

He turned and left the office with wolflike loping strides.

Nudger stood stupefied, listening to the man's descending footfalls on the wooden stairs to the street. He heard the street door open and close. The papers on the floor stirred.

Nudger went to the office door and shoved it closed. He walked to his desk, and sure enough there was an envelope, sealed. He opened it and counted out five thousand dollars in bills of various denominations. Earning this money would be a cinch, since he'd never been near any place or anyone named Chaser Heights. Then he reconsidered.

There was little doubt of a connection between the round-faced woman and the tall man. What bothered Nudger was that if these unsettling characters thought he'd been around Chaser Heights at least once when he hadn't, what was going to keep them from thinking he'd been there again? And acting forcefully on their misconception?

Now the five thousand didn't look so good to Nudger. This occupation of his had gotten him into trouble again. He put the money back into its envelope and tucked in the flap. He opened a desk drawer and got out a fresh roll of antacid tablets. He wished he knew how to paint a house.

After his stomach had calmed down, Nudger set about putting his office back together. Small as the place was, the task took the rest of the morning. Most of the time was spent matching the footprinted papers on the floor with the correct file folders. When he was finished he looked around with satisfaction, straightened the shade on his desk lamp, then went out for some lunch.

At a place he knew on Grand Avenue, Nudger drank a glass of milk, picked at the Gardener's Delight lettuce omelet special, and studied the phone directory he'd borrowed from the proprietor. Within a few minutes he found what he was looking for: "Chaser Heights Alcoholic Rehabilitation Center," with an Addington Road address way out in the country.

Nudger knew what he had to do, even if it cost him five thousand dollars.

He finished his milk but pushed his omelet away, jotted down the Chaser Heights address on a paper napkin, and put it into his pocket.

Outside, he slammed his Volkwagen's door on the tail of his topcoat, as he invariably did, reopened the door and tried again, and twisted the key in the ignition switch. When the tiny motor was clattering rhythmically, he pulled the dented VW out into traffic.

It had been a large and palatial country home in better days, with sentry-box cupolas, tall colonial pillars, and ivy-covered brick. Now it was called Chaser Heights, which Nudger gathered was a sort of clinic where alcoholics went to tilt the odds in their battle with booze. It was isolated, set well back from the narrow road on a gentle rise, and mostly surrounded by woods that in their present leafless state conveyed a depressing reminder of mortality.

Nudger parked halfway up the long gravel drive to study the house. He realized that the longer he sat there in the cosy warm car, the more difficult it would be to do what he intended. He put the VW in gear and listened to the tires crunch on the gravel as he drove the rest of the way to the house.

He entered a huge foyer with a gleaming tiled floor that smelled of pine disinfectant. There were brown vinyl easy chairs scattered about, and behind a high, horseshoe-shaped desk stood a tall elderly woman wearing a stiff white uniform. The starch seemed to have affected her face.

"May I help you?" she asked without real enthusiasm, as if she risked ripping her lips by parting them to speak.

"I'd like to see whoever's in charge," Nudger told her, removing his hat. He leaned with his elbow on the desk as if it were a bar and he was about to order a drink.

"Do you have an appointment with Dr. Wedgewick?" the woman asked.

"No, but I believe he'll want to see me. Tell Dr. Wedgewell that a Mr. Nudger is here and needs to talk with him."

"Dr. Wedge*wick*," his mannequin corrected him. She was so lifelike you expected her eyes to move. She picked up a beige telephone and conveyed Nudger's message, then without change of expression directed him down a hall and to the last door on his left.

He entered an anteroom and was told by an efficient-looking young brunette on her way out that he should go right in, Dr. Wedgewick was expecting him.

And Nudger was expecting Dr. Wedgewick to be exactly who he turned out to be: the tall, camel-coated unfriendly who had delivered the five thousand dollars. He was wearing a dark blue suit and maroon tie and was seated behind a slate-topped desk a bit smaller than a Ping-Pong table. There wasn't so much as a paper clip to break its smooth gray surface. Behind him was a floor-to-ceiling window that overlooked bare-limbed trees and brown grass sloping away toward the distant road. Probably in the summer it was an impressive view. He didn't get up.

"I am surprised to see you here," he said flatly.

"You'll be more surprised by why I came," Nudger told him.

Dr. Wedgewick arched an inquisitive eyebrow impossibly high. Obviously he'd practiced the expression, had it down pat, and knew there was no need for words to accompany it.

"I'm here to return this," Nudger said, and tossed the envelope with the five thousand dollars onto the desk. It looked as lonely as a center fielder there. "Its return should prove to you that you've made a mistake. I can't be who you think; I can't sell you whatever it is you want to buy, because I don't have it and don't know what it is."

"That is nonsense, Mr. Nudger. You've been followed from here several times by Dr. Olander, observed going to your office by the back entrance, observed emerging at times and coming here, snooping around here. Where you hid the pertinent information regarding your client, and how you managed to fool Dr. Olander when she administered her drugs, I can't say, nor do I care."

"I didn't fool her," Nudger said. "I have no client and I didn't know the answers to her questions. But I understand somewhat more of what's going on. Dr. Olander and her two silent helpers couldn't make any progress with me their way, so you came around and tried to buy me."

"We live in a mercantile society."

"The thing is, there was no reason for Dr. Olander to hassle me, and there was nothing I could tell her. I wish there were some way to get you to believe that."

"Oh, I'll bet you do."

"And I wish you'd tell me why a doctor would want to follow me to begin with, me without medical insurance."

Dr. Wedgewick smiled with large, stained, but even teeth. "Dr. Olander is not a medical doctor. You might say hers is an honorary title. She is chief of security here at Chaser Heights."

"Then I needn't expect a bill." He felt in his pocket for his tablets.

"What you should expect, Mr. Nudger, is to suffer the consequences of being stubborn."

Nudger saw Dr. Wedgewick's gaze shift to something over his left shoulder. He turned and saw the round, malicious features of Dr. Olander. She had taken a few silent steps into the office. Now she stood very still, staring through her gleaming spectacles at the bulge of the hand concealed in Nudger's coat.

He realized that she thought he had a gun.

"What's this wimp doing here?" Dr. Olander asked. "I thought he'd been taken care of."

Nudger, still with his hand inside his coat, perspiring fingers wrapped tightly around his roll of antacid tablets, backed to the door, keeping as far as possible from her. His stomach was fluttering a few feet beyond him, beckoning him on.

Dr. Wedgewick said, "He brought back the five thousand dollars." He looked somewhat curiously at Nudger. "Someone must be paying you a great deal of money," he said. His slow, discolored smile wasn't a nice thing to see. "You'll find that it isn't enough to make it worth your while, Mr. Nudger. You can't put a price on your health."

But Nudger was out into the hall and half running to the lobby. There were a few patients in the vinyl armchairs now. One of them, a ruddy old man wearing a pale blue robe and pajamas, glanced up from where he sat reading *People* and smiled at Nudger. The waxwork behind the counter didn't.

Nudger shoved open the outside door and broke into a run. He piled into his car fast, started the engine, and heard the tires fling gravel against the insides of the fenders as he drove toward the twin stone pillars that marked the exit to the road and safety.

All the way down Addington Road to the alternative highway he kept checking his rear view mirror, expecting to be followed by troops from Chaser Heights. But as he turned onto the cloverleaf he realized they didn't have to follow; they knew where to find him.

When he got back to the office he parked in front, out on the busy street, instead of in his slot behind the building. As he climbed out of the car he noticed that the tail of his topcoat was crushed and grease-stained where he'd shut the door on it again. The coattail had flapped in the wind like a flag all the way back from Chaser Heights. For once Nudger didn't care. He went up to his office, locked the door behind him, and sat for a while chomping antacid tablets.

When his stomach had untied itself, he picked up the phone and dialed the number of the Third Precinct and asked for Lieutenant Jack Hammersmith.

Hammersmith had been Nudger's partner a decade ago in a two-man patrol car, before Nudger's jittery nerves had forced him to retire from the police force. Now Hammersmith had rank and authority, and he always had time for Nudger, but not much time.

"What sort of quicksand have you got yourself into this time, Nudge?" Hammersmith asked.

"The sort that might be bottomless. What do you know about a place called Chaser Heights, out on Addington Road?"

"That clinic where drunks dry out?"

Nudger said that was the one.

"It's a second-rate operation, maybe even a front, but it's out of my jurisdiction, Nudge. I got plenty to worry about here in the city limits."

"What about the director out there? Guy named Dr. Wedgewick?"

"He's new in the area. From the east coast, I been told." Nudger heard the rhythmic wheezing of Hammersmith laboriously firing up one of his foul-smelling cigars and was glad this conversation was by phone. "Anything else, Nudge?" The words were slightly distorted by the cigar.

"How about Wedgewick's assistant and chief of security, a two-hundred-pound chunk of feminine wiles named Dr. Olander?"

"Hah! That would be Millicent Olaphant, and she's no doctor, she's a part-time bone-crusher for some of the local loan sharks."

"Isn't that kind of unusual work for a woman?"

"Yes, I would say it is unusual," Hammersmith said dryly, "and I meet all sorts of people in my job. You be careful of that crew, Nudge. The law out there is the Mayfair County sheriff, Dale Caster."

"What kind of help could I expect from Caster if I did get in the soup?"

"He'd drop crackers on you. Let's just say it would be difficult for a place like Chaser Heights to stay in business if they didn't grease the proper palms."

"And they grease palms liberally," Nudger said. He expected Hammersmith to ask him to elaborate, but the very busy lieutenant repeated his suggestion that Nudger be careful and then hung up.

Nudger sat for a long time, leaning back in the swivel chair, gazing at the ceiling's network of cracks that looked like a rough map of Illinois including major highways. He thought. Not about Illinois.

He thought until the telephone rang, then he picked up the receiver and identified himself.

"This is Danny, downstairs, Nudge," came the answering voice. "Your ex, Eileen, was by here about an hour ago looking for you. She was frowning. You behind with your alimony payments?"

"No further than with the rent," Nudger said. "Thanks for the warning, Danny."

"No trouble, Nudge. She bought half a dozen cream horns."

"Then she's doing better than I am."

When Nudger had replaced the receiver in its cradle he sat staring at it instead of Illinois, and he remembered something Danny had said this morning. "Some friends, those boys and girls," he had said. But Nudger hadn't mentioned Dr. Olander-Olaphant's gender.

Nudger put on his coat and tromped downstairs, gaining more understanding as he descended. He went outside, but instead of taking a few steps to the right and entering Danny's Donuts, he cut through the gangway and entered the building through the rear door, then opened another unlocked door and was in the aromatic back room of the doughnut shop. On a coat tree he saw Danny's topcoat, similar to the rumpled tan coat he, Nudger, was wearing, and Danny's sold-by-the-thousands brown crushproof hat that was identical with Nudger's. Nudger and Danny were about the same height, and seen from a distance and wearing bulky coats they were of a similar build. Things were making sense at last.

Nudger walked into the greater warmth of the doughnut shop proper, nodded to the surprised Danny, and sat on a stool on the customers' side of the counter. He and Danny were alone in the shop; Emil got off work at two, after the almost nonexistent lunch trade.

"I shoulda said something to you earlier, Nudge," Danny said, no longer looking surprised, nervously wiping the already gleaming counter. "I seen them people from Chaser Heights go up to your place this morning, but I couldn't figure out why until you came down here and told me you'd been roughed up."

"You've been sniffing around there, haven't you?" Nudger said.

Danny nodded. He poured a large cup of his terrible coffee and placed it in front of Nudger like an odious peace offering.

"You were spotted at Chaser Heights," Nudger went on, "and they followed you to find out who you were. You're close to my size, you were wearing a coat and hat like mine, and you came and went the back way. They checked to see who occupied the building and naturally figured it was the private investigator on the second floor. Whoever did the following probably staked out the front of the building and verified the identification when I left my office."

"It was a mistake, Nudge, honest! I didn't mean for you to come to any harm. Absolutely. I wouldn't want that."

Nudger sipped at the coffee, wondering why, if what Danny had said was true, he would serve him a cup of this. "I believe you, Danny," he said, "but what *were* you doing reconnoitering at Chaser Heights?"

Danny wiped at his forehead with the towel he'd been using on the counter. "My uncle's in there," he said.

"Is he there for the cure?"

Danny looked disgusted. "He's an alcoholic, all right, Nudge. That's how he got conned into admitting himself into Chaser Heights. But what they really specialize in at that place is getting the patients drugged up and having them sign over damn near everything they own in payment for treatment, or as a 'donation' that actually goes into somebody's pocket."

Nudger tried another sip of Danny's formidable coffee. It was easier to get down now that it was cooler. "Does your uncle have much to donate?"

"Plenty. Now don't think small of me, Nudge, but it's no secret he plans to leave most of it to me, his only living relative. And he's not a well man; on top of his alcoholism he's got a weak heart."

"And Chaser Heights is about to get your inheritance before you do. Have you tried talking to your uncle?"

"Sure. They always tell me he's in special care, under detoxification quarantine—whatever that is. So I went back there a few times in secret and hung around thinking I might get a glimpse of old Benj and get to talk to him, at least see what they're doing to him. But they've got him doped up in a locked room with wire mesh on the windows. Some quarantine. I'm worried about him."

"And his money."

"I don't deny it. But that ain't the only consideration."

Danny rinsed his towel, wrung it out, and started wiping the counter again. Nudger sat slowly sipping his coffee. *Growl,* went his stomach.

"You help me, Nudge, and I'll pay you a couple of thousand—when the inheritance comes."

Nudger eased the coffee cup off to the side. He looked at Danny. "I think it's time your Uncle Benj checked out of Chaser Heights," he said.

"You know a way to manage it?"

Nudger always figured there was a way. That was a two-edged attitude, though, because he always had to figure there was a way for the other guy, too. All of which didn't help Nudger's nervous stomach. Nor did the knowledge that he had to go back out to Chaser Heights that night and case the joint.

The next evening, Nudger and Danny parked Nudger's Volkswagen on a narrow dirt access road that ran through the woods behind Chaser Heights. Nudger was glad to see that Danny was only slightly nervous; the fool had complete faith in him. Both men put on the long black vinyl raincoats with matching hooded caps that Nudger had rented. They pinned badges on the coats and on the fronts of the caps. The sun was down and it was almost totally dark as they made their way through the trees and across the clearing to the rear of Chaser Heights.

They huddled against a brick back wall. Nudger checked the tops of the leafless trees, where the moon seemed to be nibbling at the thin upper branches, to verify which way the breeze was blowing. From a huge pocket of his raincoat he drew a plastic bag stuffed with oil-soaked rags. Danny drew a similar bag from his pocket. They laid the bags near the rear of the building, in tall dry grass that would catch well and produce a maximum

amount of smoke. Danny was smiling confidently in the fearless-
ness born of incomprehension, a kid playing a game.

Nudger used a cigarette lighter to ignite the two bags and
their contents. While Danny crept around to the side of the
building to set fire to a third bag, Nudger forced open a
basement window and lowered himself inside. He had noticed
the sprinkler system in the halls on his first visit. Following the
yellowish beam of a penlight, he made his way to the system's
pressure controls in the basement and turned the lever that
built the water pressure all the way to high, hearing an electric
pump hum to life and the hiss of rushing water.

With a hatchet strapped inside his coat, Nudger broke the
lever from the spigot with one sharp blow and then headed for
the stairs to the upper floor. He opened the door to the back
first-floor hall and then the rear door to admit Danny. Already
he could hear movement, voices. And as Danny stepped inside
and both men put on their respirator masks, Nudger saw that
the burning bags and weeds were creating plenty of smoke, all
of it drifting away from Chaser Heights.

Just then the pressure built up enough to activate the sprinkler system in the halls throughout the building, raining a cold
spray on anyone caught outside a room. There were several
startled shouts, a few curses.

Each carrying a hatchet, Nudger and Danny bustled down the
halls in their badge-adorned black slickers and hoods, the
respirators snug over their faces. They pulled the respirators
away just enough to yell, "Fire Department! Everyone remain
calm! Everyone out of the building!" They began kicking doors
open and ushering patients through the watery halls toward the
exits. Nudger was beginning to enjoy this. Not for nothing did
small boys want to be firemen when they grew up.

In the distance they could hear wails of sirens. The genuine
fire department had been called and was on the way. A white-
uniformed attendant, one of the thugs who had been in Nudger's office, jogged past them with only a worried glance.

"Where do you suppose Wedgewick and Olander are?" Danny
asked.

"You can bet they were among the first out," Nudger said.
"Go get Uncle Benj and head for the car."

Dr. Wedgewick's office was empty, as he'd thought it would be. Through the wide window behind the slate-topped desk, Nudger could see more than a dozen people gathered on the front grounds. Beyond them flashing red lights were approaching, casting wavering, distorted shadows; the sirens had built to a deafening warble. The Mayfair County fire engine even had a loud bell that jangled with a frantic kind of gaity, as if fires were fun.

The door of a wall safe was hanging open. Nudger went to it and found that the safe was empty. After glancing again out the front window, he left the office.

Everyone in front of Chaser Heights seemed to be shouting. Volunteer firemen were paying out hose and advancing on the building like an invading army. Patients and staff were milling about, asking questions. Nudger joined them. At the edge of the crowd stood Dr. Wedgewick, holding a large brown briefcase.

"Are you in charge, sir?" Nudger inquired from beneath his respirator.

Dr. Wedgewick hesitated. "Yes, I'm Dr. Wedgewick, chief administrator here."

"Could you come with me, sir?" Nudger asked. "There's something you should see." He wheeled and began walking briskly toward the side of the building. All very official.

Dr. Wedgewick followed.

When they had turned the corner, Nudger removed his respirator. "The briefcase, please," he said, not meaning the please.

"Why, you can't! . . ." Then Dr. Wedgewick's eyes darted to the hatchet Nudger had raised, and remained fixed there. He handed the briefcase to Nudger. His hand was trembling.

"Millicent!" Dr. Wedgewick suddenly whirled and ran back the way they had come, all the time pointing to Nudger.

Nudger saw the unmistakably bulky figure of Millicent Olander-Olaphant. He took off for the woods behind the building. He didn't have to look back to know Millicent and the good doctor were following.

Running desperately through the woods, Nudger shed his cumbersome coat, hood, and respirator. He kept the axe and briefcase, using both to smash through the branches that whipped at his face and arms. Behind him someone was crashing through the dry winter leaves.

Nudger had the advantage. He knew where the car was parked. He put on as much speed as he could. The pounding of his heart was almost as loud as his rasping breath.

As he broke onto the road, Nudger saw a dark form in the VW's rear seat. Still wearing raincoat and hood, Danny stood leaning against the left front fender with his arms crossed.

"Quick, get in!" Nudger shouted as he yanked open the driver's side door. He tossed the briefcase and hatchet onto the back seat next to Uncle Benj. His chest ached; his heart was trying to escape from his body.

Danny was barely into the passenger's seat when the engine caught and began its anxious clatter. As Nudger hit first gear and pulled away, he saw the fleeting shadows of pursuing figures in the rear view mirror.

"Who was chasing you?" Danny asked, straining to peer behind them into the darkness.

"My quarrelsome friends from that morning in my office."

"You think they'll get the cops, Nudge?" Danny sounded apprehensive.

Nudger snorted. "I think it's going to be the other way around." He jerked the VW into a two-wheeled turn, bounced over some ruts, and was back on the main road, picking up speed.

From behind him came a chuckle and Uncle Benj said, "Hey, young fella, where's the fire?"

Nudger thought it wise to stay in the presence of witnesses while he had the briefcase he'd taken from Dr. Wedgewick. He'd known that Dr. Wedgewick wouldn't have paid off the county sheriff, Caster, without keeping some sort of receipts. And when fire supposedly broke out at Chaser Heights and Dr. Wedgewick hurriedly cleaned out the safe, it figured that the doctor would number those receipts among his most valuable possessions.

In Danny's Donuts, Nudger examined the briefcase's contents. There was a great deal of money inside. Also some stock certificates. And among other various papers, a notebook containing the dates, times, and amounts of the payoffs to Sheriff

Caster. There also were several videocassettes, which the notebook referred to as documentation of the payoffs. Nudger had to admit that Dr. Wedgewick was thorough, but then wasn't the doctor the type?

Nudger went to the phone and called Jack Hammersmith at the Third Precinct. Hammersmith said he'd be around in ten minutes. "I don't understand how you manage to emerge from these misadventures relatively unscathed," he said. He was quite serious.

"Pureness of heart very probably is a factor," Nudger told him. Hammersmith broke the connection without saying goodbye.

"I forgot to give this to you earlier, Nudge," Danny said, holding out a small lavender envelope. "It's from Eileen. She said she could never find you and I was to deliver it."

Nudger grunted and crammed the envelope into his shirt pocket. "Ain't you gonna open it?" Uncle Benj asked, from where he sat near the end of the counter.

"I know what it is," Nudger told him. "It's from my former spouse and makes more than passing reference to neglected alimony payments."

Uncle Benj chortled. "Women can do that to you—drive you to drink if you let 'em." He sat up straighter and drew a deep breath. "You know, Danny boy," he said heartily, "despite the drugs and all the arm-twisting out at that place, I ain't had a drop of the sauce for weeks and I think my stay there did help me. I feel great, like I'll live to be a hundred!"

Danny bit his lower lip glumly, then he smiled and ducked behind the counter.

"Have a doughnut, Uncle Benj," he said.

Nudger thought about Danny's inheritance, about the rent due upstairs, about the envelope from Eileen.

"Don't forget to give him some of your coffee," he said to Danny with a meaningful nod.

If Uncle Benj was going to escape the bottle, maybe he'd fall prey to the cup.

# LAWRENCE BLOCK

# A CANDLE FOR THE BAG LADY

He was a thin young man in a blue pinstriped suit. His shirt was white with a button-down collar. His glasses had oval lenses in a brown tortoiseshell frame. His hair was a dark brown, short but not severely so, neatly combed, parted on the right. I saw him come in and watched him ask a question at the bar. Billie was working afternoons that week. I watched as he nodded at the young man, then swung his sleepy eyes over in my direction. I lowered my own eyes and looked at a cup of coffee laced with bourbon while the fellow walked over to my table.

"Matthew Scudder?" I looked up at him, nodded. "I'm Aaron Creighton. I looked for you at your hotel. The fellow on the desk told me I might find you here."

*Here* was Armstrong's, a Ninth Avenue saloon around the corner from my 57th Street hotel. The lunch crowd was gone except for a couple of stragglers in front whose voices were starting to thicken with alcohol. The streets outside were full of May sunshine. The winter had been cold and deep and long. I couldn't recall a more welcome spring.

"I called you a couple of times last week, Mr. Scudder. I guess you didn't get my messages."

I'd gotten two of them and ignored them, not knowing who he was or what he wanted and unwilling to spend a dime for the answer. But I went along with the fiction. "It's a cheap hotel," I said. "They're not always too good about messages."

"I can imagine. Uh—is there someplace we can talk?"

"How about right here?"

He looked around. I don't suppose he was used to conducting his business in bars, but he evidently decided it would be all right to make an exception. He set his briefcase on the floor and seated himself across the table from me. Angela, the new day-shift waitress, hurried over to get his order. He glanced at my cup and said he'd have coffee too.

"I'm an attorney," he said. My first thought was that he didn't look like a lawyer, but then I realized he probably dealt with civil cases. My experience as a cop had given me a lot of experience with criminal lawyers. The breed runs to several types, none of them his.

I waited for him to tell me why he wanted to hire me. But he crossed me up.

"I'm handling an estate," he said, and paused, and gave what seemed a calculated if well-intentioned smile. "It's my pleasant duty to tell you you've come into a small legacy, Mr. Scudder."

"Someone's left me money?"

"Twelve hundred dollars."

Who could have died? I'd lost touch long since with any of my relatives. My parents went years ago, and we'd never been close with the rest of the family.

I said, "Who—?"

"Mary Alice Redfield."

I repeated the name aloud. It was not entirely unfamiliar, but I had no idea who Mary Alice Redfield might be. I looked at Aaron Creighton. I couldn't make out his eyes behind the glasses but there was a smile's ghost on his thin lips, as if my reaction was not unexpected.

"She's dead?"

"Almost three months ago."

"I didn't know her."

"She knew you. You probably did know her, Mr. Scudder. Perhaps you didn't know her by name." His smile deepened. Angela had brought his coffee. He stirred milk and sugar into it, took a careful sip, nodded his approval. "Miss Redfield was murdered." He said this as if he'd had practice uttering a phrase which did not come naturally to him. "She was killed quite brutally in late February for no apparent reason, another innocent victim of street crime."

"She lived in New York?"

"Oh, yes. In this neighborhood."

"And she was killed around here?"

"Oh West 55th Street between Ninth and Tenth avenues. Her

body was found in an alleyway. She'd been stabbed repeatedly and strangled with the scarf she had been wearing."

Late February. Mary Alice Redfield. West 55th between Ninth and Tenth. Murder most foul. Stabbed and strangled, a dead woman in an alleyway. I usually kept track of murders, perhaps out of a vestige of professionalism, perhaps because I couldn't cease to be fascinated by man's inhumanity to man. Mary Alice Redfield had willed me twelve hundred dollars. And someone had knifed and strangled her, and—

"Oh, Jesus," I said. "The shopping bag lady."

Aaron Creighton nodded.

New York is full of them. East Side, West Side, each neighborhood has its own supply of bag women. Some of them are alcoholic, but most of them have gone mad without any help from drink. They walk the streets, huddle on stoops or doorways. They find sermons in stones and treasures in trashcans. They talk to themselves, to passersby, to God. Sometimes they mumble. Now and then they shriek.

They carry things around with them. The shopping bags supply their generic name and their chief common denominator. Most of them seem to be paranoid, and their madness convinces them that their possessions are very valuable, that their enemies covet them. So their shopping bags are never out of their sight.

There used to be a colony of these ladies who lived in Grand Central Station. They would sit up all night in the waiting room, taking turns waddling off to the lavatory from time to time. They rarely talked to each other, but some herd instinct made them comfortable with one another. But they were not comfortable enough to trust their precious bags to one another's safekeeping, and each sad crazy lady always toted her shopping bags to and from the ladies' room.

Mary Alice Redfield had been a shopping bag lady. I don't know when she set up shop in the neighborhood. I'd been living in the same hotel ever since I resigned from the NYPD and separated from my wife and sons, and that was getting to be quite a few years now. Had Miss Redfield been on the scene that long ago? I couldn't remember her first appearance. Like so many of the neighborhood fixtures, she had been part of the scenery. Had her death not been violent and abrupt I might never have noticed she was gone.

I'd never known her name. But she had evidently known mine, and had felt something for me that prompted her to leave money to me. How had she come to have money to leave?

She'd had a business of sorts. She would sit on a wooden soft-drink case, surrounded by three or four shopping bags, and she would sell newspapers. There's an all-night newsstand at the corner of 57th and Eighth, and she would buy a few dozen papers there, carry them a block west to the corner of Ninth, and set up shop in a doorway. She sold the papers at retail, though I suppose some people tipped her a few cents. I could remember a few occasions when I'd bought a paper and waved away change from a dollar bill. Bread upon the waters, perhaps, if that was what had moved her to leave me the money.

I closed my eyes, brought her image into focus. A thick-set woman, stocky rather than fat. Five-three or -four. Dressed usually in shapeless clothing, colorless gray and black garments, layers of clothing that varied with the season. I remembered that she sometimes wore a hat, an old straw affair with paper and plastic flowers poked into it. And I remembered her eyes, large guileless blue eyes that were many years younger than the rest of her.

Mary Alice Redfield.

"Family money," Aaron Creighton was saying. "She wasn't wealthy, but she had come from a family that was comfortably fixed. A bank in Baltimore handled her funds. That's where she was from originally, Baltimore, though she'd lived in New York for as long as anyone can remember. The bank sent her a check every month. Not very much, a couple of hundred dollars, but she hardly spent anything. She paid her rent—"

"I thought she lived on the street."

"No, she had a furnished room a few doors down the street from where she was killed. She lived in another rooming house on Tenth Avenue before that but moved when the building was sold. That was six or seven years ago and she lived on 55th Street from then until her death. Her room cost her eighty dollars a month. She spent a few dollars on food. I don't know what she did with the rest. The only money in her room was a coffee can full of pennies. I've been checking the banks and there's no record of a savings account. I suppose she may have spent it or lost it or given it away. She wasn't very firmly grounded in reality."

He sipped at his coffee. "She probably belonged in an institution," he said. "But she got along in the outside world, she functioned well enough. I don't know if she kept herself clean, and I don't know anything about how her mind worked, but I think she must have been happier than she would have been in an institution. Don't you think?"

"Probably."

"Of course she wasn't safe, not as it turned out, but anybody can get killed on the streets of New York." He frowned briefly, caught up in a private thought. Then he said, "She came to our office ten years ago. That was before my time." He told me the name of his firm, a string of Anglo-Saxon surnames. "She wanted to draw a will. The original will was a very simple document leaving everything to her sister. Then over the years she would come in from time to time to add codicils leaving specific sums to various persons. She had made a total of thirty-two bequests by the time she died. One was for twenty dollars—that was to a man named John Johnson whom we haven't been able to locate. The remainder all ranged from five hundred to two thousand dollars." He smiled. "I've been given the task of running down the heirs."

"When did she put me into her will?"

"Two years ago in April."

I tried to think what I might have done for her then, how I might have brushed her life with mine. Nothing.

"Of course, the will could be contested, Mr. Scudder. It would be easy to challenge Miss Redfield's competence, and any relative could almost certainly get it set aside. But no one wishes to challenge it. The total amount involved is slightly in excess of a quarter of a million dollars—"

"That much."

"Yes. Miss Redfield received substantially less than the income which her holdings drew over the years, so the principal kept growing during her lifetime. Now, the specific bequests she made total thirty-eight thousand dollars, give or take a few hundred, and the residue goes to Miss Redfield's sister. The sister, her name is Mrs. Palmer, is a widow with grown children. She's hospitalized with cancer and heart trouble and I believe diabetic complications, and she hasn't long to live. Her children would like to see the estate settled before their mother dies, and they have enough local prominence to hurry the will through probate. So I'm authorized to tender checks for the full amount of the specific bequests on the condition that the legatees sign quitclaims acknowledging that this payment discharges in full the estate's indebtedness to them."

There was more legalese of less importance. Then he gave me papers to sign and the whole procedure ended with a check on the table. It was payable to me and in the amount of twelve hundred dollars and no cents.

I told Creighton I'd pay for his coffee.

I had time to buy myself another drink and still get to my bank before the windows closed. I put a little of Mary Alice Redfield's legacy in my savings account, took some in cash, and sent a money order to Anita and the boys. I stopped at my hotel to check for messages. There weren't any. I had a drink at McGovern's and crossed the street to have another at Polly's Cage. It wasn't five o'clock yet, but the bar was doing good business already.

It turned into a funny night. I had dinner at the Greek place and read the *Post,* spent a little time at Joey Farrell's on 58th Street, then wound up getting to Armstrong's around ten-thirty or thereabouts. I spent part of the evening alone at my usual table and part of it in conversation at the bar. I made a point of stretching my drinks, mixing my bourbon with coffee, making a cup last a while, taking a glass of plain water from time to time.

But that never really works. If you're going to get drunk, you'll manage it somehow. The obstacles I placed in my path just kept me up later. By two-thirty I'd done what I had set out to do. I'd made my load and I could go home and sleep it off.

I woke around ten with less of a hangover than I'd earned

and no memory of anything after I'd left Armstrong's. I was in my own bed in my own hotel room. And my clothes were hung neatly in the closet, always a good sign on a morning after. So I must have been in fairly good shape. But a certain amount of time was lost to memory, blacked out, gone.

When that first started happening I tended to worry about it. But it's the sort of thing you can get used to.

It was the money, the twelve hundred bucks. I couldn't understand the money. I had done nothing to deserve it. It had been left to me by a poor little rich woman whose name I'd not even known.

It had never occurred to me to refuse the dough. Very early in my career as a cop I'd learned an important precept. When someone put money in your hand, you closed your fingers around it and put it in your pocket. I learned that lesson well and never had cause to regret its application. I didn't walk around with my hand out, and I never took drug or homicide money, but I grabbed all the clean graft that came my way and a certain amount that wouldn't have stood a white-glove inspection. If Mary Alice thought I merited twelve hundred dollars, who was I to argue?

Ah, but it didn't quite work that way. Because somehow the money gnawed at me.

After breakfast I went to St. Paul's, but there was a service going on, a priest saying Mass, so I didn't stay. I walked down to St. Benedict the Moor's on 53rd Street and sat for a few minutes in a pew at the rear. I go to churches to try to think and I gave it a shot, but my mind didn't know where to go.

I slipped six twenties into the poor box. I tithe. It's a habit I got into after I left the department, and I still don't know why I do it. God knows. Or maybe He's as mystified as I am. This time, though, there was a certain balance in the act. Mary Alice Redfield had given me twelve hundred dollars for no reason I could comprehend. I was passing on a ten percent commission to the church for no better reason.

I stopped on the way out and lit a couple of candles for various people who weren't alive any more. One of them was for the bag lady. I didn't see how it could do her any good, but I couldn't imagine how it could harm her, either.

I had read some press coverage of the killing when it happened. I generally keep up with crime stories. Part of me evidently never stopped being a policeman. Now I went down to the 42nd Street library to refresh my memory.

The *Times* had run a pair of brief back-page items, the first a report of the killing of an unidentified female derelict, the second a followup giving her name and age. She'd been forty-seven, I learned. This surprised me, and then I realized that any specific number would have come as a surprise. Bums and bag ladies are ageless. Mary Alice Redfield could have been thirty or sixty or anywhere in between.

The *News* had run a more extended article than the *Times*, enumerating the stab wounds—twenty-six of them—and describing the scarf wound about her throat—blue and white, a designer print, but tattered at its edges and evidently somebody's castoff. It was this article that I remembered having read.

But the *Post* had really played the story. It had appeared shortly after the new Australian owner took over the paper and the editors were going all out for human interest, which always translates out as sex and violence. The brutal killing of a woman touches both of those bases, and this had the added kick that she was a character. If they'd ever learned she was an heiress, it would have been page-three material, but even without that knowledge they did all right by her.

The first story they ran was straight news reporting, albeit embellished with reports on the blood, the clothes she was wearing, the litter in the alley where she was found, and all that sort of thing. The next day a reporter pushed the pathos button and tapped out a story featuring capsule interviews with people in the neighborhood. Only a few of them were identified by name, and I came away with the feeling that he'd made up some peachy quotes and attributed them to unnamed nonexistent hangers-on. As a sidebar to that story, another reporter speculated on the possibility of a whole string of bag lady murders, a speculation which happily had turned out to be off the mark. The clown had presumably gone around the West Side asking shopping bag ladies if they were afraid of being the killer's next victim. I hope he faked the piece and let the ladies alone.

And that was about it. When the killer failed to strike again, the newspapers hung up the story. Good news is no news.

I walked back from the library. It was fine weather. The winds had blown all the crap out of the sky, and there was nothing but blue overhead. The air actually had some air in it for a change. I walked west on 42nd Street and north on Broadway, and I started noticing the number of street people, the drunks and the crazies and the unclassifiable derelicts. By the time I got within a few blocks of 57th Street I was recognizing a large percentage of them. Each mini-neighborhood has its own human flotsam and jetsam, and they're a lot more noticeable come springtime. Winter sends some of them south and others to shelter, and there's a certain percentage who die of exposure, but when the sun warms the pavement it brings most of them out again.

When I stopped for a paper at the corner of Eighth Avenue, I got the bag lady into the conversation. The newsie clucked his tongue and shook his head. "The damnedest thing. Just the damnedest thing."

"Murder never makes much sense."

"The hell with murder. You know what she did? You know Eddie, works for me midnight to eight? Guy with the one droopy eyelid? Now, he wasn't the guy used to sell her the stack of papers. Matter of fact that was usually me. She'd come by during the late morning or early afternoon and she'd take fifteen or twenty papers and pay me for 'em, then she'd sit on her crate down the next corner and she'd sell as many as she could, and then she'd bring 'em back and I'd give her a refund on what she didn't sell."

"What did she pay for them?"

"Full price. And that's what she sold 'em for. The hell, I can't discount on papers. You know the margin we get. I'm not even supposed to take 'em back, but what difference does it make? It gave the poor woman something to do is my theory. She was important, she was a businesswoman. Sits there charging a quarter for something she just paid a quarter for, it's no way to get rich, but you know something? She had money. She lived like a pig, but she had money."

"So I understand."

"She left Eddie seven-twenty. You believe that? Seven hundred and twenty dollars, she willed it to him, there was this lawyer come around three weeks ago with a check. Eddie Halloran. Pay to the order of. You believe that? She never had dealings with him. I sold her the papers, I bought 'em back from her. Not that I'm complaining, not that I want the woman's money, but why Eddie? He don't know her. He can't believe she knows his name. He tells this lawyer, he says maybe she's got some other Eddie Halloran in mind. It's a common Irish name, and the neighborhood's full of the Irish. I'm thinking to myself, Eddie, schmuck, take the money and shut up, but it's him all right because in the will it says Eddie Halloran the news dealer. That's him, right? But why Eddie?"

Why me? "Maybe she liked the way he smiled."

"Yeah, maybe. Or the way he combed his hair. Listen, it's money in his pocket. I worried he'd go on a toot, drink it up, but he says money's no temptation. He says he's always got the price of a drink in his jeans, and there's a bar on every block, but he can walk right past 'em, so why worry about a few hundred dollars? You know something? That crazy woman, I'll tell you something, I miss her. She'd come, crazy hat on her head, spacy look in her eyes, she'd buy her stack of papers and waddle off all businesslike, then she'd bring the leftovers and cash 'em in, and I'd make a joke about her when she was out of earshot, but I miss her."

"I know what you mean."

"She never hurt nobody," he said. "She never hurt a soul."

"Mary Alice Redfield. Yeah, the multiple stabbing and strangulation." He shifted a cud-sized wad of gum from one side of his mouth to the other, pushed a lock of hair off his forehead, and yawned. "What have you got, some new information?"

"Nothing. I wanted to find out what you had."

"Yeah, right."

He worked on the chewing gum. He was a patrolman named Andersen who worked out of the Eighteenth. Another cop, a detective named Guzik, had learned that Andersen had caught the Redfield case and had taken the trouble to introduce the two of us. I hadn't known Andersen when I was on the force. He was younger than I, but then most people are nowadays.

He said, "Thing is, Scudder, we more or less put that one out of the way. It's in an open file. You know how it works. If we get new information, fine, but in the meantime I don't sit up nights thinking about it."

"I just wanted to see what you had."

"Well, I'm kind of tight for time, if you know what I mean. My own personal time, I set a certain store by my own time."

"I can understand that."

"You probably got some relative of the deceased for a client, wants to find out who'd do such a terrible thing to poor old Cousin Mary. Naturally you're interested because it's a chance to make a buck and a man's gotta make a living. Whether a man's a cop or a civilian, he's gotta make a buck, right?"

Uh-huh. I seem to remember that we were subtler in my day, but perhaps that's just age talking. I thought of telling him that I didn't have a client, but why should he believe me? He didn't know me. If there was nothing in it for him, why should he bother?

So I said, "You know, we're just a couple of weeks away from Memorial Day."

"Yeah, I'll buy a poppy from a Legionnaire. So what else is new?"

"Memorial Day's when women start wearing white shoes and men put straw hats on their heads. You got a new hat for the summer season, Andersen? You could use one."

"A man can always use a new hat," he said.

A hat is cop talk for twenty-five dollars. By the time I left the precinct house, Andersen had two tens and a five of Mary Alice Redfield's bequest to me, and I had all the data that had turned up to date.

I think Andersen won that one. I now knew that the murder weapon had been a kitchen knife with a blade approximately seven and a half inches long. That one of the stab wounds had found the heart and had probably caused death instantaneously. That it was impossible to determine whether strangulation had taken place before or after death. That *should* have been possible to determine—maybe the medical examiner hadn't wasted too much time checking her out, or maybe he'd been reluctant to commit himself. She'd been dead a few hours when they found her—the estimate was that she'd died around midnight and the body wasn't reported until half-past five. That wouldn't have ripened her all that much, not in winter weather, but most likely her personal hygiene was nothing to boast about, and she was just a shopping bag lady and you couldn't bring her back to life, so why knock yourself out running tests on her malodorous corpse?

I learned a few other things. The landlady's name. The name of the off-duty bartender heading home after a nightcap at the neighborhood after-hours joint who'd happened on the body and had been drunk enough or sober enough to take the trouble to report it. And I learned the sort of negative facts that turn up in a police report when the case is headed for an open file—the handful of nonleads that led nowhere, the witnesses who had nothing to contribute, the routine matters routinely handled. They hadn't knocked themselves out, Andersen and his partner, but would I have handled it any differently? Why knock yourself out chasing a murderer you didn't stand much chance of catching?

In the theater, SRO is good news. It means a sellout performance, Standing Room Only. But once you get out of the theater district it means Single Room Occupancy, and the designation is invariably applied to a hotel or apartment house which has seen better days.

Mary Alice Redfield's home for the last six or seven years of her life had started out as an old Rent Law tenement, built around the turn of the century, six stories tall, faced in redbrown brick, with four apartments to the floor. Now all of those little apartments had been carved into single rooms as if they were election districts gerrymandered by a maniac. There was a communal bathroom on each floor, and you didn't need a map to find it.

The manager was a Mrs. Larkin. Her blue eyes had lost most of their color, and half her hair had gone from black to gray,

but she was still pert. If she's reincarnated as a bi
house wren.

She said, "Oh, poor Mary. We're none of us safe,
the streets full of monsters? I was born in this n
and I'll die in it, but please God that'll be of natural causes. Poor
Mary. There's some said she should have been locked up, but
Jesus, she got along. She lived her life. And she had her check
coming in every month and paid her rent on time. She had her
own money, you know. She wasn't living off the public like
some I could name but won't."

"I know."

"Do you want to see her room? I rented it twice since then.
The first one was a young man, and he didn't stay. He looked all
right, but when he left I was just as glad. He said he was a sailor
off a ship, and when he left he said he'd got on with another
ship and was on his way to Hong Kong or some such place, but
I've had no end of sailors and he didn't walk like a sailor so I
don't know what he was after doing. Then I could have rented
it twelve times but didn't because I won't rent to colored or
Spanish. I've nothing against them, but I won't have them in the
house. The owner says to me, Mrs. Larkin, he says, my instruc-
tions are to rent to anybody regardless of race or creed or
color, but if you was to use your own judgment, I wouldn't
have to know about it. In other words, he don't want them
either, but he's after covering himself."

"I suppose he has to."

"Oh, with all the laws, but I've had no trouble." She laid a
forefinger alongside her nose. It's a gesture you don't see too
much these days. "Then I rented poor Mary's room two weeks
ago to a very nice woman, a widow. She likes her beer, she
does, but why shouldn't she have it? I keep my eye on her and
she's making no trouble, and if she wants an old jar now and
then, whose business is it but her own?" She fixed her blue-gray
eyes on me. "You like your drink," she said.

"Is it on my breath?"

"No, but I can see it in your face. Larkin liked his drink and
there's some say it killed him, but he liked it and a man has a
right to live what life he wants. And he was never a hard man
when he drank, never cursed or fought or beat a woman as

ᴊome I could name but won't. Mrs. Shepard's out now. That's the one took poor Mary's room, and I'll show it to you if you want."

So I saw the room. It was kept neat.

"She keeps it tidier than poor Mary," Mrs. Larkin said. "Mary wasn't dirty, you understand, but she had all her belongings— her shopping bags and other things that she kept in her room. She made a mare's nest of the place, and all the years she lived here it wasn't tidy. I would keep her bed made but she didn't want me touching her things, and so I left the rest cluttered. She paid her rent on time and made no trouble otherwise. She had money, you know."

"Yes, I know."

"She left some to a woman on the fourth floor. A much younger woman, she'd only moved here three months before Mary was killed. If she exchanged a word with Mary, I couldn't swear to it, but Mary left her almost a thousand dollars. Now, Mrs. Klein across the hall lived here since before Mary ever moved in, and the two old things always had a good word for each other—all Mrs. Klein has is the welfare and she could have made good use of a couple of dollars, but Mary left her money to Miss Strom instead." She raised her eyebrows to show her bewilderment. "Now, Mrs. Klein said nothing, and I don't even know if she's had the thought that Mary might have mentioned her in her will, but Miss Strom said she didn't know what to make of it. She just couldn't understand it at all, and what I told her was you can't figure out a woman like poor Mary who never had both her feet on the pavement. Troubled as she was, daft as she was, who's to say what she might have had on her mind?"

"Could I see Miss Strom?"

"That would be for her to say, but she's not home from work yet. She works part-time in the afternoons. She's a close one, not that she hasn't the right to be, and she's never said what it is that she does. But she's a decent sort. This is a decent house."

"I'm sure it is."

"It's single rooms and they don't cost much so you know you're not at the Ritz Hotel, but there's decent people here and I keep it as clean as a person can. When there's not but one toilet on the floor it's a struggle. But it's decent."

"Yes."

"Poor Mary. Why'd anyone kill her? Was it sex, do you know? Not that you could imagine anyone wanting her, the old thing, but try to figure out a madman and you'll go mad your own self. Was she molested?"

"No."

"Just killed, then. Oh, God save us all. I gave her a home for almost seven years. Which it was no more than my job to do, not making it out to be charity on my part. But I had her here all that time and of course I never knew her, you couldn't get to know a poor old soul like that, but I got used to her. Do you know what I mean?"

"I think so."

"I got used to having her about. I might say hello and good morning and not get a look in reply but even on those days she was someone familiar and she's gone now and we're all of us older, aren't we?"

"We are."

"The poor old thing. How could anyone do it, will you tell me that? How could anyone murder her?"

I don't think she expected an answer. It's just as well. I didn't have one.

After dinner I returned for a few minutes of conversation with Genevieve Strom. She had no idea why Miss Redfield had left her the money. She'd received eight hundred and eighty dollars, and she was glad to get it because she could use it, but the whole thing puzzled her. "I hardly knew her," she said more than once. "I keep thinking I ought to do something special with the money, but what?"

I made the bars that night, but drinking didn't have the urgency it had possessed the night before. I was able to keep it in proportion and to know that I'd wake up the next morning with my memory intact. In the course of things I dropped over to the newsstand a little past midnight and talked with Eddie Halloran. He was looking good and I said as much. I remembered him when he'd gone to work for Sid three years ago. He'd been drawn then, and shaky, and his eyes always moved off to the side of whatever he was looking at. Now there was confidence in his stance and he looked years younger, though it hadn't all come back to him and maybe some of it was lost forever. I guess the booze had him pretty good before he got it kicked once and for all.

We talked about the bag lady. He said, "Know what I think it is? Somebody's sweeping the streets."

"I don't follow you."

"A cleanup campaign. A few years back, Matt, there was this gang of kids found a new way to amuse themselves. Pick up a can of gasoline, find some bum down on the Bowery, pour the gas on him, and throw a lit match at him. You remember?"

"Yeah, I remember."

"Those kids thought they were patriots. They thought they deserved a medal. They were cleaning up the neighborhood, getting drunken bums off the streets. You know, Matt, people don't like to look at a derelict. That building up the block, the Towers? There's this grating there where the heating system's vented. You remember how the guys would sleep there in the winter. It was warm, it was comfortable, it was free, and two or three guys would be there every night catching some Z's and getting warm. Remember?"

"Uh-huh. They they fenced it."

"Right. Because the tenants complained. It didn't hurt them any, it was just the local bums sleeping it off, but the tenants pay a lot of rent and they don't like to look at bums on their way in or out of their building. The bums were outside and not bothering anybody but it was the sight of them, you know, so the owners went to the expense of putting up cyclone fencing around where they used to sleep. It looks ugly as hell and all it does is keep the bums out, but that's all it's supposed to do."

"That's human beings for you."

He nodded, then turned aside to sell somebody a *Daily News* and a *Racing Form*. Then he said, "I don't know what it is exactly. *I* was a bum, Matt. I got pretty far down. You probably don't know how far. I got as far as the Bowery. I panhandled and slept in my clothes on a bench or in a doorway. You look at men like that and you think they're just waiting to die, and they are, but some of them come back. And you can't tell for sure who's gonna come back and who's not. Somebody coulda poured gas on me, set me on fire. Sweet Jesus."

"The shopping bag lady—"

"You'll look at a bum and you'll say to yourself, Maybe I could get like that and I don't wanta think about it. Or you'll look at somebody like the shopping bag lady and say, I could go nutsy like her, so get her out of my sight. And you get people who think like Nazis—you know, take all the cripples and the lunatics and the retarded kids and give 'em an injection and good-bye, Charlie."

"You think that's what happened to her?"

"What else?"

"But whoever did it stopped at one, Eddie."

He frowned. "Don't make sense," he said. "Unless he did the one job and the next day he got run down by a Ninth Avenue bus, and it couldn't happen to a nicer guy. Or he got scared. All that blood and it was more than he figured on. Or he left town. Could be anything like that."

"Could be."

"There's no other reason, is there? She musta been killed because she was a bag lady, right?"

"I don't know."

"Well, Jesus Christ, Matt. What other reason would anybody have for killing her?"

The law firm where Aaron Creighton worked had offices on the seventh floor of the Flatiron Building. In addition to the four partners, eleven other lawyers had their names painted on the frosted glass door. Aaron Creighton's came second from the bottom. Well, he was young.

He was surprised to see me, and when I told him what I wanted, he said it was irregular.

"It's a matter of public record, isn't it?"

"Well, yes," he said. "That mean you can find the information. It doesn't mean we're obliged to furnish it to you."

For an instant I thought I was back at the Eighteenth Precinct and a cop was trying to hustle me for the price of a new hat. But Creighton's reservations were ethical. I wanted a list of Mary Alice Redfield's beneficiaries, including the amounts they'd received and the dates they'd been added to her will. He wasn't sure where his duty lay.

"I'd like to be helpful," he said. "Perhaps you could tell me just what your interest is."

"I'm not sure."

"I beg your pardon?"

"I don't know why I'm playing with this one. I used to be a cop, Mr. Creighton. Now I'm a sort of unofficial detective. I don't carry a license, but I do things for people and I wind up making enough that way to keep a roof overhead."

His eyes were wary. I guess he was trying to guess how I intended to earn myself a fee out of this.

"I got twelve hundred dollars out of the blue. It was left to me by a woman I didn't really know and who didn't really know me. I can't seem to slough off the feeling that I got the money for a reason. That I've been paid in advance."

"Paid for what?"

"To try and find out who killed her."

"Oh," he said. *"Oh."*

"I don't want to get the heirs together to challenge the will, if that was what was bothering you. And I can't quite make myself suspect that one of her beneficiaries killed her for the money she was leaving him. For one thing, she doesn't seem to have told people they were named in her will. She never said anything to me or to the two people I've spoken with thus far. For another, it wasn't the sort of murder that gets committed for gain. It was deliberately brutal."

"Then why do you want to know who the other beneficiaries are?"

"I don't know. Part of it's cop training. When you've got any specific leads, any hard facts, you run them down before you cast a wider net. That's only part of it. I suppose I want to get more of a sense of the woman. That's probably all I can realistically hope to get, anyway. I don't stand much chance of tracking her killer."

"The police don't seem to have gotten very far."

I nodded. "I don't think they tried too hard. And I don't think they knew she had an estate. I talked to one of the cops on the case, and if he had known that, he'd have mentioned it to me.

There was nothing in her file. My guess is that they waited for her killer to run a string of murders so they'd have something more concrete to work with. It's the kind of senseless crime that usually gets repeated." I closed my eyes for a moment, reaching for an errant thought. "But he didn't repeat," I said. "So they put it on a back burner and then they took it off the stove altogether."

"I don't know much about police work. I'm involved largely with estates and trusts." He tried a smile. "Most of my clients die of natural causes. Murder's an exception."

"It generally is. I'll probably never find him. I certainly don't expect to find him. Hell, it was all those months ago. He could have been a sailor off a ship, got tanked up and went nuts, and he's in Macao or Port-au-Prince by now. No witnesses and no clues and no suspects and the trail's three months cold by now, and it's a fair bet the killer doesn't remember what he did. So many murders take place in blackout."

"Blackout?" He frowned. "You don't mean in the dark?"

"Alcoholic blackout. The prisons are full of men who got drunk and shot their wives or their best friends. Now they're serving twenty-to-life for something they don't recollect at all."

The idea unsettled him, and he looked especially young now. "That's terrifying," he said.

"Yes."

"I originally gave some thought to criminal law. My Uncle Jack talked me out of it. He said you either starve or you spend your time helping professional criminals beat the system. He said that was the only way you made good money out of a criminal practice and what you wound up doing was unpleasant and basically immoral. Of course, there are a couple of superstar criminal lawyers, the hotshots everybody knows, but the other ninety-nine percent fit what Uncle Jack said."

"I would think so, yes."

"I guess I made the right decision." He took his glasses off, inspected them, decided they were clean, put them back on again. "Sometimes I'm not so sure," he said. "Sometimes I wonder. I'll get that list for you. I should probably check with someone to make sure it's all right, but I'm not going to bother. You know lawyers. If you ask them whether it's all right to do

something they'll automatically say no. Because inaction is
always safer than action and they can't get in trouble for giving
you bad advice if they tell you to sit on your hands and do
nothing. I'm going overboard. Most of the time I like what I do
and I'm proud of my profession. This'll take me a few minutes.
Do you want some coffee in the meantime?"

I let him have his girl bring me a cup, black, no sugar. By the
time I was done with the coffee he had the list ready.

"If there's anything else I can do—"

I told him I'd let him know. He walked out to the elevator
with me, waited for the cage to come wheezing up, and shook
my hand. I watched him turn and head back to his office, and I
had the feeling he'd have preferred to come along with me. In
a day or so he'd change his mind, but right now he didn't seem
too crazy about his job.

The next week I worked my way through the list Aaron
Creighton had given me, knowing what I was doing was essen-
tially purposeless but compulsive about doing it all the same.

There were thirty-two names on the list. I checked off my
own and Eddie Halloran and Genevieve Strom. I put additional
check marks next to six people who lived outside of New York.
Then I had a go at the remaining twenty-three names. Creighton
had done most of the spadework for me, finding addresses to
match most of the names. He'd included the date each of the
thirty-two codicils had been drawn, and that enabled me to
attack the list in reverse chronological order, starting with
those persons who'd been made beneficiaries most recently. If
this was a method, there was madness to it; it was based on the
notion that a person added recently to the will would be more
likely to commit homicide for gain, and I'd already decided this
wasn't that kind of a killing to begin with.

Well, it gave me something to do. And it led to some interesting conversations. If the people Mary Alice Redfield had chosen
to remember ran to any type, my mind wasn't subtle enough to
discern it. They ranged in age, in ethnic background, in gender
and sexual orientation, in economic status. Most of them were
as mystified as Eddie and Genevieve and I about the bag lady's
largesse, but once in a while I'd encounter someone who

attributed it to some act of kindness he'd performed, and there was a young man named Jerry Forgash who was in no doubt whatever. He was some form of Jesus freak and he'd given poor Mary a couple of tracts and a Get Smart—Get Saved button, presumably a twin to the one he wore on the breast pocket of his chambray shirt. I suppose she put his gifts in one of her shopping bags.

"I told her Jesus loved her," he said, "and I suppose it won her soul for Christ. So of course she was grateful. Cast your bread upon the waters, Brother Matthew. You know there was a disciple of Christ named Matthew."

"I know."

He told me Jesus loved me and that I should get smart and get saved. I managed not to get a button, but I had to take a couple of tracts from him. I didn't have a shopping bag so I stuck them in my pocket.

I didn't run the whole list. People were hard to find, and I wasn't in any big rush to find them. It wasn't that kind of a case. It wasn't a case at all, really, merely an obsession, and there was surely no need to race the clock. Or the calendar. If anything, I was probably reluctant to finish up the names on the list. Once I ran out of them I'd have to find some other way to approach the woman's murder, and I was damned if I knew where to start.

In the meantime, an odd thing happened. The word got around that I was investigating the murder, and the whole neighborhood became very much aware of Mary Alice Redfield. People began to seek me out. Ostensibly they had information to give me or theories to advance, but neither the information nor the theories ever seemed to amount to anything substantial, and I came to see that they were merely a prelude to conversation. Someone would start off by saying he'd seen Mary selling the New York *Post* the afternoon before she was killed, and that would serve as the opening wedge of a discussion of the bag woman, or bag women in general, or various qualities of the neighborhood, or violence in American life, or whatever.

A lot of people started off talking about the bag lady and wound up talking about themselves. I guess most conversations work out that way.

A nurse from Roosevelt said she never saw a shopping bag lady without hearing an inner voice say there but for the grace of God. She was not the only woman who confessed she worried about ending up that way. I guess it's a spectre that haunts women who live alone, just as the vision of the Bowery derelict clouds the peripheral vision of hard-drinking men.

Genevieve Strom turned up at Armstrong's one night. We talked briefly about the bag lady. Two nights later she came back again, and we took turns spending our inheritances on rounds of drinks. The drinks hit her with some force, and a little past midnight she decided it was time to go. I said I'd see her home. At the corner of 57th Street she stopped in her tracks and said, "No men in the room. That's one of Mrs. Larkin's rules."

"Old-fashioned, isn't she?"

"She runs a daycent establishment." Her mock-Irish accent was heavier than the landlady's. Her eyes, hard to read in the lamplight, rose to meet mine. "Take me someplace."

I took her to my hotel, a less decent establishment than Mrs. Larkin's. We did each other little good but no harm, and it beat being alone.

Another night I ran into Barry Mosedale at Polly's Cage. He told me there was a singer at Kid Gloves who was doing a number about the bag lady. "I can find out how you can reach him," he offered.

"Is he there now?"

He nodded and checked his watch. "He goes on in fifteen minutes. But you don't want to *go* there, do you?"

"Why not?"

"Hardly your sort of crowd, Matt."

"Cops go anywhere."

"They do, and they're welcome wherever they go, aren't they? Just let me drink this and I'll accompany you, if that's all right. You need someone to lend you immoral support."

Kid Gloves is a gay bar on 56th, west of Ninth. The decor is just a little aggressively gay lib. There's a small raised stage, a scattering of tables, a piano, and a loud jukebox. Barry Mosedale and I stood at the bar. I'd been there before and knew better than to order their coffee. I had straight bourbon. Barry had his on ice with a splash of soda.

Halfway through the drink, Gordon Lurie was introduced. He wore tight jeans and a flowered shirt, sat on stage on a folding chair, sang ballads he'd written himself with his own guitar for accompaniment. I don't know if he was any good or not. It sounded to me as though all the songs had the same melody, but that may just have been a similarity of style. I don't have much of an ear.

After a song about a summer romance in Amsterdam, Gordon Lurie announced that the next number was dedicated to the memory of Mary Alice Redfield. Then he sang:

She's a shopping bag lady who lives on the sidewalks of
    Broadway,
Wearing all of her clothes and her years on her back,
Toting dead dreams in an old paper sack,
Searching the trashcans for something she lost here on
    Broadway—
Shopping bag lady.

You'd never know, but she once was an actress on Broad-
    way,
Speaking the words that they stuffed in her head,
Reciting the lines of the life that she led,
Thrilling her fans and her friends and her lovers on Broad-
    way—
Shopping bag lady.

There are demons who lurk in the corners of minds and of
    Broadway
And after the omens and portents and signs
Came the day she forgot to remember her lines,
Put her life on a leash and took it out walking on Broad-
    way—
Shopping bag lady.

There were a couple more verses and the shopping bag lady in the song wound up murdered in a doorway, dying in defense of the "tattered old treasures she mined in the trashcans of Broadway." The song went over well and got a bigger hand than any of the ones that had preceded it.

I asked Barry who Gordon Lurie was.

"You know very nearly as much as I," he said. "He started here Tuesday. I find him whelming, personally. Neither over-whelming nor underwhelming but somewhere in the middle."

"Mary Alice never spent much time on Broadway. I never saw her more than a block from Ninth Avenue."

"Poetic license, I'm sure. The song would lack a certain something if you substituted Ninth Avenue for Broadway. As it stands it sounds a little like 'Rhinestone Cowboy.' "

"Does Lurie live around here?"

"I don't know where he lives. I have the feeling he's Canadian. So many people are nowadays. It used to be that no one was Canadian, and now simply everybody is. I'm sure it must be a virus."

We listened to the rest of Gordon Lurie's act. Then Barry leaned forward and chatted with the bartender to find out how I could get backstage. I found my way to what passed for a dressing room at Kid Gloves. It must have been a ladies' lavatory in a prior incarnation.

I went in thinking I'd made a breakthrough, that Lurie had killed her and now he was dealing with his guilt by singing about her. I don't think I really believed this, but it supplied me with direction and momentum. I told him my name and that I was interested in his act. He wanted to know if I was from a record company. "Am I on the threshold of a great opportunity? Am I about to become an overnight success after years of travail?"

We got out of the tiny room and left the club through a side door. Three doors down the block we sat in a cramped booth at a coffee shop. He ordered a Greek salad and we both had coffee.

I told him I was interested in his song about the bag lady.

He brightened. "Oh, do you like it? Personally I think it's the best thing I've written. I just wrote it a couple of days ago. I opened next door Tuesday night. I got to New York three weeks ago, and I had a two-week booking in the West Village, a place called David's Table. Do you know it?"

"I don't think so."

"Another stop on the K-Y circuit. Either there aren't any straight people in New York or they don't go to nightclubs. But I was there two weeks, and then I opened at Kid Gloves. Afterward I was sitting and drinking with some people and somebody was talking about the shopping bag lady and I'd had enough amaretto to be maudlin on the subject. I woke up Wednesday morning with the first verse of the song buzzing in my splitting head, and immediately wrote it down. As I was writing one verse, the next would come bubbling to the surface and before I knew it I had all six verses." He took a cigarette, then paused in the act of lighting it to fix his eyes on me. "You told me your name," he said, "but I don't remember it."

"Matthew Scudder."

"Yes. You're the person investigating her murder."

"I'm not sure that's the right word. I've been talking to people, seeing what I can come up with. Did you know her before she was killed?"

He shook his head. "I was never even in this neighborhood before. *Oh.* I'm not a suspect, am I? Because I haven't been in New York since the fall. I haven't bothered to figure out where I was when she was killed, but I was in California at Christmastime and I'd only gotten as far east as Chicago in early March, so I do have a fairly solid alibi."

"I never really suspected you. I think I just wanted to hear your song." I sipped some coffee. "Where did you get the facts of her life? Was she an actress?"

"I don't think so. Was she? It wasn't really *about* her, you know. It was inspired by her story, but I didn't know her or anything about her. The past few days I've been paying a lot of attention to bag ladies, though. And other street people."

"I know what you mean."

"Are there more of them in New York, or is it just that they're so much more visible here? In California everybody drives, you don't see people on the street. I'm from Canada, rural Ontario, and the first city I ever spent much time in was Toronto, and there are crazy people on the streets there but it's nothing like

New York. Does the city drive them crazy, or does it just tend to draw crazy people?"

"I don't know."

"Maybe they're not crazy. Maybe they just hear a different drummer. I wonder who killed her."

"We'll probably never know."

"What I really wonder is *why* she was killed. In my song I made up the reason that somebody wanted what was in her bags. I think that works in the song, but I don't think there's much chance it happened like that."

"I don't know."

"They say she left people money—people she hardly knew. Is that the truth?" I nodded. "And she left me a song. I don't even feel that I wrote it. I woke up with it. I never set eyes on her, and she touched my life. That's strange, isn't it?"

Everything was strange. The strangest part of all was the way it ended.

It was a Monday night. The Mets were at Shea and I'd taken my sons to a game. The Dodgers were in for a three-game series which they eventually swept as they'd been sweeping everything lately. The boys and I got to watch them knock Jon Matlack out of the box and go on to shell his several replacements. The final count was something like thirteen to four. We stayed in our seats until the last out. Then I saw them home and caught a train back to the city.

So it was past midnight when I reached Armstrong's. Trina brought me a large double and a mug of coffee without being asked. I knocked back half of the bourbon and was dumping the rest into my coffee when she told me somebody'd been looking for me earlier. "He was in three times in the past two hours," she said. "A wiry guy, high forehead, bushy eyebrows, sort of a bulldog jaw. I guess the word for it is underslung."

"Perfectly good word."

"I said you'd probably get here sooner or later."

"I always do. Sooner or later."

"Uh-huh. Are you okay, Matt?"

"The Mets lost a close one."

"I heard it was thirteen to four."

"That's close for them these days. Did he say what it was about?"

He hadn't, but within the half hour he came in again and I was there to be found. I recognized him from Trina's description as soon as he came through the door. He looked faintly familiar, but he was nobody I knew. I suppose I'd seen him around the neighborhood.

Evidently he knew me by sight because he found his way to my table without asking directions and took a chair without being invited to sit. He didn't say anything for a while and neither did I. I had a fresh bourbon and coffee in front of me, and I took a sip and looked him over.

He was under thirty. His cheeks were hollow and the flesh of his face was stretched over his skull like leather that had shrunk upon drying. He wore a forest-green work shirt and a pair of khaki pants. He needed a shave.

Finally he pointed at my cup and asked me what I was drinking. When I told him, he said all he drank was beer.

"They have beer here," I said.

"Maybe I'll have what you're drinking." He turned in his chair and waved for Trina. When she came over, he said he'd have bourbon and coffee, the same as I was having. He didn't say anything more until she brought the drink. Then, after he had spent quite some time stirring it, he took a sip. "Well," he said, "that's not so bad. That's okay."

"Glad you like it."

"I don't know if I'd order it again, but at least now I know what it's like."

"That's something."

"I seen you around. Matt Scudder. Used to be a cop, private eye now, blah blah blah. Right?"

"Close enough."

"My name's Floyd. I never liked it, but I'm stuck with it, right? I could change it, but who'm I kidding? Right?"

"If you say so."

"If I don't somebody else will. Floyd Karp, that's the full name. I didn't tell you my last name, did I? That's it, Floyd Karp."

"Okay."

"Okay, okay, okay." He pursed his lips, blew out air in a silent whistle. "What do we do now, Matt, huh? That's what I want to know."

"I'm not sure what you mean, Floyd."

"Oh, you know what I'm getting at, driving at, getting at. You know, don't you?"

By this time I suppose I did.

"I killed that old lady. I took her life, stabbed her with my knife." He flashed the saddest smile. "Steee-rangled her with her skeeee-arf. Hoist her with her own whatchacallit, petard. What's a petard?"

"I don't know, Floyd. Why'd you kill her?"

He looked at me, he looked at his coffee, he looked at me again.

He said, "Had to."

"Why?"

"Same as the bourbon and coffee. Had to *see*. Had to taste it and find out what it was like." His eyes met mine. His were very large, hollow, empty. I fancied I could see right through them to the blackness at the back of his skull. "I couldn't get my mind away from murder," he said. His voice was more sober now, the mocking playful quality gone from it. "I tried. I just couldn't do it. It was on my mind all the time, and I was afraid of what I might do. I couldn't function, I couldn't think, I just saw blood and death all the time. I was afraid to close my eyes for fear of what I might see. I would just stay up, days it seemed, and then I'd be tired enough to pass out the minute I closed my eyes. I stopped eating. I used to be fairly heavy and the weight just fell off of me."

"When did all this happen?"

"I don't know. All winter. And I thought if I went and did it once I would know if I was a man or a monster or what. So I got this knife, and I went out a couple nights but lost my nerve. Then one night—almost couldn't do it, but I couldn't *not* do it, and then I was doing it and it went on forever. It was horrible."

"Why didn't you stop?"

"I don't know. I think I was afraid to stop. That doesn't make any sense, does it? I just don't know. It was insane, like being in a movie and being in the audience at the same time. Watching myself."

"No one saw you do it?"

"No. I went home. I threw the knife down a sewer. I put all my clothes in the incinerator, the ones I was wearing. I kept throwing up. All that night I would throw up even when my stomach was empty. Dry heaves, Department of Dry Heaves. And then I guess I fell asleep, I don't know when or how but I did, and the next day I woke up and thought I dreamed it. But I didn't."

"No."

"No. But it was over. I did it and I knew I'd never want to do it again. It was something crazy that happened and I could forget about it."

"Did you forget about it?"

A nod. "For a while. But now everybody's talking about her. Mary Alice Redfield, I killed her without knowing her name. Nobody knew her name and now everybody knows it and it's all back in my mind. And I heard you were looking for me, and I guess, I guess . . ." He frowned, chasing a thought around in his mind like a dog trying to capture his tail. Then he gave it up and looked at me. "So here I am," he said. "So here I am."

"Yes."

"Now what happens?"

"I think you'd better tell the police about it, Floyd."

"Why?"

"I suppose for the same reason you told me."

He thought about it. After a long time he nodded. "All right," he said. "I can accept that. I'd never kill anybody again. I know that. But—you're right, I have to tell them."

"I'll go with you if you want."

"Yeah. I want you to."

"I'll have a drink and then we'll go. You want another?"

"No. I'm not much of a drinker."

I had it without the coffee this time. After Trina brought it I asked him how he'd picked his victim. Why the bag lady?

He started to cry. No sobs, just tears spilling from his deepset eyes. After a while he wiped them on his sleeve.

"Because she didn't count," he said. "That's what I thought.

She was nobody. Who cared if she died? Who'd miss her?" He closed his eyes tight. "Everybody misses her," he said. "Everybody."

So I took him in. I don't know what they'll do with him. It's not my problem.

It wasn't really a case and I didn't really solve it. As far as I can see, I didn't do anything. It was the talk that drove Floyd Karp from cover, and no doubt I helped some of the talk get started, but much of it would have gotten around without me. All those legacies of Mary Alice Redfield's had made her a nine-day wonder in the neighborhood. They ran to no form known to anyone but the bag lady herself, and they had in no way led to her death, but maybe they led to its resolution, since it was one of the legacies that got me involved.

So maybe she caught her own killer. Or maybe he caught himself, as everyone does. Maybe no man's an island and maybe everybody is.

All I know is I lit a candle for the woman, and I suspect I'm not the only one who did.